FLIGHT TIME

DARCY FLYNN

ACKNOWLEDGMENTS

This story has been on my heart for years and since it was my first attempt at young adult fiction, I knew I'd need an editor suited to that genre. I have to say Deirdre Lockhart's love for YA fiction, as well as her insightful edits, made my story sing. Thank you, Deirdre, for fitting me into your busy schedule. I so enjoyed working with you.

To my creative team—Jesse Gordon, my formatter—Rae Monet, for the gorgeous cover design, and Karen Duvall for creating the flat. Thank you.

Sometimes a writer needs expert council. This book concerns flying a Cessna 172 and when I couldn't find the answers on Bing, I called a pilot . . . well, two, actually. Thanks Billy King for answering my questions concerning single engine aircraft. I also wish to thank Jake Morris, at Wings of Eagles flight school in Nashville, Tennessee for clarifying specific state and national aviation law, for me.

Finally, many thanks to my incredible, hard working, critique partners, Cindy Brannam and Jeanne

Hardt. Your thoughtful insight and creative input are, as usual, spot on. And I'm most grateful for your encouragement during the many tough, heartbreaking days of 2020. Your friendship means the world to me.

For Warren
And for Alexandra
In loving memory

On Friday the 13th in October of 1944, my uncle, Lt. Henry W. Robison climbed into his P-40 Warhawk Fighter and departed, along with his squadron, from Eglin Air Force Base for a training mission, before being deployed overseas.

During that mission, he was lost on the Gulf of Mexico off Alligator Point, Florida, leaving behind his young wife who was expecting their first child.

Although he disappeared years before I was born, I grew up hearing wonderful stories about him from my mother and grandmother. When they spoke of Henry, I gleaned their sorrow, as well as their joy, in their *tellings*. I learned he was a man of character who loved and honored his family and his country. I got to know him through their tales and anecdotes and grew to love him with each story told.

Fascinated by his life, I created scenarios of my own concerning his disappearance. Until, as a twelve-year-old, I was convinced he was not dead, but merely stranded on a deserted island.

Henry was fun and outgoing, respected by both his commanding officers and his peers. Dearly loved by his family, he was the golden boy and the brave one.

On that fateful day, he was flying the aircraft that pulled the target for the other planes to shoot at, and his plane may have been accidentally shot, catching fire. If it did, my family never knew if he'd had time to bail out.

The Air Force redacted the other pilot's testimony, as well as other details, and to date has never released the full documents concerning that training mission.

Henry and his aircraft were never found, and his disappearance is still a mystery.

He was twenty-two years old.

I lovingly dedicate *Flight Time* to him.

"We must not allow the clock and the calendar to blind us to the fact that each moment of life is a miracle and mystery."

—H. G. Wells

CHAPTER 1

Rylee Dean rested her arm along the Piper PA-28 Cherokee's left wing and squinted through the lingering haze hovering over the tarmac. Having completed her preflight check, she waited for her instructor's final approval.

What was it about waiting that made time slow down? Just ten after eleven according to the large clock mounted on the face of the municipal airport. These ten minutes had felt like an hour. She brushed sweat from her forehead.

Ryan "Coop" Cooper, well known in middle Tennessee's small plane community and the best flying instructor at Jaxon C. Scott Airport, *finally* approached. Planting his hands on his hips, he shook his head. "Sorry, Ry, but you missed one thing."

Her stomach tightened. He had to be kidding. "Again?" She groaned and tucked dark hair behind her ears, but the wavy strands wouldn't stay put. "What was it this time?"

"You forgot to double-check the fuel filler caps."

"They looked fine."

"You have to do more than look. You must physically check if they're properly attached. If something's loose on the ground, it will loosen even more in the air. That, and yesterday's low tire, add up to two misses this week and three in total since you passed the written exam."

He handed her the FAA manual. "Study the book. Get it right. We don't go up again until you do."

"That's not fair. Of the eight steps to getting a private pilot license, I'm *on* number six—flying."

"And I'm the instructor, so what I say goes."

She waved the book, the movement fanning her. "That's not in the manual."

"It's in mine." He spun on his heel and strode away.

"Come on, Coop." She hurried alongside him. "I've aced the written exam. Doesn't that count for anything?"

"Yes, it got you to me. Now you have to pass me."

"I can do it. I've taken the controls many times without mishap."

He stopped midstride. "I know you have. You're the youngest and best student pilot I've ever had. As a sixteen-year-old, you have amazing instincts—right on the money. But it's not just about what your gut tells you. There're reasons for rules. Your head's in the clouds, Rylee, and if you plan on getting the rest of your body up there, memorize the preflight list. No one passes without getting it *all* correct. Including the granddaughter for whom this airport is named. The rules are for your safety."

The tightness in her stomach threatened to push up her breakfast. "But your rules expect me to be a mechanic."

"Not a mechanic, observant. Besides, I promised your mother I'd take no chances where you're concerned."

Of all the . . . "You've never taken chances with me or anyone."

"I know that and you know that. But your mother—"

"Doesn't get it."

"She pays me, so she's the boss." Coop put his back to her and strode across the tarmac.

Rylee slapped the manual against her thigh as he made his way to the single-story building. She blew out a frustrated breath, tipping her head back. Soft clouds billowed as a jet stream penciled across the blue expanse. That's where she wanted to be—where she *should* be—right now.

How'd she mess up again? Huffing, she stomped to her powder-blue Schwinn bicycle, then stuffed the manual into her backpack. She flicked up the kickstand and mounted the bike. *Coop and his stupid rules.* If she'd obeyed the rules, specifically her mother's, she wouldn't be flying at all.

She pulled her cell phone from her jeans back pocket and group texted Lizzy and Frank.

Lesson cut short. Heading to the Dip now. See you soon.

With the phone in her pocket, she pedaled over to Billy's Dairy Dip on Fourth and Main. The oval red-and-blue sign hovered over the flat-roofed, single-story diner like a flying saucer.

After securing her bike, she pushed through the metal and glass doors to the smell of fried onion rings and sweet cakes. Shawn Mendes's "Stitches" rocked the diner with its upbeat rhythm as she slid into the last booth on the left, the vinyl seat sticky in the heat. It had the best view of the parking lot—perfect for monitoring approaching cars and having private conversations.

Liam flicked his dark hair away from his brown eyes and straightened his T-shirt with the Dip's logo embossed under his right shoulder. "Hey, I'm Liam. What can I get you?"

Like he had to introduce himself to her *every time* —as if he'd never seen her before. Apparently, *he* had never *seen* her before. She'd crushed on him since eighth grade. And except for this moment, he had no idea she existed. Everyone knew Liam Whitefield, an upperclassman and Harpeth High's track-and-field star. And little wonder when the guy oozed hotness and athleticism like some modern-day Adonis.

Her heartbeat skyrocketed, her mouth went dry, and she swallowed. "Water right now. Oh, and there'll be three of us."

"You got it." He passed her a menu and flipped two more onto the table.

While she waited, she wrestled the flight manual from her overstuffed bag and opened it to the precheck section. Before she'd finished the first paragraph, familiar laughter distracted her.

She waved as her friends approached. Lizzy, wearing a blue-and-white madres skirt and a blue ribbed blouse, beamed a bright smile. Frankie, always two steps ahead of his petite girlfriend, reached the booth first and stood waiting for her to slide in before he took his seat.

"What did you forget this time?" Lizzy laughed again.

"To double-check the fuel filler caps."

"You didn't," Frankie said.

"Oh, like you would know." Rylee tossed her straw at him.

He flinched, laughing. "Maybe not, but I sure do like giving you a hard time."

Lizzy resettled in her seat, adjusted her off-the-shoulder fitted top, and flicked her long blond hair back. "Aren't you supposed to memorize that stuff?"

"I *have* memorized it. Well, most of it. Coop sabotages something. If it's not in the engine, it's with the landing gear."

"Sabotage?"

"Nothing too serious. He loosens bolts, wires—disconnects things. He creates a scenario that could be a problem if overlooked. I didn't notice either one he did this week. That makes three in total."

Lizzy slipped the straw from its paper and plunged it into her water. "And he won't let you fly until you catch them all?"

"Yep."

"Sounds like he's trying to keep you safe." Frankie draped one arm over the back of the booth and twirled the straw she'd thrown at him in his other hand. "Especially after what happened to your grandfather."

Great. Like she needed *that* brought up again. Rylee glared at him and drummed her fingers against the Formica.

"What?" He shrugged. "He's a legend."

Exactly. Couldn't they—her best friends—see that? "One I'm trying my best to live up to."

"Are you saying you'd rather not?" He waved the straw at her.

"Heck, no. I adore the man."

"Speaking of adore . . . Liam," Lizzy whispered. "One o'clock."

Liam approached the booth. "You guys ready to order?"

"Yeah." Frankie gathered up their menus. "I'll have the double cheeseburger, fries, and a real Coke."

"Same," Lizzy said.

One brow rising, Frankie eyed his petite girlfriend.

"I'm hungry, okay?"

While her friends placed their order, Rylee allowed her wayward heart to crush on the teenage dream, all broad-shouldered and gorgeous, mere inches from her table, oblivious to her racing heart. His wavy dark hair fell near his left eyebrow. Her gaze moved from his brown eyes, to his perfect lips . . . . He was saying something.

"And you? Do you want anything?" he repeated. His eyes held a lazy and somewhat impatient regard.

Her heart stopped. She blinked, swallowed, and handed over her menu. "I'll have the BLT, fried onion rings, and a small vanilla shake."

"Good choice." He stacked the menus, then strode toward the counter. All too soon, he disappeared through the swinging door into the kitchen. Ugh. Both her friends were watching her with humorous grins.

"You've got it bad." Frankie waved the straw again. "This is his table, isn't it? And the *real* reason you insist on sitting here every time we come in?"

"Not true. He just started last week."

Leaning forward, Lizzy braced both elbows on the table, her blond hair draping her shoulders. "And if his table ends up being changed to somewhere else?"

Well, duh! "Then we'll move, of course." Rylee gave a quick nod and a slow grin.

Chapter 2

With a tall glass of sweet, iced tea in each hand, Rylee pushed through the screened door and stepped onto the covered back porch. She placed them on the wicker table. Condensation already streaked the glasses. Man, was it usually this hot and humid the first week of summer break?

She dropped down onto the love seat and settled next to her grandmother, Tessa Scott, squishing the faded yellow-and-white striped cushion. "You coming over for dinner tonight?"

"Not tonight." A crisp leather smell drifted in the stifling air as Tessa opened a leather album.

"This album's new?"

"I put it together specifically for you to commemorate your solo flight. Don't forget to take it when you leave."

"Grandma . . . thank you." Rylee inched closer. "I see you started with one of my favorites." She smiled. "So... Tell me again about that photo?"

Tessa slid her finger over Jax's image, tapping his clean-shaven face, then outlining his officer's uniform as he stood next to his F-16 Falcon. "As if you haven't heard it a hundred times, already."

"Every time you tell it, I learn something new about Jax." Rylee looped their arms together, nearly jostling the iced tea.

And a wistful smile curved her grandmother's soft pink lips. "I love how you call him that."

"Jaxon Scott. It's a great name. I guess if he'd lived, I'd have called him something like Grandpa or Pops."

"Speaking of names"—Tessa unhooked their arms and reached for the iced tea—"Jax was always giving people nicknames. He's the one who came up with the Dragon for his mother."

She'd heard it all before, but seeing her grandmother smile always warmed something inside Rylee. She curled her own fingers around the cool glass, condensation dripping on her jeans as she hoisted it. "Did he have one for you?"

"Peaches." Ice cubes tinkled as Tessa swirled them. "Unless he was cross with me. Then he called me Tessa Jane."

"And Mom?"

Her eyes twinkling, Tessa saluted with the glass. "He had a few ideas he kept to himself. He said none of them seemed quite right, but he would know it when he laid eyes on her."

"What about names for people he didn't like?"

"Oh, he had some of those, too, but not at all appropriate for your young ears."

Rylee bent over the album again. "I love the photos of him next to his airplanes. I wish the color and clarity were sharper."

"It's not bad, considering we couldn't afford an expensive camera back then. The photos you've taken with your phone are so much better." Tessa sipped her tea. "Jax would be amazed by today's technology. He was always tinkering with gadgets. He spent many late nights in that very barn—designing, creating. If you could name it, he was building it."

"Really?" Rylee's hand jerked, nearly sloshing liquid from her glass. "How come I never heard about that before now?"

"I'd forgotten, I guess. This many years later—it's hard to remember everything."

"I so get that." She braced an elbow on her knee and plunked her chin in her hand, her misses with Coop still fresh on her mind. "What kind of things did Jax work on?"

"Mostly work he did for the military and the aeronautics firm. Very hush-hush, you know."

Rylee shifted even closer as if she'd be able to hear more clearly. "Wow, I didn't know!" Her heartbeat skittered. Who'd have guessed she'd be hearing a new story—especially about something secretive her grandfather did?

"How long was it . . . you know . . . before he . . .?"

"Disappeared in the Atlantic?"

She nodded, almost afraid to speak as a lump caught in her throat. Funny how you could feel an emptiness for someone you'd never had a chance to meet.

"Not long after we married. I'm not sure if I've ever told you, but I'd just found out I was pregnant with your mother. He was so happy." The tears vanished, and Tessa's eyes brightened. "At least he knew."

Tessa flipped the page over.

"I don't recall this picture," Rylee said. "Who's that?"

"Doris Scott, my mother-in-law, the Dragon."

"Seriously?" The gruff-looking woman fit her nickname.

"I was terrified to meet her. But as I got to know her, I learned she was indeed tough—in a 'mama bear' sort of way. According to her, she practically raised the football team. With teenage boys coming and going, it's no wonder she had to be tough. She wouldn't tolerate any nonsense from any of them, especially her son." Tessa tipped the photo away from the sunlight's glare. "It about killed her when Jax disappeared. She never got over it."

"How awful." Rylee stared at her grandmother's profile, waiting for her to say something more until Tessa flipped the page. In the next photo, Jax leaned against his single-engine Cessna. "Oh, I love this one."

"Me, too."

Laughter bubbled up in Rylee's chest. With the casual indifference in his stance, the photo looked like a movie poster. "Jaxon Scott was totally and completely cool, Grandma."

"He was, wasn't he?" Tessa's laughter joined hers. "He was crazy about his airplane. Speaking of . . . Are you and Mark Jenkins close to getting it airworthy?"

"*He* thinks so."

"But not you?"

Rylee sipped her tea, giving herself time to answer. "It's hard to say. I mean, it's taking forever. I can't wait to get it started and taxi out of their barn."

"You can't expect miracles when you two only work the occasional weekend."

"But since summer break has started, I'm hoping to change it to every day."

"I wouldn't get your hopes up. Mark has a regular job, you know."

Tessa rubbed shaky fingers over her forehead, wiping away sweat, then fingered the album's top corner, flipping the page to their wedding photo. "It's one of the few professional pictures taken of us. And to think he almost married Sylvia Lockley. Talk about gorgeous. She had it all—beauty, position, wealth."

"Wait a minute. How come I've never heard this story?"

"Timing is everything." She winked. "I'd had a crush on Jax all during high school, but he never noticed me. Then one Sunday, after he'd returned from flight school, he and I volunteered to chaperone the youth at a Wednesday all-night church event. And all I can say is he finally noticed me."

Something warmed inside Rylee. "So did he ask you out?"

"What do *you* think?" Tessa's softly painted lips parted, and a mischievous twinkle lit her eyes. "I'm the one in the picture, aren't I? Stealing the best-looking man in town from someone like Sylvia was quite the heady experience."

"So how'd you do it?"

"That story is for another day." Tessa's mouth curved as she ran her hand over the page as if savoring every memory.

Rylee eyed the last photo in the album. "This is where you stop the telling."

"This is where the photos end." Tessa gave Rylee a measured look and laid her hand over Rylee's. "What are you hoping to find out? Your eyes hold more questions than I can answer."

Rylee turned her hand to hold her grandmother's and laced their fingers together. "Even though your words bring him to life, I long to know so much more. He's such a mystery—especially his disappearance. Do you know what it's like growing up, hearing these wonderful stories, and not knowing what happened? There's more to know. So. Much. More."

Tessa's eyes clouded, reflecting a sadness Rylee rarely saw in her grandmother.

"He was the kind of man who, once the decision was made, never looked back, never second-guessed. I admired that in him, but it led to his disappearance. When I voiced my concerns, he just laughed, cupped my face with his hands, and kissed me. Said there was no talking him out of it. It's the last time I saw him. Stubborn, stubborn man."

"Talking him out of what?"

"That's enough for today."

As Tessa lifted the cover to close the album, Rylee took note of the date below the photo. 6/11/81.

"That last photo brings back too many painful memories for me," Tessa continued.

"Why?"

"It was the last picture I took of him. He disappeared not long after."

*　*　*

With the album tucked under her arm, Rylee maneuvered her Schwinn to the cottage's back steps, turning her grandmother's obscure remark over and over in her mind. "Talk him out of what?" She dismounted, lowered the kickstand, then pushed through the front door.

"That you, Rylee?" Her mom, Felicity, yelled from the kitchen.

"It's me."

Rylee placed the album on the coffee table, then entered the homey, pine and white kitchen to the aroma of baked bread, beef barley, and candy. She moved across the room as her mother removed hot biscuits from the oven.

"You hungry?"

"Starved." Rylee breathed in deeply, her steps echoing on the wide plank flooring. "Need any help?" She jumped up and landed seat first on the counter. Then she plucked up a leftover spring of carrot and popped it between her lips.

"Ladle the beef stew into the bowls while I set the table."

Rylee pushed off the counter, then lifted the ladle from a wall hook. "How was work today?"

"Great." Her mom placed a soupspoon and a butter knife at each place setting. "The Jenkins love the drawings I did for their patio garden."

"That's good."

Once done, they sat at the farmhouse-style table, stirring hot stew. Today seemed too hot to be eating something so steamy. No wonder Tessa didn't come over. Still, Rylee inhaled a deep breath. "This smells great, Mom. Grandma's missing out."

"I'll fix her a bowl. You can take it over later if you want."

"I hate knowing she's all alone in her big rambling house. How come we don't live with her?"

"I like my privacy."

Yep. She'd heard that excuse so many times. It was more than that. Dipping her spoon into the stew, Rylee gave her mother a *look*.

Mom huffed. "When your dad left us for that . . . for Monica, I didn't want to see the 'I told you so' in Mom's eyes."

At least she was being real about it. Keeping her head down, Rylee feigned intense interest in the stew, potatoes and carrots twirling over her spoon.

"I want you to know, what happened between David and me wasn't your fault. But I do blame him for not keeping up with you—as if he thinks his monthly child support check is enough."

Rylee slouched back in her chair, not quite pushing the bowl of stew away, but ducking away from the steamy scents as her stomach twisted further. "It's probably why I love Jax so much—well, Jax the phantom, anyway. Grandma makes him sound *so* wonderful." What fatherless girl wouldn't be enamored? And he was her own flesh and blood—a flyboy. Maybe she could eat a biscuit. She plucked one from the basket, heat searing her fingertips. "Ouch."

"Careful."

She tossed the hot biscuit from one hand to the other before letting it fall to the bread plate, pried the biscuit apart with her fingers, then cut a wedge of butter.

"Speaking of flying, how'd your lesson go today?"

Couldn't she guess? She knew Coop sabotaged her. Rylee shrugged. "You'll be happy to know I didn't get to fly."

Mom's head jerked up, and she rested her spoon along the edge of the bowl. "Don't say that."

Heat tingled up Rylee's neck and burned her ears as she stiffened in her chair. "Well, it's true, isn't it?"

"I know you wanted to take your solo flight on your sixteenth birthday. It's only been two weeks since then. I worry about you up there, but I want you to be happy."

"Then why do you do your best to block my efforts?" Rylee nearly slapped the table. Instead, she took a deep breath and glared at her mother, letting out the truth. "Because of you, Coop boxes me in with every turn."

Every bit of her mother stilled. Seconds ticked past as her wide eyes peered at Rylee—shocked? Hurt? What? Why couldn't Rylee ever read her mother the way she could understand Grandma? "What"—the word came slowly, as if drug from somewhere deep inside Mom—"are you talking about?"

"I'm talking about this deal you two cooked up."

A wave of her hand brushed the words away. She refocused on her stew. "Keeping you safe is our job."

"Suffocating, more like, and last I heard, that kills people." Rylee slumped back in her chair, arms crossed. A heat now hotter than the biscuits surged through her chest. Why couldn't Mom get it? "Flying makes me happy. It's *everything* to me. Why can't you see it?"

"I never knew my father *because* of flying." Mom's voice rose—her voice never rose. "He was obsessed with it."

Rylee slammed her napkin onto the table. "How would you know?"

Mom stared—speechless, her face losing all of its color.

"Mom, I . . . I didn't mean that. It's just, well, he *loved* it."

"First, you're going to have consequences for talking like you did, young lady. Next, it's the same thing. I wish my mother would stop regaling you with those stories. It adds to the romance. There's nothing romantic about disappearing over the Atlantic, lost forever, never to be found, no closure."

A pang shot through Rylee's heart. "Grandma tells me about him because I ask her to. Didn't *you* ever ask her?"

"Of course, I asked her. Then she'd cry and I'd feel guilty. How do you think that makes a ten-year-old girl feel? I wanted to know everything about him. But it upset her—and then I'd get upset." Rubbing her forehead, Mom pushed away from the table and stood, carrying her half-full stew bowl to the sink. "I stopped asking because my questions only brought pain."

"And you denying me mine hurts, too." Rylee held her breath. Maybe Mom would finally say something about her father. But all she got was silence. "Grandma showed me the last photo she took of him. Said he disappeared not long after."

Mom paused in her cleaning and stood perfectly still. "I know the picture. And for your information, just because I never knew him doesn't mean I haven't missed having him in my life." She rinsed her bowl in the sink. "I've never denied you your questions, Ry. I simply don't know the answers because *my* questions were never answered."

"You could ask them now. Grandma would tell you whatever you wanted to know."

"I'll leave the question asking to you."

Rylee stood and gathered the rest of the dishes. They cleaned in silence. After she wiped the last plate, she left her mom with her evening cup of coffee.

As she made her way down the short hallway, she thought of her grandmother, all alone in a big rambling house a few hundred yards across the field. How could two people from the same family be so different? The time she spent with her grandma was wonderful, but conversations with her mother usually ended in an argument.

Even though her grandmother was just as concerned about her flying, she didn't put up walls. Sometimes Rylee wished she could live with her grandmother, but the mere suggestion would devastate her mother.

Once in her room, she threw herself on the bed, the airplane-patterned comforter fluffing under her, and picked up the FAA manual. Tomorrow she'd get everything right. She'd make it to the next level if it killed her. She wasn't Jaxon C. Scott's granddaughter for nothing.

CHAPTER 3

While Rylee waited for Coop to grade her performance, she leaned against the Piper's fuselage, heat waves swirling around her. With a deep breath, she reached into her back pocket for an old photo of Jax. She wanted it with her on her solo flight. As Coop sauntered over, she tucked the photo on the Piper's instrument panel.

"Congratulations, young lady."

"Really?" The photo slipped loose as she clapped and let out a faint squeal.

"Really. But no solo flight today. There's a front coming in. High winds and rain."

The thrill deflated like hot air from a balloon.

"Tomorrow's forecast looks good, though. I'll monitor the weather and text you in the morning."

"Okay." Thunderclouds *had* gathered in the western sky. She blew out a breath, scooped up the photo, and slipped it back into her pocket.

"Hey, be happy. You not only passed—you passed *me*."

"Right." Although she forced a smile, she was far from happy. "What's one more day?"

"That's the spirit." Coop slapped her back.

As Rylee mounted her bike, her phone dinged a message. She slipped it from her pocket. It was Lizzy.

How'd your flight go?
Postponed!
Bummer!
Tell me about it!

Rylee parked her bike and glanced at the big house. Grandma's car was gone, so her news would have to wait. Once inside the cottage, she flopped onto the sofa, kicked off one sneaker, then the other, and curled up on the cushions. She'd just started looking through the photo album when she heard Lizzy's shout.

"Ry!"

When Rylee sprang up and rushed to open the front door, Lizzy clipped up the steps, a large canvas bag slung over her shoulder. She waved behind her. "Surprise! I brought reinforcements."

Two friends from Harpeth High bounded up onto the porch.

"Becky, Rach, hey. Come on in, y'all." The small entourage crossed the foyer into the living room.

"So what happened with the flight?" Lizzy slipped the satchel off her shoulder.

"Bad weather. Coop thinks it'll clear up by tomorrow morning."

"In the meantime, maybe this will cheer you up." Grinning, Lizzy jiggled the white bag.

Rylee grabbed the canvas and peered inside the opening. "Whatcha got there?"

"My mom gave me a ton of last year's Mary Kay makeup." Lizzy unloaded an assortment of cosmetics—lipsticks, eye shadow, blush, and a collection of skin care products—on the coffee table as Rylee snatched the photo album out of the way and set it on the hearth.

"Oooh, fun. A makeover. Just what I need. You guys organize the loot, and I'll grab some eats," Rylee hollered over her shoulder, headed for the kitchen. Arms full, she returned with chips, dip, lemonade, and water bottles. "Hey, Alexa, play 'Who Says' by Selena Gomez."

The girls hit the floor to the opening strains of the song, settling themselves on four sides of the low table. They spent the next few minutes pulling off lipstick caps and inspecting various blush shades. Then Becky instructed Alexa for the next song, and they moved to eye shadow. Rylee flicked open one of the four eye shadow compacts in the stack and tipped the little mirror to focus on her eyes while she imagined them highlighted by some of the eight different colors.

"There's one for each of us," Lizzy announced, her shoulders rocking to the music.

"Your mom thought of everything," Becky said.

"Let's try the avocado mask first." Lizzy's nose hovered over the open jar. "Mmm, citrus. It'll ready our faces for the makeup."

Becky scrunched her nose. "I'll pass."

"Ick. Me, too." Rach pushed the gunky thing away.

While Becky and Rachel settled themselves with an assortment of cosmetics, Rylee copied her friend and smeared an ample portion of avocado mask on her face. Once done, they relaxed next to each other before the fireplace.

Lizzy rolled onto her stomach and grabbed the album from the hearth. "What's this?"

Rylee stretched out on the plush cream rug too, kicking her legs up behind her, and grabbed a handful of chips. "My grandma made it for me. It's mostly pictures of my grandfather and his flyboy years."

"Cool." Liz flipped it open and perused the old photos. "Wow, he's a real hottie in this one. I *do* love a man in uniform."

"I know." Rylee grinned. "He was so cute, wasn't he?" She popped a potato chip between her lips, savoring the salty yumminess.

While Rach picked the next song—another Selena Gomez, of course—Liz stopped flipping pages at one of Rylee's favorites. This one had faded over the years, but as always, he seemed to speak to her as he gazed up from the album.

"He's wearing a jumpsuit." Lizzy twisted up her lips. "Not near as impressive as his uniform."

"I don't think so," Rylee said. "I like him in this. They're practical—made with plenty of pockets—and keep the pilot warmer."

"Of course, *you* would know that." Lizzy rolled her eyes and snagged the last chip from Rylee's open palm.

Rylee brushed the salt from her hands, then slipped the black-and-white photograph from the album's four triangular corners for closer inspection.

"What are you looking for?" Lizzy edged closer on her elbows.

"For the scar at the side of his left eye. My grandma said he got it fishing on the Harpeth River. When his buddy, Rick, cast his line—the fishhook caught Jax near his eye."

"Ouch." Lizzy swiped the photo from Rylee's hand and peered at the image. "Sorry. I don't see it."

"Let me." Becky scooted around the low table over to them on the floor, the carpet rustling beneath her knees. After Liz handed her the photo, she held it up to the lamplight. "I think I do see something—"

"No, you don't." Lizzy reared up and snatched the photo.

"Hey, careful with that." Rylee took it from Liz and inserted it safely back in its spot. "Come on, Liz." She pushed herself off the floor and offered Lizzy her hand. "Time to wash this stuff off. I don't know about you, but my face is starting to feel like a prune."

When they returned, faces glowing, Becky and Rachel were already applying polish to their fingernails.

Lizzy winked at Rylee. "Ready for the good stuff?"

"You bet."

They rummaged through the cosmetics, starting with base, then blush, followed by liner and mascara. Rylee took great care in applying liner to her upper and lower lids. After finishing up with a pretty summer pink on her lips, she pulled out her phone.

"You ready for the glamor shot?"

When Lizzy stood, Rylee tucked their heads together, and they pursed their lips, striking several sultry poses. As she snapped their picture, Becky and Rachel blew on their nails and watched from the sofa.

"Silly pose!" Lizzy yelled, then crossed her eyes, and stuck out her tongue. They laughed as Rylee struck a crazy contortion of her own. Giggling, they collapsed on the sofa next to Rach and Beck.

"If Liam could see you now, Ry," Lizzy said.

Rylee snorted. "I doubt he'd recognize me."

"More fool him." Lizzy took a swig of water. "You look like Millie Bobbie Brown."

"Oh, I love her," Rachel gushed.

Did she? Rylee grabbed the compact mirror and lifted it to her face. She tilted her head right, then left. Warmth surged through her. "I do kind of."

"Who do I look like?" Becky asked.

"Amy Adams."

"Amy Adams?" she wailed. "She's old enough to be my mother!"

"Okay, then a young Amy Adams. It's your red hair. Besides, she's adorable."

"And me?" Lizzy asked.

"Jennifer Lawrence. And Rachel's got those Selena Gomez vibes going."

"I'll take it." Rach shrugged. "Just wish I could sing like her."

Lizzy propped her feet on the coffee table and rested her head against the cushions. "This was fun."

Rylee tucked her legs underneath on the far end and surveyed her friends. "You guys rock, you know that?"

"We know." Becky winked at the others.

"Alexa, play 'New Wings' by Alyssa Bonagura."

"Who's that?" Rylee's three friends said in unison.

"Up-and-coming star. Her music's awesome." She took a swig of water. "No joke, you guys should follow her on Instagram."

" 'New Wings,' huh," Lizzy said. "Sounds like your very own theme song."

"Yeah, I like that." Rylee nodded her approval as she swathed dip on a chip. "So, Liz, how's it going with Frankie?"

"It's great." She took the chip bowl from Rylee and passed it on to Rachel. "Frankie is Frankie, and I wouldn't have it any other way."

"I'm glad."

Rachel balanced the bowl in her lap, then squinted, and stared ahead. "Who's that photo of on your mantle—the teenager by the airplane?"

"That's Jax next to a Rockwell Thrush Commander."

"That's a funny name for a plane."

"It's for crop-dusting."

"He flew that?"

"Yeah, flew it and was crop-dusting three counties by the time he was thirteen."

"Wow, that's young." Rachel twirled a chip in dip, lifted it to her mouth, and bit down. A dollop of dip landed on her shirt.

"The rules were a lot different back then." Rylee huffed an exaggerated sigh, then passed over a napkin. "Not like today."

"I'd be terrified to do something like that," Lizzy said.

"You're terrified of everything."

Liz picked up a striped pillow and flung it at her as the other two snickered and Rylee laughed, swatting it to the floor. Then Lizzy glanced at her wristwatch. "My dad's picking us up around fourish. We'd better clean this mess up before your mom gets home from work."

CHAPTER 4

Thirty minutes later, Rylee stood on the front porch and waved goodbye to her friends. She glanced at her watch—four o'clock—plenty of time to visit before her mom got home. After passing the massive oak tree and crossing the manicured lawn to Grandma's front yard, she mounted the front steps and entered the single-story farmhouse. "Grandma!"

"In here!" Tessa yelled.

"I passed Coop's—" Rylee entered the parlor and stopped midstride.

With a self-satisfied expression, her grandmother stood by the mantel, hands folded at her waist. "I already know. Coop called."

"What's going on? You look—"

"I've been holding this in for over a week now." She stepped forward. "I have something to show you. Well, two things, actually. Have you seen the late edition of today's paper?"

Rylee sucked in a breath. "It's out already?"

Giggling, Tessa waved the paper in the air above her head. "And on the front page, too."

"Boy, that was fast." Rylee hurried to her grandmother's side.

"Coop contacted the reporter with the news. They just needed that final piece for the article." Tessa unfolded the newspaper and handed it to her.

Granddaughter of Jaxon C. Scott Qualifies for Solo Flight.

The bold headline ran above two photos, one depicting her by the Cessna and the other Jaxon Scott in his air force uniform. A smaller photo of her and Coop in his Piper nestled amid the article itself.

Rylee clutched the newspaper to her heart, then tucked it on the seat next to her. "I'll always treasure it. So, what's the other thing? No way are you this excited over the newspaper article."

A broad smile spread Tessa's lips and bunched up her cheeks. "It's in the big barn. Come on."

Her grandmother practically bounced down the front steps before flitting across the yard. At the rustic outbuilding, she slid a skeleton key from her apron and unlocked the sliding doors.

Sunlight streaming through slits in the wallboards fought the darkness. In the center stood Jax's Cessna.

Rylee sucked in air and flattened her hands to her heart, then darted across the concrete floor. "How long has it been here?"

"Mark had it moved while you were in finals. We wanted a surprise for your solo flight."

"What do you mean?"

"It took some convincing, but Coop agreed to let you take your solo flight in your grandfather's plane. He's already checked it out and even flew it to ensure it's safe. He flew it here—landed on the old airstrip next to the farm, then taxied here across the field."

"But how did Mr. Jenkins get it fixed? The last time I worked with him, the plane needed parts and—"

"We hired a professional company to take care of the repairs."

Air whistled past her lips as her chest swelled. Unable to hold all the emotion in, Rylee flung her arms up and spun around, "flying" like she had as a little girl. "Oh, Grandma, that must have cost a fortune."

"I have the money. I could either will it to you or spend it on you now with the added blessing of watching you enjoy it." She nodded toward the Cessna. "The only thing we didn't do was have it repainted."

Who needed paint? This was the way Jax flew it! "She'll fly the way she is."

"That's what we thought."

"I can't believe it." A strange sensation tingled through Rylee's limbs. "I can't believe it." She threw her arms around Tess, then stepped away. Just one thing . . . "Does Mom know?"

"Of course."

"How'd she handle it?"

"Not well, at first. But when I reminded her of your determination to fly it, she realized the importance of having it professionally refurbished."

"So . . ." Rylee's lips flattened, her chest deflating. But the words burst out anyway. "You pulled the safety card on her?"

"Call it whatever you want. Your safety is important to both of us. She even helped pay for it."

Wow. Something warmed her chest, heated the backs of her eyes. Rylee swallowed the clog in her throat. "That's . . . huge. I'd better thank her."

Not quite ready to face her mom or surrender the special moment, she stood staring at the plane. Then she hooked her arm with her grandma's, resting her head against her shoulder. "How does it make you feel when you look at her?"

"Sad because it reminds me of what I've lost. And happy because of what it means to you."

"If you could change anything about your last day with him, what would it be?"

"If you only knew how many times I've pondered that very thing—questioned my actions. Wondering if I could have done or said anything more? All these years later and I still don't know the answer."

Tessa hugged Rylee's arm to her side and tipped her head against Rylee's. "But, if I'd known that was going to be our final day, I'd have held on a lot longer to that last kiss, clung to him with my entire being, but beg him not to go? No . . . Oh, I wanted to, but my asking would have been like a knife to his heart."

They stood there in silence until her grandmother straightened her spine, released Rylee's arm, and stepped away.

"The military chose him to work with this aeronautics firm. There was so much he wasn't at liberty to tell me. It was all flying and more science than military, but he was a warrior just the same."

"And of course you wouldn't ask him to give that up, not even for you." Rylee gave her grandmother's sleeve a little tug. "What do you think he'd have said, had you asked?"

"I don't know, but if he'd have given it up, stayed for me, our relationship would have never been the same. To have him wondering if he'd made the right decision—to be the reminder of the thing he'd loved and lost—I didn't want that. I only had him for a short time, but we were great together." Tess wrapped an arm around Rylee's waist and drew her close. "I'm so thankful he left me with the gift of your mom and you."

Rylee tucked her head in the crook of her grandmother's neck. Then a childish declaration burst from her lips. "I wish I could go back in time and save him."

"If only our wishes could come true." Tessa cupped her hand to Rylee's head and slid a strand of hair through her fingers. "And he and I would grow old together—live happily ever after. . . ."

"And Mom and I would know him . . . If only."

* * *

Minutes later, Rylee found her mother ironing in their mudroom.

"Mom."

Her mom lifted the iron and raised a brow. "By the look in your eye, you saw it."

Rylee hugged the folded newspaper to her chest. "The article or the Cessna?"

"The airplane."

"Yes." She ran a finger down the side of the doorjamb. "It was quite a surprise—and would've been better had you been there."

"It's yours and your grandmother's thing. I didn't care to intrude."

Intrude? Hugging the newspaper like a shield to her chest, Rylee edged toward her. "But you helped pay for it."

Mom's suit pants sizzled as she pressed the iron to perfect their crease. "I paid for your protection, nothing more. Since you're determined to go up in a relic, what else was I supposed to do?"

Why couldn't she just say she loved her and wanted her to be happy? Why couldn't she try to share Rylee's joy? Her hold on the newspaper loosened. "Thank you, Mom."

Her mom gave a slight nod, adjusted the slacks on the ironing board, then slid the iron over the crisp fabric.

Rylee so wanted to give her mom a hug—to make up from the previous night. But more than the ironing board blocked their way. The not-so-subtle irony wasn't lost on her. Something always stood between them. She refocused, waiting for any sign of further acknowledgment. When none came, she slumped onto the back porch, leaned against the railing, and peered into the dark sky. Rain clouds had moved in, and the distant rumble signaled the storm Coop had referred to.

"Go ahead and come. But don't stay too long, because tomorrow I plan to fly solo."

She headed to her room, sat at her desk, and opened up the editorial. Warmth swelled through her chest. How incredible to be related to this man.

She'd spent much of her life learning about him, so this article offered nothing new. But it proved she wasn't the only one who admired him. If this man—her grandfather and her hero—had lived, her life and her mom's life would have been amazingly different.

She grabbed a pair of scissors and cut the article free, then folded it into a small square, and slid it into her jeans back pocket. She'd keep it with her as a reminder that her destiny would always be linked to his.

CHAPTER 5

The rains came during dinner. After Rylee finished her meal, she grabbed a rain slicker. Ducking into the wind, she dashed across the yard to the barn and struggled with the heavy sliding doors. Bracing both feet and ignoring the rain stinging her face, she finally slid them from end to end. Inside, she shook off the wet.

Breathlessness caught up her chest as she approached the red-and-white Cessna. Clamping her teeth over her lower lip, she ran her hand along the left wing. She stepped around to the front, placed her left hand on the propeller, and touched the nose with her right. It was finally fly-worthy . . . and it belonged to her!

Along the barn wall, her grandmother's roll-top trunk reminded her of playing dress-up.

It had to be the same one. When she lifted the lid, she scrunched her nose against the musty odor, then rummaged through the clothing and trinkets. She laid her hand on an old-fashion magazine and held it up. Below a pub date in 1980, the cover photo displayed a gorgeous blond in a swimsuit. She sported a great smile and a mass of long, multilayered blond hair. The caption declared her Farrah Fawcett. Rylee shrugged and dropped the magazine at her side. "Never heard of her."

Setting aside dresses and boots, she unfolded a green jumpsuit just about her size. These were back in style. She took off the slicker and tossed it toward the corner. She slipped the jumpsuit over her jeans, wiggled it around her hips, then shrugged the top half around her white cotton shirt.

Deeper in the trunk, she touched something leather. It couldn't be? She yanked it from underneath a striped, double-breasted suit jacket with shoulder pads and red suede boots and leg warmers and bangles and bright sunglasses, then held it up for a closer look. A low whistle slid past her lips. It *was* a brown leather flight jacket. It had to have been Jax's. She shoved one arm through, then the other. It was too big for her, but no matter. She spread her arms wide, twirled across the floor, then stopped in front of the wide double doors.

The rain had slackened. She clamped her teeth over her lower lip. She wouldn't fly, but she *could* taxi out of the building—get a feel for her. After all, she needed to practice her preflight check.

She stepped around the plane, noting its general condition. After checking that the wings and tires were all level, she turned on the beacon switch, then moved to the cabin. Back at the house, all was quiet, so she opened the door and climbed into the red-and-white seat.

Once inside, she flipped on the lights and checked the operating handbook. All documents appeared to be in order. She flicked the master switch and checked the fuel gauges.

Satisfied, she secured the seat harness. This was it. She opened the throttle a quarter inch and turned the key. The propeller sputt-sputtered to life—the engine noise deafening as the prop whirled.

Shivers coursed through her veins as she throttled the plane forward and taxied into the night.

Ten minutes later, she had maneuvered the Cessna onto the abandoned runway next to their property. She pumped her foot to the brake and studied the instrument panel.

She hadn't noticed the unusual compass-like dial next to the clock. Come to think of it, the aircraft she flew with Coop had no such instrument. But this Cessna was over fifty years old, so it must be some outdated thing or one of the add-ons her grandmother mentioned. She'd have to ask Coop about it.

She checked the time on her watch. Nine thirty. She tapped the dial's face. It emitted a series of low clicks, as if it had gone through some kind of reset.

Odd.

She shrugged, eased her foot from the brake, and continued to taxi. As she did so, the clicks returned.

Then the dial's needle moved clockwise, slowly at first, before picking up speed.

When she stepped on the brake, the needle stopped. Heart pounding, she taxied again. The needle began to spin again.

Her fingertips tingled as she studied the instrument. "What are you for?"

Maybe she should fly to find out?

An inner quest, a curiosity she couldn't ignore, kept her foot on the accelerator. But the needle stopped moving.

This is totally weird.

She scanned the rest of the panel to make sure everything else was accurate. Satisfied and with the runway beckoning, she pressed her foot on the accelerator. *Just a few minutes in the air. What could it hurt?*

Rylee stifled a squeal, increased her speed, going full throttle. Then the Cessna lifted, and the ground fell away.

She was barely airborne when lightning cut through the air, splitting the night sky in two. She sucked in a sharp breath and gripped the yoke. The needle on the strange instrument started spinning again.

But this time . . .

Backward.

What an odd sensation traveling forward and upward, while watching the needle spin in the opposite direction. Goose bumps pebbled her flesh. Something wasn't right. She should land.

To approach the runway, she banked the Cessna. As she began her descent, the aircraft shuddered. The needle spun backward even faster. Her thudding heart was beating out of her chest—the desire to get safely on the ground her only thought.

Stay calm. Stay steady. She focused and slowed her airspeed to sixty knots. With her limbs shaking, it was all she could do not to fly the Cessna into the ground. At touchdown, she applied the brakes, but the shaking only increased. Violent tremors juddered the ground, the aircraft, and her.

An internal earthquake erupted from her core. She clung to the yoke—aware she'd have to ride out whatever was happening. As the plane rolled forward, the needle on the weird dial continued to turn backward, as if in sync with the Cessna's movement.

The aircraft stopped with a jerk, and dizziness overwhelmed her. She shook her head to dispel the heady sensation, but a dark haze blurred her vision. As the needle stopped, her world went black.

Rylee opened her eyes and inhaled a ragged breath. Having lost all sense of time, she sat perfectly still, hoping doing so would slow her erratic heartbeat. Hair stood up on her nape, sending a prickly sensation down her spine. Her hands clung to the yoke. She righted herself and stared straight ahead. The rain had stopped, and a dense fog now surrounded the plane. How long had she been un-conscious?

Lifting a shaky hand to her forehead, she took several more steadying breaths. As her head began to clear, she scanned the gauges on the instrument panel, then the clock. Nine thirty. That couldn't be right? She'd started taxying from the shed at nine thirty.

The needle on the dial had spun backward. That had to mean something, but what? Whatever it was left her feeling uneasy. She squeezed her eyelids together and shook her head again. The strange compass could wait.

She was in big trouble. Once Coop found out what she'd done, he'd ground her indefinitely. So much for taking a short flight without anyone noticing. What had she been thinking?

She swallowed and glanced in the side mirror. Her heart stopped.

A line of trees, thick and dense, spanned as far left and right as she could see. She spun around. Where was the barn? And the farm? She hadn't gone that far, and an airplane, even as small as the Cessna, couldn't make it through those woods. She checked the GPS for her location. The map showed she was near the farm, but her view out the window said otherwise.

An eerie sensation overwhelmed her, and her flesh crawled. Had she missed something? And did the spinning needle have anything to do with her landing in the wrong place? It was nighttime after all, and maybe the compass had taken more of her attention.

Whatever she'd done, she needed to undo—right now.

She started the engine. As the Cessna crept through the tall brush, she focused on the dial, expecting the needle to turn. It didn't. The plane rolled forward, but not the needle. She tapped on the instrument. "Come on, *move!*"

Hysteria rose in her throat. She slammed on the brake.

Mouth dry, she swallowed. Man, she needed a bottle of water. She opened the door. A warm mist brushed her face as she climbed from the fuselage. Trembling, she hopped to the ground.

Where am I?

Next to the Cessna, she faced the field opposite the trees and squinted into the mist. A light appeared in the distance. Some protective instinct told her to put space between her and the plane. She sprinted left along the tree line, keeping her eye on the light.

As it came closer, the light thinned, forming a horizontal line, then split into two lights. She stopped and clutched her hand to her heart to ward off her rising panic.

An engine rumbled into her anxious thoughts. The lights grew closer. It was a car—no, a Jeep—and it was approaching way too fast. She jumped back as it stopped mere feet from her.

Two men in uniform got out. The short one brushed his dark hair away from his forehead. The other one, who had the same coloring, stopped in front of her but stood much taller than her and his companion.

"You're trespassing on government property," the tall man said. "Who are you?"

Rylee licked her lips. *Trespassing?* "I believe it's you who are trespassing." Although her voice shook, she stood her ground. "This is the Scott farm."

The two men exchanged a look.

"Listen, my name is Rylee . . . Rylee Dean. And this is my family farm." She glanced over her shoulder to where the farmhouse and outbuildings should be standing, but weren't. "At least, I think it is."

The shorter man leveled his flashlight beam to her face. She squinted and raised a hand to shield her eyes.

"Wait a minute. I think it's her," he said.

The tall guy panned her with his flashlight. "How did you get way out here?"

Her heart raced. "I just—"

"Sorry if we frightened you. I'm Buck and this is Simpson." Buck spoke in a rush. "You were supposed to meet Rick by the side door. That's where the party is."

"Party?"

"Yeah." The man ran his gaze over the green jumpsuit and flight jacket. "That's a little big for you, isn't it?"

"It's hiding her costume, idiot," Simpson said.

Costume? Maybe this was how Alice felt when she fell down the rabbit hole.

"Hop in," the tall man said.

Hop? A nervous laugh escaped her lips.

"We're late, and we still have to sneak you inside."

Inside where?

The men bundled her into the Jeep. She couldn't rally quick enough to protest and found herself gripping the side of the open-air vehicle as they sped toward a flat-roofed building. If the man drove any faster, they'd become airborne.

Then the driver pulled the Jeep to a screeching halt, spitting gravel in all directions. Before he could put the gear in park, Simpson got out with an impatient grunt. "Let's go, miss." He grabbed her hand. The three pushed through a side door into the building they'd been so eager to reach.

"I'm sorry, but where are we going? I don't think I should—"

"The rec center," Simpson said.

She followed them down a hall, through a set of double doors, stopping at the entrance to a small stage.

"I'm confused. Is this some sort of military reenactment?"

The two men exchanged another baffled stare.

Buck pushed her forward. "No time, miss."

"You're the surprise." Simpson winked and gave a cagy grin. "You know, the guest of honor."

"You're on," Buck said.

With a second push, this time from Simpson, Rylee stumbled onto the stage to whoops and whistles from men in the audience. A spotlight from the back of the auditorium cast a focused stream of light onto her.

She stood still, staring speechless at the audience until one young man escorted another onto the stage. He wore a blindfold, and his entry sparked more shouts and whistles.

Rylee swallowed hard and licked her suddenly dry lips. The escort untied the other man's blindfold, then left the stage.

In keeping with the military feel, this man was dressed in khaki pants and shirt. His short dark hair held just a hint of wave. He squinted in the spotlight, and when his gaze fell on her, one corner of his mouth quirked.

Something about him seemed familiar. She stuffed the thought away for later and focused on the immediate, like *how* she ended up here.

As the officer stepped toward her, he looked at the audience and winked. Laughter fell across the room while he took his time walking around her, as if performing a uniform inspection. He crossed between her and the audience, stopped, and tugged on the jacket sleeve.

"Take it off!" someone from the audience yelled.

The officer continued strutting around her until he stopped on her right.

"Maybe she needs some help!" another soldier yelled.

Rylee clutched the front of the flight jacket.

"Looks a bit young." The officer smiled. "Maybe she has an older sister."

For the first time since she'd been pushed out on stage, she got a good look at the man's face. Maybe it was the way the spotlight hit him in that instant, or maybe it was the to-die-for smile and his near-black hair.

It couldn't be.

A soft gasp escaped her. She shook her head as if doing so would deny his identity. "How is this possible?" she whispered.

* * *

Jaxon Scott tried not to smile, but the wide-eyed young woman's gaping expression almost doubled him over. She was totally out of her element. He'd been to his share of bachelor parties, and no way had this girl ever been to one, much less been the so-called guest of honor.

"All right." He held his hand toward the audience. "You men have had enough fun. I believe the young lady has no clue what she's signed up for."

Laughter rang from the audience.

He turned toward her. "I take it, the sergeant must not have . . . sufficiently explained your role here."

More chuckles from the men as she shook her head.

"So. What's your name, sweetheart?"

The girl merely stared, tongue-tied. About to say something else, he spotted one of his men waving from the wings. The man pointed to the woman at his side and twisted his face up in an apologetic expression of one who'd screwed up big time.

From her spiked heels, mesh stockings, and skimpy skirt and blouse, the woman was obviously the stripper his men had hired. So, if she was tonight's entertainment, then who was the young woman next to him?

"R–Rylee," she stammered.

His humor vanished. Jaxon led the girl off the stage and stopped her in a narrow hallway. "First of all, let me apologize for the mix-up. Rest assured, I *will* get to the bottom of this."

The young woman gazed at him with awe. Poor kid must be in shock.

"Rylee?"

She nodded and continued to gape.

Huh, the girl underneath the heavily applied makeup was probably no more than fifteen or sixteen.

"There's a phone in the office." He placed his hand on her back. "Why don't I call your parents? I'm sure you're ready to get out of here."

"You look so much like him." She scrutinized his face, tilting her head. "The resemblance . . . It's uncanny."

"Like who?"

"Jaxon Scott."

"Well, that's because I am Jaxon Scott."

Her face lost all of its color. What on earth? Was she going to faint? He caught her arm to steady her and led her to the office.

"Here. Sit while I get you something to drink." He returned with a bottle of Coke.

"Drink this," he said. "The sugar should help."

He should recognize her, know her family. About five six, she flicked wavy dark hair away from blue eyes—both uncannily like his. She gulped a sip and lifted her stunned gaze.

"The way you keep staring is beginning to make me uncomfortable." He said it as a joke, but her awestruck stares *were* making him uneasy. She obviously knew him or *of* him. But he had no earthly idea who she was. Maybe his mother knew her family.

"Feel better?" he asked.

"Yes . . . I mean, no. Not really." She pressed her fingertips to her temples—her face pale under all that goop. "How are you here?"

The question, although innocent, seemed to hold a deeper meaning.

"I work here." He cupped his hand over hers and brought the Coke to her mouth. "Take another sip."

As she did, he continued. "It seems you have me at a disadvantage." Maybe if he engaged her in conversation he'd get her to relax. "You know me, but I don't recall ever meeting you."

"You have the kindest eyes. I just *knew* you would."

Oookay, a definitive swoon added an extra pitch to her young voice. This was getting creepy. He caught the movement of someone standing in the doorway. Rick braced a shoulder against the jamb, watching them, his smile mirroring the laughter in his eyes. Jax shot him a quelling glance, then turned back to Rylee.

"Do our families know each other?"

Still staring at him, she licked her lips and swallowed.

Somehow, his presence had caught her off guard. "That's okay—if you don't want to tell me."

She gave her head a shake as if his words broke some kind of spell he'd had over her. "I believe my grandmother has spoken of your family," she said.

Her grandmother must have done more than *speak* of his family. He should challenge her, but he'd let it go for now. Instead, he gave a quick nod, perched his hip against the metal desk, and picked up the phone receiver. "What's your number?"

She clutched the Coke bottle, and her eyes rounded bigger than its cap.

"Or I can have one of my men drive you home, if you'd prefer."

"That's all right." She shot to her feet. "I'll call an Uber."

"A what?"

Her wide-eyed gaze darted around the room as if seeking inspiration. "A–a taxi."

He gnawed the inside of his lip and held out the receiver.

She took it from his hand. "Do you happen to know the number?"

Eyeing her, he stood, grabbed a thick phone book from a shelf, and flipped through it. "Yellow Cab all right with you?"

She nodded.

"Let me." He took the receiver. Once he secured her ride, he motioned for her to follow him, and she trailed him to a wooden bench near the entrance.

"Wait here," he said. "The taxi should arrive soon. And again, I'm sorry for the misunderstanding."

When she dropped onto the bench, he slid a business card from his pocket. "If your folks want to speak with me about what happened tonight, here's how they can reach me."

The side of her mouth quirked upward, revealing the hint of a dimple. "It's okay."

"All right, then. Private Simpson will stay with you until your cab arrives."

She glanced over her shoulder, mounting desperation contorting her face.

"Take care." Jax put his back to her and strode across the parking lot.

He hadn't taken ten steps when he felt the presence behind him. When Rylee skidded to a halt a few feet away, he raised a brow.

"You're leaving?"

"No." He jerked his thumb over his shoulder. "I'm getting something from my car. You'll be all right with Simpson."

"I messed up your party, didn't I?"

"That's okay. I wasn't too keen on it and was just as surprised as you were to be thrust on stage. I only participated because I didn't want to disappoint the men." He focused beyond her. "Your taxi's here."

She tossed a glance over her shoulder, then back at him, the most deflated expression sagging her young face.

"I . . ." She clutched her hands to her stomach. "Goodbye, then."

A glistening mist filled her eyes. She stuck out her hand.

He took her hand and gave it a slight shake. The way she stared at him tugged at his heart in much the same way his mother did two years ago when she'd learned of his deployment overseas to thwart a rising conflict in the Middle East. Desperate and pleading, yet somehow accepting the inevitable. The whole thing left him with the craziest notion he should be protecting this girl.

"Come on. I'll see you to the cab."

After securing her in the yellow vehicle, he braced a hand on the door and another on the roof as he leaned into the backseat. "Do you have any money?"

She padded her jumpsuit pockets. "I, um, think so."

"Never mind. Do you live nearby?"

When she nodded, he handed the driver a twenty. "This should cover it."

"Yes, sir," the driver said.

As the taxi drove away, a pair of blue eyes locked onto his. Jaxon watched until the vehicle turned off the base. He brushed a palm across his chin. Maybe he should've been the one taking her home. There were still questions to be answered. He should have kept her here, asked those questions, dug deeper into how she'd gotten onto the base. It couldn't have been deliberate, and yet . . . The entire incident was odd. She knew who he was. But stranger still was her reaction—as if she'd seen a ghost.

Chapter 6

"Where to, miss?"

That was a very good question to which Rylee had no immediate answer. Man, her head hurt. But it was more than that. Things were all twisted up inside her—outside too.

"Um, where's the nearest hotel?"

The driver glanced at her through the rearview mirror. "About eight miles."

"What day is it?"

"Wednesday. June third."

"Today's Wednesday?"

"Yeah, June third."

But it's Thursday.

Something shivered through her. "What year?"

"Is this a joke?"

"No." Yes! It had to be. Some kind of prank played on her. But how? She twisted her hands in her lap.

"It's 1981."

Her heart took a nosedive. "Take a left here."

"What?"

"Just go left and let me off at the corner."

The best thing right now was to get back to her airplane.

"Aren't you a little young to be—"

"I live close by. It's late, and I don't want to get into trouble."

He shrugged. "Have it your way." He stopped the vehicle, then started to give her change for the twenty.

"Keep it," she said as she got out.

She waited for him to leave, then doubled back to the base. She made her way across the field to where she'd left the Cessna. Finding the area took a while. Her sense of direction wasn't the best, and the terrain was different from in her time.

She pulled herself up short. *Her time?*

That was crazy. This whole thing was nuts. There had to be an explanation. Maybe she'd hit her head harder than she thought. Maybe she was still dreaming. Yes—she'd wake up in the Cessna, and all would be okay. Well, everything except the trouble she'd be in. Right now, she wouldn't even mind being grounded in all senses of the word as long as she was in her room.

When the plane came into view, she ran the rest of the way. Finally. The one familiar thing and more importantly the one thing promising she hadn't lost her mind.

She placed her foot on the step, gripped the door handle, and climbed into the pilot's seat. Closing her eyes, she took a slow steadying breath, then blew it out. How could it be Wednesday, June 3, 1981? She glanced at the clock. It still read nine thirty.

Heart thudding, she started the ignition. The hum of a thousand locusts filled the cabin. A sweet sound normally, except this time she was in trouble and the propeller's deafening roar would only bring attention to her whereabouts. That said, the sound comforted her, and so she sat staring ahead.

Now what?

She ran her gaze over the instrument panel, specifically the strange dial. Then she taxied forward. "Okay, do your thing. Get me back home."

The needle didn't budge. Maybe there was an order to this? Her mind raced through the steps she'd made in the barn, then afterward.

"Start engine—check. Taxi forward—check." Pressing her right foot on the pedal, she maneuvered the plane until it faced the wooded tree line. As the Cessna rolled forward, she tried to recall how far she'd taxied from the shed before reaching the runway. Three, four hundred yards? The dial needle still did not move. She tapped on the glass, but got nothing. And if the needle didn't move, taking off could end in disaster.

Maybe it was the lightning that had come out of nowhere. The rain had lessened, and yet the weather brought on lightning.

As the Cessna rolled through the tall brush, she craned her neck and peered through the windshield.

Nothing to check off here. Stars twinkled in the heavens, clearly visible. Cassiopeia, the Big and Little Dippers, Draco, and many others she could easily identify.

She pressed the brake, gripped the wheel, and sat back. "So what? Do I stay somewhere in the eighties and wait for bad weather?"

But it couldn't have been the weather. The needle had spun backward long before the lightning bolt.

Hopelessness gathered in the pit of her stomach. Tears heated her eyes. She blinked them away and checked her wristwatch. Eleven o'clock. The sickening sensation grew. Mom and Grandma had to be concerned over her absence. By now, her mom had already called Lizzy and Frankie to see if she was with them.

Guiding the Cessna forward, Rylee put as much distance between the aircraft and the base as she could, then circled right to a small clearing in the woods.

Woods. How were there woods? This should be an open field with the shed in the distance and the cottage and the main house beyond that. Something cold wound around her heart and squeezed. She'd have to hide the Cessna until she could figure out what to do and where she was.

She taxied forward as far as the space would allow, freaked out by the nagging fear that someone would find it, then have it moved. Although she had no idea how this had happened, the Cessna had to be part of the equation. Without it, she'd never get back home.

She shut off the engine and jumped to the ground. She stood next to the plane, shivering. Since she had no idea what to do, the wisest thing was to make her way back to the base.

She marched back, putting distance between her and the Cessna, and did her best to enjoy the beautiful summer night. Even though it was a different year, the warm weather meant she'd traveled back to the same date—as the instrument panel and the taxi driver had confirmed.

About halfway to the base, she stopped. What would Jax think if she showed up again? Even she knew how odd that would be. She stared at the lights glowing from the building. Jax was the only person she knew, and with no one else to trust, what else could she do but go to him? He was, after all, her grandfather. Well . . . not yet, exactly.

She squeezed her eyes shut and pressed her forehead into her hands. When she lifted her head, a set of headlights barreled across the tarmac toward her.

* * *

Jaxon knew the female's identity as soon as the headlights caught her. Which made him question her story.

Within seconds, the Jeep lights had Rylee in full view. She stood blinking against the brightness as he jumped from the vehicle. While he strode toward her, her panicked expression twisted his gut.

"*What* are you still doing here? I put you in a taxi less than an hour ago."

"I know." She clutched her hands together, gaping at him.

"Well?"

"I live too far away for a taxi."

"Did you need more money? Why didn't you say so? I could've given him more."

"That wouldn't have helped." Her small voice almost squeaked.

He ran his hand across the back of his neck. "Look, it's after eleven. I'll take you home with me."

"Oh, but—"

"No buts. I live on a farm with my mother. It's about a mile from here. Just on the other side of those trees. She'll be happy to put you up for the night. Tomorrow we'll get you home. In the meantime, we'll go back to the office so you can call your parents—let them know you're all right."

Chapter 7

Rylee followed Jax through the side door, down the hall, and back into the office. Cigarette smoke hung heavily in the air. Strange to have smoke in an indoor workplace.

"Have a seat."

"What is this place?" With her legs wobbling, she dropped into the chair near his desk.

His head jerked up. "We call it a base, but it's more of an outpost."

"Like a military outpost?"

"It's not military, but it has a military presence."

"I see."

He folded his arms and gave her a measured look. "I doubt it."

Uncomfortable under his intense scrutiny, she shifted in her seat.

As if sensing her awkwardness, he added, "It's an overflow office for an aeronautics firm here in town."

She nodded, unsure if she should speak. After all, her coming back here had aroused his suspicions.

"I have to make a call." With an abrupt move, he headed for the door. "I'll be in the office across the hall. Use my phone." He nodded toward his desk. "It'll give you some privacy. Then we can go."

As he left her sitting there, she tried to steady her breathing. How could this young man, not much older than she was, be her grandfather? Being with him was totally wonderful. His searching looks aside, she was in no hurry to get back. She wanted to stay in 1981 and get to know him. This man, the greatest mystery in her life, who'd been a ghost of someone else's memories, was flesh and blood here . . . and very, very much alive.

She examined the office. There was nothing modern, at least not by 2021 standards, only the basics, including a desk, four chairs, and some shelving. A bulky, black rotary dial phone near the corner of the desk boasted the name Bell South on the dial plate.

On a hunch, she brought the receiver to her ear and dialed the farm number. The result was nothing more than a weird high/low-beeping signal. She lowered the receiver to its cradle, clueless as to what would happen next.

As she waited, she tried to work through the events leading her here. Some combination of those events had to have sent her back in time. Since her earlier attempt to retrace those steps hadn't been successful, then the weather or some astronomical event might've been the key.

The only thing she hadn't been able to duplicate had been the rain and the lightning. An electrical current, maybe? That could move a compass needle, right? But if so, then she may never get home. Or maybe it was none of those things. Could the settings on one or more of the control panel instruments, particularly those of the strange compass have done something? She hadn't noticed anything else unusual.

She swiveled in her chair to find Jax standing in the doorway, arms folded, watching her. Unnerved by his scrutiny, she rubbed the shivers on her arms. Just how long had he been standing there?

"You're back," she said.

"Did you make your call?"

"Yes."

"Good. Let's go."

She followed him down the hallway to another outside door.

"That's my Chevy over there," he said. "The blue one."

Rylee had to take two steps for every one of his to keep up. Seated beside him, she ran her hand to her hip then behind her.

"What are you looking for?"

"The seat belt."

"This is a '69 Chevelle. No seat belts here." He shifted gears. "As a pilot, I think they're an important safety feature. At some point, I'll have them installed. But for now, Tennessee only recently made them mandatory. It's been a long time coming."

What a cool car. She ran her gaze over the padded door and leather dash. Something was appealing about the simple design, with nothing digital and automated, so unlike the cars in 2021. "Is that a phone?"

"Yeah, it's Radiophone. This particular model has been around for about ten years."

"I had no idea phones like this were in cars." She traced her index finger along the handset.

"They're pretty expensive. The aeronautics company I fly for pays for this one."

They passed the road that should have taken them to the farm. "Where are we going? I thought you said your farm was a mile from the facility."

"I have to make a slight detour. It shouldn't take long."

* * *

Jax pulled up in front of the sheriff's station and stopped. He put the gear in park, then turned toward Rylee.

The kid squirmed. "Why are we stopping here?"

He braced his arm across the back of the bench seat. "You and I are going to have a little talk."

"Okay." Her questioning gaze searched him.

"You can tell me—or them." He nodded toward the station.

"Tell you what?" Something glittered in her eyes— fear?

"How you got on the base?"

She licked her lips. "A couple of your men brought me to the hall."

Nice try. A set of motorcycles whizzed past, roaring their engines like the street was a runway. They were gonna hurt themselves or someone else. He refocused, shook his head. "Your name was not on the list. You didn't come through the gate. No one checked you in. I put you in a taxi, and then you showed up again. And those clothes . . ."

She fiddled with the jacket zipper. Odd. The thing was scuffed on the right shoulder just like his.

"The flight jacket is military issued, and that green thing looks like something my mother would wear, not a teenage girl."

"Would you believe me if I told you I was playing dress-up and this jumpsuit was my grandmother's?" Her eyebrows wobbled, those big black rings around her eyes making them look creepy.

"I would not. So, let me ask you again. How did you get on the base?"

"I came from that side field, by the tree line." She pointed over her shoulder.

"A barbed wire fence runs all along that field."

She cleared her throat. "I didn't see any barbed wire."

He shrugged, turned off the ignition, and got out. In seconds, he had the passenger door open and stood waiting for her. He motioned her ahead of him. "After you."

She held his gaze, swung her legs to the ground, and stood. Eyeing the front of the building, she let out a shaky breath and stepped forward. Seconds later, they entered Harpeth Sheriff's Department's brightly lit entrance and approached the front desk.

"Sheriff Carney. Good evening."

"Jaxon. Good evening to you. What's up?"

Jaxon clamped a hand on the girl's shoulder. "I may have found a runaway."

Her head snapped sideways. Mouth gaping, she stared at him.

Carney ran his gaze over her. "Is that so? What's your name, young lady?"

"Rylee Dean."

"Let me check our files for any recent reports. Be just a moment."

"I'm not a runaway." Brow furrowed, she lifted pleading eyes to Jax's. "Please, please don't do this. Just take me to your mother."

The officer returned. "Sorry, but no one in our database matches her description."

"See? I told you."

"What about her parents?" the officer asked.

Jaxon tightened his grip on her shoulder. "Good question."

Jerking her shoulder free, the girl sidestepped him and drew herself up to her full height. "I called them from Jaxon's office."

"And?" The sheriff came around the desk.

"They're"—she swallowed—"coming to get me to-morrow."

"Would you like to try that one more time?" Jaxon crossed his arms.

Her face flushed a dull pink.

"You see," he continued, "I was listening in from another phone."

"Oh." Her spine sagged, and her chin dipped.

Carney joined him, blocking her exit, not that the kid looked like she'd run. "If you'd like, I can call Child Services."

Her head snapped up. All color faded from those pinked cheeks, and her wounded frown somehow slammed Jaxon in the gut.

"That's probably a good idea." Even as he said the words, he couldn't be certain he was doing the right thing. She was lying and most likely had been since she set foot on the base.

"Have a seat along the wall there, young lady." Sheriff Carney pointed to an orange vinyl bench.

She shuffled across the room and plopped down—an all-is-lost expression crumpling her features as her shoulders curved inward. She lowered her head and stared at her feet while twisting her hands in her lap.

Closing his eyes, Jax drew in a deep breath. It didn't lift the weight from his chest. "Keep me posted on her whereabouts."

"Having second thoughts?"

"Something about her . . . I don't know." Something felt off inside him. Reopening his eyes, he rubbed the back of his neck. "It's only been a few hours, but . . ."

"You feel bad. I get it. No one likes to put a kid with the state if they don't have to."

The phone's shrill ring interrupted. Sheriff Carney picked up the receiver. "Carney here. . . . Yes. I see. . . . Of course. Thank you."

As Jax strode toward the exit, the girl stared at him from across the room.

The receiver clattered back onto its base. "Because of the late hour, Child Services can't get here until tomorrow morning."

Tomorrow? As the word shot through him, Jaxon's hand slipped from the door. "Tomorrow?"

"That's what they said."

Rylee cocked her head at him—her big blue eyes pleading, her shoulders and back rigid.

"She can stay here until then," Carney said.

"And what, sleep in a cell?" His every muscle tightening, Jaxon threw the words over his shoulder.

"There are worse places."

And that anxious, imploring gaze continued to assail him.

"Don't bother." He gave her a nod. "Tonight, she can stay with my mother."

"You sure? The cots are comfortable."

"No need." With a jerk of his head, he signaled for her to join him.

She sprang to her feet like she'd been sitting on a spring.

"Don't make me regret this." He pushed open the door, cringing as a wave of heat hit him.

"I won't." Relief warbled in her voice while she scooted through the door ahead of him. "I promise."

He took hold of her arm and led her to his Chevy.

"Would he have locked me in a cell?"

"He was offering you a bed. And no, he wouldn't have locked you in." A pink hue had returned to her cheeks. "Another thing. You lie to me one more time, and you'll be back here faster than you can think. Got it?"

Nodding, she gazed at him with the same expression he'd witnessed on stage—the fixated look of an adoring and somewhat anxious puppy. Sure, he was a good-looking guy, and it wouldn't be the first time an adolescent girl leveled him with adoration. But there was something more in her searching gaze. Anxiety.

He huffed. "All right, Kitten, let's go."

Her lips quirked, and she glanced at her feet. Probably best not to ask what amused her. She would soon be his mother's problem, and with her propensity for taking in strays, a teenage girl should be a nice change.

"Thank you so much," she said.

"Don't thank me yet. You haven't met my mother."

Chapter 8

Rylee scrambled into the Chevy and settled next to this young man who was her grandfather. If there was any proof Jaxon Scott was indeed *the* Jaxon Scott and her grandmother's husband, the kitten comment sealed it.

A thrill shivered up her spine again. Her grandfather had given her a nickname.

Kitten.

That alone would've been worth her trip. Of course, it might be a bit early to attribute the giving of a nickname as confirmation of his identity, but she allowed herself to believe it. It was also way too soon for any real affection on his part, but she'd still count it as such.

A pang jabbed her heart. He'd never had the chance to give her mother an affectionate name. Maybe in some small way, this one would count. She hoped to tell her mom this when she got back to her time.

Back to her time.

Her heart thudded. How was she going to manage that? Jaxon had to be the key to all of this—him *and* his Cessna.

She twisted in her seat. He seemed deep in thought, focused on the road. He looked to be somewhere in his early to midtwenties.

Such a cute guy and much better looking than his old photos. Hair cut short and skin slightly tanned, her grandfather was totally—

Huh. She was going to say *hot,* but that was creepy. What girl refers to her grandfather that way?

They don't.

But then again, how many get to travel back in time to see one of their grandparents? A grandparent who is young, with their whole life in front of them. Except Jaxon did not have his entire life in front of him. He only had months or weeks or even *days.* Urgency thrummed through her blood, her heartbeat picking up. She had to find out how old he was and how much time he had left.

* * *

Jaxon's shoulders stiffened. He'd caught her staring—again. A sweet smile curved her mouth, and her eyes sparkled. She held her smile as she faced the road ahead.

What was it with this kid? And *what* had he been thinking to bring her home? He rubbed the back of his stiff neck. The last time he'd succumbed to a wide-eyed innocent was when his mom brought home the golden retriever pups. This girl had given him the same, heart-tugging, woeful expression.

And here he was bringing her home like one of Mom's stray cats. He stifled a groan. The apple didn't fall far from the tree.

"Is your mom expecting me?" Rylee broke into his thoughts.

"She is." He slowed and hooked a left.

Rylee craned her neck, swiveling to look behind her.

"You looking for something?"

"Oh, um, I thought . . . there'd be a gas station there."

"Really?"

"Uh-huh."

"Well, Texaco isn't planning to start construction until later this summer. They're not too fast once they get approval."

"Texaco?"

Huh? Why'd she think there'd be a gas station if she hadn't heard what company was putting it up? His gaze jerked from the road, even as his forehead knotted up painfully. "Yeah, you know—'You can trust your car to the man who wears the star.'"

"Sorry, I don't know that one."

"You're kidding." This time the wheel almost jerked in his hands. What kind of liar was she? "The whole world knows that TV jingle."

Rylee had pressed her lips together, and her face held a pensive, secretive expression—as if she'd said something she shouldn't have.

If she didn't know about Texaco . . . "So how *did* you know?"

That wide-eyed stare blinked his way.

"About the gas station."

"I must have read about it online."

"Online? Never heard of it. Is it a new publication?"

"I mean, in the paper."

Right.

She swiveled her head away, taking interest in the open fields. He still hadn't ruled out the possibility that she was a local runaway. It wouldn't be the first time a teenager wrangled a friend to cover for them while they made their escape. Database or not, she didn't belong here. Of that, he was certain.

As he turned onto the family farm, he caught the glow and expectancy from her. Such blatant anticipation said she was hiding something, so it better not be anything unlawful. Was she a stalker? A sucker punch struck his gut. No. That's crazy talk. He wasn't a celebrity or anything. But she held a particular interest in him—and now in the farmhouse. He shouldn't have brought her home.

* * *

There it is! Rylee leaned forward. Her heartbeat soared as the rambling, single-story white farmhouse came into view. She hadn't realized how worried she'd been these past hours. But there was *the house*, and looking at it made her feel hugged, safe, *home*.

Jax stopped his car and got out. She joined him in front of the vehicle.

"Okay, let's get this meet and greet over with. Ready?"

She grinned, thinking of Grandma's mama-bear remark about Doris Scott.

"Aren't we confident all of a sudden?"

Him mocking her in a teasing way touched her, giving her a glimpse of all she'd missed by not having him in her life—all her mother had missed. Mom would most likely have turned out differently had he lived, wouldn't she have?

Wow. She and her mom had a lot in common, having been deserted by their fathers. If she ever got home, she'd cut her some major slack.

When she followed Jax through the kitchen entrance, a woman at the farm table pushed pink-framed glasses up the bridge of her nose and eyed them. As she stood, the light caught on streaks of gray running through her wavy dark hair like silver ribbons.

"The Dragon," Rylee whispered.

Jax's head snapped around. He'd been about to speak when two dogs bound into the kitchen in a mad, tail-wagging frenzy.

Laughing, Rylee dropped to her knees.

"That's Kitty and Hawk. They like you," the Dragon said.

"Kitty." Rylee stroked the golden retriever's head. "That's an odd name for a dog."

"The dogs are mine and named for the Wright brothers," Jax told her. "I thought about naming them after the brothers themselves, but Orville and Wilbur didn't do it for me. The cats you see wandering around the place are my mother's."

"There's only one now," the Dragon said. "I found homes for Baskin and Button this morning."

A furry orange, white, and black creature rubbed against Rylee's side.

Jax chuckled. "And that's Redo."

Rylee stroked the calico's soft fur, then stood and held out her hand. "Hi. I'm Rylee Dean. Thank you so much for letting me stay with you."

"And I'm Doris Scott." She took hold of Rylee's hand. "Say, why don't you take Rylee to the church for the youth lock-in tonight?"

"Too late. I've already canceled."

"Oh, well, maybe another time then."

Rylee slid her hand free. "I thought I was going to have to spend the night in jail."

"Jail?" Doris shook her short hair away from her face and planted her fists on each hip. "That sounds like something Pat Carney would suggest."

"In his defense, it is late, and Child Services can't come until tomorrow morning."

"He called Child Services?"

"Well, yeah."

She slipped off her glasses and began cleaning them with her apron hem. "Men and their rules," she mumbled, then pointed her eyewear at her son. "You never should've taken her there, much less let him call them."

"You can stop fretting. She's here now, isn't she?"

"And quit talking about the child as if she isn't standing right here in this room."

Rylee stifled a laugh. No wonder this forceful woman was called the Dragon.

"I'll talk to Pat in the morning," Doris continued, becoming her champion, her very own protective mama bear, "and get this all sorted out. Child Services indeed."

Rylee glanced from one to the other. These were her ancestors. Her grandfather and great-grandmother. Living, breathing, and full of life and spirit. Both gone in her own time, and one far too soon. Soon Jax's disappearance would devastate this bold, bigger-than-life woman. A rush of tears heated her eyes.

"Good heavens. Now, look what you've done." Doris Scott jammed her glasses back in place.

"Me?" Jax widened his stance, scowling at both of them.

"Don't cry, dear."

"Oh no. Please," Rylee said. "I'm fine, really. It's not either one of you."

"Come here, darlin'."

When Doris opened her arms, Rylee couldn't think of anything more wonderful than stepping into them. She hugged her great-grandmother close, resting her head against the woman's ample shoulder, finding comfort during this strange turn of events. She caught the fragrance of lavender and fresh mint. Just like the mint in her grandmother's garden. She breathed deeply and pulled away.

* * *

Jax eyed the two women. One his mother and the other a stranger. A stranger who now gazed at his mother with the same awe-filled expression that had freaked him out. She was only a cute teenager, but still . . . Something about the whole thing bothered him. Fishy didn't begin to describe it.

He gnawed his inner lip. *Where* had she come from? Her explanation didn't satisfy him at all.

Could she be a plant from a competitor—a spy? That sounded too crazy. Still, the entire thing held a peculiar ring, and having her in his home was either a brilliant move or a foolish one.

She knew things—his name and "the Dragon" comment. Only family and a few close friends used that endearment.

What kind of intelligence agency or competitor could ferret out such intimate details? Had the project been infiltrated higher up? Most involved were former military—all who knew the importance of keeping a secret. And then she'd used that word—*online*. It'd tripped off her tongue as if she'd said it a million times. He'd heard it before, but couldn't recall where.

"My wonderful guest room happens to have your name on it," his mom said.

The girl beamed up at her with a smile that would stop a young man's heart, much less a woman's whose only weaknesses were stray cats and dogs—and now homeless girls.

As his mother escorted Rylee down the hallway, he lifted the receiver from the kitchen wall phone and dialed the airstrip. Something was off about this girl and her story, and the sooner he found out what it was, the better.

CHAPTER 9

The smell of bacon woke Rylee. She pushed herself to her elbows. The morning light streamed in through the venetian blinds, casting a soft glow throughout the small bedroom. The yellow-and-green floral curtains and matching bedspread cheered her until she remembered where she was and how she'd gotten here. She hugged her knees to her chest and glanced at the creamy white dresser and matching bedside tables.

She sucked in a breath. *My mother grew up here.* Or *would* grow up here? Which way was she supposed to think of it anyway? Grinning, she shook her head, then slid her cell phone from under her pillow. Last night, she'd turned it off to save her battery, and since no one would be able to call her, she'd better keep it off.

After she showered and dressed, she pocketed her phone and headed to the kitchen. Except for the window curtains—now a soft checkered yellow—nothing much had changed here. The wall calendar said it was Thursday, June 4. Yesterday had been Thursday, too. Maybe she *had* gone down that rabbit hole.

Iron frying pan in hand, Doris turned when she entered. "Good morning. Breakfast is about ready. Take a seat."

A rush of heat built behind Rylee's eyes, and something clogged her throat. But she pushed both back. "Thank you. It smells wonderful."

"I hope you like pancakes and bacon." Doris nodded a stack of cakes on the table.

Licking her lips, Rylee pulled out a chair. She hadn't realized how hungry she was.

"I phoned Pat Carney this morning. He agreed to postpone Child Services until you reach your parents."

"Thank you, Miss Doris."

As she sat, Jaxon came in through the screen door. "Morning. This looks great, Mom."

"Thanks, hon. Would you get my rooster-shaped cutting board?"

"Where is it?"

"It's in the narrow cabinet by the sink," Rylee said.

As Jax's eyes widened, he became suddenly still. He glanced from her to his mom, who also stood with the same question in her eyes.

Oops! Rylee dropped her gaze and gnawed the inside of her lip.

"Rylee, how did you know where to find that?" Doris stepped forward and placed a hand on Rylee's shoulder.

Rylee gave an anxious cough. "Lucky, I guess. The long thin cabinet and its location near the sink sort of gave it away." She shrugged. "It . . . seemed the logical place for a cutting board." As the Dragon's hand fell away, Rylee focused on eating her breakfast.

Jaxon handed his mom the board and took his seat. Eyeing her, he brought a piece of bacon to his mouth and bit down. He watched her a moment longer, then turned his attention to his mother. "I've got to go into town today. You need anything while I'm there?"

"No, I've got plenty for the next few days. Why don't you take Rylee? Show her around some."

He forked a bite of pancake, scowling. So he wasn't happy with her suggestion.

Rylee wiggled forward in her seat. "I'd like that . . . if you're sure you don't mind."

Okay, so she was sure he *would* mind. But she could pretend otherwise, couldn't she?

"I don't mind, but what about your parents? What time are they coming to get you? That is, assuming you called them this morning."

Uh-oh. Here goes. She blinked and swallowed. "They won't be coming today."

He paused with his fork midair. "What do you mean?"

Rylee dabbed her mouth with her napkin, then set it beside her place. "My mom has the flu, and my dad . . . is not in the picture. If I could stay until she's better—one or two more nights . . . Or I can take the bus home."

They exchanged glances.

"I'm so sorry to hear that," Doris said. "Of course you can stay until your mother's better. We'd love to have you."

Jax twirled his fork between his fingers. "And just when were you going to let us know?"

"Jaxon, don't badger the child."

"Well?" he said.

"I didn't find out until I called this morning to co-ordinate today's schedule."

"How efficient of you."

Doris tsked. "Jaxon, for goodness sakes."

"Just don't put me with Child Services," Rylee said.

"And I've already handled that this morning." Doris shot Jaxon something close to an evil eye. "Sheriff Carney knows she's here with us. And if I have to go through the approval process until her mother gets here, then I will."

"Fine." Jax released a heavy breath. "You can come with me. We'll leave in an hour."

He didn't say anything else during breakfast. Neither one spoke, amplifying the tension. Rylee cringed, sinking deeper into her seat. She'd caused the rift between him and his mom. Their silence mirrored those between her and her own mother. Maybe this sort of thing was hereditary?

She forked a bite of cold pancake and stole as many glances at him as she could, finding it hard not to look. His blue eyes darkened when he was angry—man, he was amazing!

And he'd caught her staring. Groan. Both he and his mother exchanged glances as Doris smothered a smile.

What must they think of her gazing at him like some lovesick puppy? As much as she wanted to go to town with him, maybe she ought to offer to stay behind. She at least needed to *try* to be cool.

"If Jaxon has other plans, I'm happy to stay and help you, Miss Doris."

"Nonsense. You only have a day or two. Go and have fun."

"No, really." Rylee sat up higher in her chair and stacked her utensils on her plate. "If it's all right with you, I'd like to hang around the farm. Explore a bit."

"Well, of course you can stay if you want to."

"I do."

At least Jax's stiff stance relaxed. She couldn't blame him. Someone her age was a nuisance to someone like him. She so wanted to get to know him, but she'd have to be patient. Not an easy thing to do when she had no idea how long she'd be in this time or what chain of events would get her home, but at least she'd have two more days here at the farm—if she stayed in this time. But no way could she risk becoming a ward of the state. She'd camp out in the Cessna if she had to. That ship was her lifeline to her future, most likely to her very existence.

After breakfast, she excused herself and went into the living room. The mantel over the fireplace held an assortment of family photos. She picked up one of her great-grandmother and Jax when he was a teenager. After stealing a glance over her shoulder, she slipped out her cell phone, pressed the power button, then snapped a picture. She turned it back off and hid it in her pocket. Then she crossed the room to a long side table holding a collection of model airplanes—the same ones from her grand-mother's den in the future. She examined the P-40 jet used during World War II.

"Hey, be careful with that."

When she swung around, still holding the air-plane, Jax strode to her and took the model. "This took an entire weekend to put together."

"It's beautiful. The paint job is right on."

He grinned, nodding. "It is, isn't it?"

"You've got some collection. That's for sure. Did you build them all?"

"I did."

"The yellow biplane is awesome."

"Awesome, huh?"

"Do you have a favorite?"

"The Spitfire MK11 is cool. Then there's the Re-public P-47D Thunderbolt, the Razorback version." He eased a model from its place, balancing it be-tween two fingers, and held it before her. "So nicknamed for the ridge behind the cockpit. See?"

She peered closely. "But later the P-47Ds had a bubble canopy."

A particular glow lit his eyes—maybe a growing respect?

"Right." His head cocked to one side, his brow furrowed. "Where do get your knowledge and love for aircraft?"

You. I get it from you.

"My grandfather." She swallowed. "Nice job on the black-and-yellow checkerboard tail wing."

"Thanks. That took one steady hand."

"I bet." She stood, almost holding her breath, reveling in this moment with him. Seeing the kid in him —the man with his toys—was wonderful.

He set the model back in its stand and checked his watch. "Time for me to go."

She watched him leave the room. Too bad, she'd agreed to stay behind.

A few minutes later, he pushed through the kitchen door and clipped down the back steps to his car. He offered a quick wave before leaving.

Doris had just started washing up. Rylee stepped to the sink and grabbed a dishtowel. "I'll dry."

"Why, thank you." Doris handed her a freshly washed, blue willow plate. "Tell me. What's the real reason why your parents haven't come to get you? If you were my daughter, I'd have been frantic to get here."

Her question shouldn't have caught her off guard. Her direct approach probably helped earn this formidable woman her Dragon title.

To come up with a convincing answer, Rylee lowered her gaze and wiped off the back of the plate. "So, you noticed. Even I thought it was pretty lame."

"I've raised a boy and half of his friends, so I've heard it all."

Rylee set the plate aside. "The last time I was with my mom, we had a fight. She thinks I'm staying with one of my friends through the weekend."

"I see. And you're in no hurry to get back home?"

She nodded.

"I'd feel better if you phoned her so I could let her know you're here."

She nodded, again. "My parents are divorced. My dad's remarried and lives overseas. As for my mom, we don't always get on. She loves me, of course, and I hate it when we argue. But . . ."

"You're what, fifteen, sixteen?"

"Sixteen."

Doris stacked one plate over another. "I wouldn't let it worry you too much. It's natural at your age to start breaking away." She handed Rylee a mug. "And trust me, she knows it, too."

With the last of the dishes washed and put away, Rylee lingered by the sink, gazing out of the window.

"There's a bicycle out back," Doris said. "You're welcome to use it."

Thankful for the change in subject, Rylee smiled at her great-grandmother. She so hated lying. "I'd love that, but only if you're sure you don't need me for anything."

Doris flitted her hand in the air. "Off with you, girl. I have a full day at the church. I'm head of the committee for next month's summer bazaar."

Kitty and Hawk greeted Rylee on the porch. She gave each a pat on the head, then continued down the steps.

Even though the house had been built in the early 1900s, it looked almost new. The porch rail, the wide wooden steps to the yard, and the shrubs were in pristine condition.

She'd love to grab another photo, but dared not. The Dragon could be watching from a window, and it wouldn't do to give her anything else to quiz her about.

Finding the bike took only a few seconds. Getting to her plane—making sure it was still there—had to be her priority. The Cessna was her link to sanity. If anything happened to it . . .

No. She couldn't let her mind go there. *Just find the plane—keep it secure.*

She pedaled across the property to the tree line, then dismounted, and pushed through the tall grass and low tree limbs, stopping at the barbed wire. After securing the bike next to a tree, she walked the fence line for an opening.

Hiking over and around the thick brush was more difficult than she'd thought. On the verge of turning back, she spotted a break. Bending at the waist, she stepped through, careful to clear the metal barbs. On the other side, the woods opened up, and then she spotted the Cessna's familiar red-and-white markings. Ten minutes later, she flattened both palms on the plane, her pulse thrumming through them as though coming from the machine itself. "Am I glad to see you."

In daylight, it was far more visible than she'd thought. Amazing no one had noticed it. It wouldn't be long before someone patrolling from the base spotted it.

She climbed in and taxied through an opening surrounded by a thickly wooded area. It wasn't perfect, but it would have to do.

* * *

Normally, Jax wouldn't mind the tagalong, but he was meeting Sylvia for lunch. He hadn't seen her in days, and with the upcoming series of test flights—one longer mission, in particular—he needed to speak to her privately.

He couldn't tell her or his mom some things about his work, but he *could* offer assurances before he left.

He pulled into his parking space at the base. As he entered the building, Rick met him in the hallway. "Just the man I wanted to see," Jax said.

"What's going on?"

"Let's go to my office." After they entered, Jax removed a small notebook and pencil from his breast pocket. "I need you to check a name." He scribbled across the pad, then tore off the sheet, and handed it to Rick. "See if there's anything on a Rylee Dean—age sixteen."

"The girl who got on the base last night?"

"Yep." Jax rested his hip on the corner of his desk. "Something's off with her." The girl knew where that cutting board was stored—as if she'd been there many times.

Rick fingered the note, then creased it in his methodical manner. "In what way?"

"She knows things."

"Things about the project?"

"No, nothing that obvious." Creepy things. Jax shoved the notebook back into his pocket.

"Then what?"

"Personal things about me and my mother."

"Like . . .?"

"My name for one."

His friend's eye roll asked what was surprising about that. Which was true, but . . .

"Nothing." Folding his arms across his chest, Jax let out a long low breath. Time to say it. "Except we've never heard of her, and now she's staying at the farm."

Rick's head jerked up. "You're kidding."

"I wish. I didn't have the heart to put her with Child Services. Then Mom got involved, and now one night at our house has turned into a long weekend."

A grin crinkled up Rick's cheeks. "That sounds just like your mother."

"Don't I know it?" Jax tapped the pencil against his knee.

"All kidding aside, I've never known you to sweat the small stuff. But you're serious about this. You suspect the girl to be what, some sort of plant?"

What did he suspect? His fingers clutched the pencil so tightly it pinched them. That was the whole trouble with this. "Well, when you put it like that, it does sound crazy."

"I'll see if headquarters has anything on her in our database. It doesn't hurt to be proactive. I'll also check with the local police and sheriff's department —see if they can find out anything."

"Forget the sheriff. He's already checked." He tossed the pencil aside and stood. "In the meantime, you and I are going to take a drive. I want to know where Buck and Simpson found her."

Minutes later, they parked the Jeep and got out.

"This is about where they spotted her." Rick waved ahead of them. "They saw her jogging somewhere along there."

"Could they tell which direction she'd come from?"

"Hard to say. They thought she might have come from the far left." Rick stepped closer to the tree line.

"She could've cut straight through these woods, any-where along here."

This wasn't helping. Jax rubbed the pulse at his temple. "Did she say anything that might help us?"

"When they informed her she was trespassing, she told them this was the Scott farm, insinuating they were the ones trespassing."

His heart gave a strange jerk. "Sounds like her destination may have been my farm all along."

"As the crow flies, your place is close. Maybe she got lost."

"Maybe."

Jax canvassed the ground, inspecting for any clear markings or signs. A difficult task since it hadn't rained in over a week.

He flicked back his cuff and checked his watch. "I need to leave for a lunch appointment. Drop me off at the gate, then get Buck and Simpson out here to scour for any disturbances. Rylee came from some-where along here, and there has to be evidence of that. She didn't just drop out of the sky."

* * *

Jax spotted Sylvia the minute he entered Billy's Dairy Dip. Her chestnut hair fell loose around her shoul-ders the way he liked it. As he crossed the black-and-white tile floor, she glanced up with a pair of hazel eyes—her face lighting up. He slid into the seat oppo-site and took her hand.

"Hey, beautiful."

"Hey, yourself."

"Sorry I'm a bit late. Have you already ordered?"

Her nod rippled her chestnut hair and wafted him with her warm and spicy perfume, something she called Opium. "For both of us."

"Today's special, I hope."

"Of course. You love Billy's country-fried steak."

"You know me so well." Breathing in deeply, he gave her hand a gentle squeeze.

"So." She wiggled forward on her bench and lowered her voice to a teasing whisper. "What's all the secrecy about?"

Allowing himself one more deep breath, he gazed at her. "My work may take me away sooner than I'd thought."

The light in her eyes clouded over. "Don't tell me that."

He leaned toward her. "What would you think of our moving up the wedding?" His heartbeat picked up speed in keeping with his rush of words.

And her features crumpled. She tugged her hand from his and sat back.

"Look," he said. "I know how important all the wedding stuff is, but—"

"Stuff? Seriously?"

"Okay, that came out all wrong." He'd never understand why it all the pomp mattered so much to her. "But isn't it more important that we're married?"

"Of course, but I've dreamed of my wedding since I was a little girl. Marriage is forever, so a wedding only happens once. And I want the one of my dreams. Surely, you can understand that."

Not really. He exhaled, tamping down the disappointment. He'd expected her reaction, of course, but he'd thought she'd think about it.

Her expression softened. "I mean, if this were war, with the possibility of never seeing each other again, *then* a ceremony in front of Judge Carlyle would be appropriate."

"You're right. What was I thinking?" Forcing a smile he didn't feel, he glanced around the crowded restaurant for something else to say. Maybe if he were at liberty to tell her the dangers of his work, she'd move up their wedding. But she didn't know, and he couldn't expect her to give up her dreams on a whim.

Rylee pushed through the glass door. How'd she get into town? Had his mother accompanied her? One glance behind the girl told him she'd come alone. She slid into a seat at the counter before he turned his attention back to Sylvia.

"Are we okay?"

"Of course." Her cherry-red lips parted. "You do understand, don't you?"

"Yes. And I . . . I shouldn't have asked."

"You can always ask, darling." She reached across the Formica table and rubbed her thumb over the back of his hand.

CHAPTER 10

With Dolly Parton singing in the background and a group of girls in halter-tops with sweatbands holding back their fluffy hair, it felt like some crazy eighties-night party. Trying not to gawk at the diners, Rylee pulled a menu from between the metal napkin holder and the condiment rack as the waitress set a water glass in front of her.

"Welcome to Billy's." The pretty blonde with her Farrah Fawcett hair behind the counter smiled. "New in town, or just visiting?"

"Yeah, I'm here for a . . . visit. But how'd you know?"

"Very small town, plus all the kids come here. It's the best hangout."

"Oh, right."

"Today's special is country-fried steak. The soup of the day is chicken noodle. Would you like something to drink besides water?"

"A Coke."

"Great. Take a minute to look at the menu. I'll be back in a jiffy."

Other than the menu's neon colors, not much had changed. Billy still sold all the basics—hamburgers, fries, shakes, and standard sandwiches. Even the daily specials were pretty much the same.

The waitress returned with Rylee's Coke and set it on the counter. "So, what'll it be?"

"I'll have a grilled cheese with fries."

The waitress didn't respond as she stood with her pencil hovering over the ordering pad, gawking over Rylee's left shoulder. With such an enamored expression, she must be enjoying the view. Recognizing the look, Rylee couldn't help but smile. Half the girls at Harpeth High had crushed on Liam and displayed that same goofy expression, herself included.

Curious, she swiveled the red vinyl stool left to see who caught the blonde's attention. Her body stiffened. Jax. He sat holding hands with a pretty brunette as if he couldn't get enough of her.

Her smile faded. "She's gorgeous." *No wonder he didn't want her tagging along.*

She spun the stool back toward the waitress. "He's cute."

"I'll say." The waitress sighed and rested her chin in her hands.

She stared at the pretty blonde who seemed so enamored with Jax. She looked oddly familiar. Could she be . . . ? Her gaze slid to the woman's uniform. No name tag, and without it, Rylee couldn't be certain. Except for that wedding photo, she hadn't seen any old pics of her grandmother in months.

As for the woman with Jax, she pretty much knew her identity, but for the sake of clarity, she asked, "Who's he with?"

"Sylvia Lockley."

Her grandmother's words heralded through her brain—"And to think he almost married Sylvia Lockley." Rylee swallowed. "So that's Sylvia Lockley."

"It is. The Lockleys live in the big house just outside of town."

"The big house?"

"Yeah, that's what we locals call it. They moved here about a year ago. Her father is some bigwig with an aeronautics firm."

A burly man approached the waitress. "Tess, enough gossiping. You have two customers who still haven't gotten their water."

"I'm on it, boss."

It *was* her! An almost electric jolt charged through Rylee, and her jaw dropped. "What did he just call you?"

"Tess." She shook her curly head. "I'm sorry. I forgot my name tag today." She held out her hand over the counter. "I'm Tessa Blake. If you've moved here, I'm sure we'll see a lot of each other."

Rylee inhaled and took the young woman's hand—Tessa Blake's hand, her grandmother's hand.

"Listen, I work with the teens at Calvary Baptist Church. We have tons of fun, and I'd love for you to join us sometime. Our next get-together is Saturday night at the skating rink—seven o'clock."

Before Rylee could reply, Tess excused herself and made her way to the opposite end of the counter to take an order.

Grandma, you are so adorable.

Rylee pivoted the stool for a better look at her grandmother's competition. Easy to see why Jax would be into her. The gorgeous Sylvia Lockley smiled and chatted as if they'd already shared many hours together, known each other for years, and with a concerning intimacy. Even though he'd break up with her and go out with Tess, seeing him so besotted was unnerving.

Oh, Grandma, how *did you ever break through that*?

Jax must have felt her focus on him, because he suddenly gazed across the diner as if he'd known she'd been staring. Stilling her first instinct to look away, she waved. He lifted his hand, then focused on the brunette.

As she turned back to the counter, she stole a furtive glance at Sylvia, who seemed annoyed at the interruption. Rylee focused once again on her Coke and thought about her lame attempts to attract Liam's attention, only to be ignored. Oh, he'd looked at her many times, but without *seeing* her.

If the timeline on her grandfather's demise was correct, why wasn't he already going out with her grandmother? Shouldn't they be dating by now? What if her arrival had already messed that up? Her insides plummeted. She'd only been here a day and a half. How could she have altered anything?

Since her arrival, she'd contemplated what her being here could do to her future like some time-continuum thing those movies and books always discussed. Would her presence alter events? Lead Jax to marry Sylvia? And had she unwittingly set something else into motion?

She had no idea what any of that meant. But if it was real, then had she already messed up big time? Her heart stopped. If so, her mother would never be born. And neither would she.

* * *

Jax drummed his fingers on the tabletop as Sylvia opened a sugar packet, then emptied the contents into her iced tea.

"She's rather young for you, isn't she?"

Her sharp tone and cynical stare failed to move him.

"It was just a wave, Sylvia."

"So, who is your little darling?" Her sarcasm was an unlovely trait he'd chosen to ignore, but lately, she seemed more and more inclined to use it.

He scooped up her hand. Distraction usually worked its charm. "Jealous?"

She tossed back her wavy brown hair, her scent more cloying this time. "Of that child? Don't be silly."

"She's my mother's guest for a few days."

"One of her pet projects, you mean." She withdrew her hand.

"I guess you could say that." He shrugged. "You know my mother."

"Do I ever." She flicked a fly away from her dress as the waitress approached and set two, blue-plate specials in front of them. Unfortunately, the mouth-watering beef and gravy dish had lost some of its appeal. For the rest of the meal, his attempts to engage Sylvia fell flat, so he gave up. Man, he hated this silent treatment.

As he ate, laughter came from the grill's other side—Rylee and a pretty blonde behind the counter. His little houseguest had a way with people. His mother wasn't the only person she'd charmed.

He glanced over at Sylvia, sulky and toying with her mashed potatoes. Stifling a groan, he attacked a piece of country-fried steak.

After another minute of silence, he set his fork aside. "Sweetheart, how many ways can I say I'm sorry? We'll keep the wedding date as planned. Okay?"

"I'm surprised you're not suggesting we postpone the thing. Your mother's made it quite clear how she feels about us."

"My mother has no say in whom I wed, nor am I worried about what she thinks when it comes to you."

"You still live with her."

He stiffened. Since when had she become so bad-tempered? "How many times do I have to say that arrangement is temporary? Even though my mother's still a young woman, I don't like her living alone on that farm. That said, when we're married, you and I will have a place of our own. But right now, my living there is practical, and if that bothers you, then I'm sorry."

When she refused to look at him, he slid from his seat and stepped around the table to sit beside her. "It's like this." He tilted her chin upward. "If we ever have a son and I'm not around anymore, then I'd expect him to take care of you. All right? Now, quit worrying about my mother. She'll come around once we're married." He took hold of her hands and squeezed them. "She'll have to."

Then he lowered his head to kiss her. Before he claimed her lovely pout, she turned her head sideways, and his lips landed on her cheek.

With a huff, she folded her arms and tipped up her chin, shaking her hair down her back. "And is that another reason for this rushed wedding you've proposed? Hurry and get married so your mother has no choice, but to accept it?"

"It's not. But aren't *we* more important than the time and date of our wedding?" Oops. As soon as the words left his mouth, he knew it had to have been a mistake.

"We've already been over that." Narrowing her eyes, she snatched up her purse to signal her desire to leave.

With a twinge of disappointment, he got up and stepped aside, allowing her to slide from the booth. He stuffed his hands in his pockets and watched her exit Billy's as the Bee Gees's melodious "How Deep Is Your Love" played from the jukebox. Just how deep *was* Sylvia's love? If today's display was an example, then it wasn't near deep enough.

This wasn't the first time she'd withheld her affection because she was miffed. Most instances were due to some silly nonsense, but this—*this*—was a serious matter and not a time for female manipulation. He'd thought her better than this.

Speaking of manipulating little females—Rylee was polishing off a french fry. In four strides, he was standing beside her.

"I see you have an appetite."

Mouth full, she swiveled her seat toward him, chewed, swallowed, then took a long swig of her Coke. "I know. My friends back home tell me I eat like a field hand."

"Well, that explains it."

She rewarded him with her dimpled smile. She was a cute kid, but it wouldn't be long before she, too, would deny some Joe a kiss and break his heart.

"So. You here by yourself?" He knew the answer, but couldn't think of what else to say. He shifted his feet. The adoration in her eyes still made him a bit uncomfortable. Handling a teenage crush was not in his wheelhouse. It was all he could do to manage the merry-go-round called Sylvia.

"Yeah. I explored your farm and somehow ended up here."

"Smelled the french fries, did ya?"

She giggled. "Something like that."

"Since you walked, how about I give you a lift back?"

"I didn't walk. I rode your mother's bike."

"That relic still works?"

"It got me here." She shrugged and pulled out several bills and some loose change.

"My treat." He laid a five-dollar bill on the counter.

"Thanks, but you and your mom have already done so much for me."

"Not to worry."

"At least take the change. It's a pain to carry without a purse."

"All right." He dropped the coins in his pocket. "Let's go."

Once outside, he wedged the old bike inside his trunk. On the drive back, she stared out the window. He'd known her less than forty-eight hours, but something troubled her.

"How was lunch?" he asked.

"Good. Yours?"

"Good."

She traced a finger along the silvery SS embossed above the glove compartment. "Who was that girl you were with?"

"My girlfriend."

"She's *very* pretty."

"That she is."

Her finger stopped moving. Her hand dropping to the roll crank for the window, she shifted in her seat to face him. "Been dating long?"

"Long enough."

"Is it serious?"

"What?" He eyed her. "Are you my mother?"

A rosy hue flooded her cheeks. "Sorry, I'm just curious."

"Is that what you call it?" He flipped on the blinker and turned right.

Her flush deepened even more. "You don't look very happy," she said. "Come to think of it, neither did your girlfriend when she left."

"My mother put you up to this?"

"No."

He gripped the steering wheel. "It's just . . . my mom doesn't like her very much."

"How come?"

A chuckle rumbled through his chest. "What is it with you?"

And those big faux-innocent blue eyes blinked at him. At least, she'd washed the black junk away from them. "What do you mean?"

"Forget it."

CHAPTER 11

Since he was a kid, Jax enjoyed building aircraft models, and the hobby had yet to lose its appeal. The sun had set, and a cool breeze now fluttered the curtains beside him. Outside, cicadas reveled in the coming evening while inside the scent of pot roast drifted all the way from the kitchen. Relaxing into the moment, he held the small plastic fuselage of a P-51D Red Tail in one hand and stroked the fine-tipped paintbrush over it with his other hand. Then he sat back and gazed at his handiwork.

"Hi."

He swiveled in his seat toward Rylee. "Hey."

"You're not out with Sylvia tonight?" She crossed the living room to join him at the table.

A half smile quirked his mouth. This must be what it's like to have an annoying little sister? "That's one of the things I like about you."

"What?"

"You come right to the point. No subtleties with you."

"Mind if I watch?"

"Why watch when you can help?"

Her eyes goggled. "Really?"

"That's another thing I like." He laughed. "It doesn't take much to make you happy."

"Only everything aircraft and flying." She pulled out the chair opposite him and plunked down.

"Here." He set the yellow paint vial, along with the left wing, in front of her. "You'll need a steady hand for this. Just follow the photo on the box."

"Don't you glue the plane together before painting it?"

"Sometimes, but because of its size, it's easier to paint the individual pieces first."

She picked up the brush, then dipped the tip into the paint. "My grandfather . . . he was into airplanes, too."

"So you said." He selected the tail end of the fuselage to inspect his work. "Tell me about him."

"He was a pilot . . . like you."

"Was?" Replacing the fuselage, he scooted his chair closer to the table.

The hand holding the paintbrush shook, but she had the smarts not to let it touch the wing. She braced the tip of the brush back in the paint vial and drew in a deep breath, then seemed to use it to push the words out. "He took off one day and never came back."

He winced. "That had to be tough."

She ducked her head and nodded.

"Were you two close?"

"He disappeared before I was born, but"—that gaze of hers latched onto him again—"he's everything I want to be."

Man, the kid looked at him as if she wanted to make him stay there forever. "I'm sure he'd be very proud of you." He shifted in his chair and scooted it a bit further away from her. "How did it happen?"

"We never knew for certain." She shrugged. "He was on a test flight, and his plane went down over the Atlantic. The air force never found him or his plane. I spent years wondering—asking questions."

"Years, huh? You must have started when you were about *five*." He let another half smile quirk his mouth.

"Well, maybe not years."

"What about your father?"

She picked up the brush again. Her hand steady now as she bent over her work. "He left me and my mom when I was little."

"Sounds like your mom married a real loser."

"My grandmother thought so."

"I can't imagine ever leaving my kid." He swished his brush in water. "You close?"

"He lives overseas." She held the wing near her mouth and blew over the fresh paint. "He's remarried and has another family. You know how it is."

"And most likely the reason your grandfather became a substitute."

"Substitute?"

"You know, father figure."

She rested her forearms on the table. "I grew up hearing all these wonderful stories about him, so that makes sense."

"*And* he never left you."

"At least not on purpose."

Something about the way she said it gave him pause. When he glanced up, she was staring at him in an odd way.

"I should show you—"

"Jaxon," Sylvia called out, interrupting him from the front door.

"Excuse me, Rylee." He gestured to the wet brushes and paint. "Would you mind cleaning some of this up for me?"

She beamed. "Not at all."

* * *

When Jax returned home from an early morning meeting the next day, he found Rylee working on the same model. She seemed so at home here. There had to be a discreet way to find out more about her. She certainly had a thing for aircraft. Maybe he could garner more information through her interest in that.

Folding his arms, he leaned against the doorjamb and watched her, caught up in the task and oblivious to him. When he stepped into the room, she glanced up.

"That's looking great," he said.

"Thanks. I hope you don't mind me continuing. I've never built a model before."

"It can get in your blood for sure." He took a seat opposite and started on the model he'd begun yesterday.

"How was your date with Sylvia?"

When he paused midstroke, Rylee finished swishing her brush in the water cup, then fixed her not-so-innocent gaze on his.

He gnawed the inside of his lip to keep from smiling. Setting his brush aside, he sat back and folded his arms. His invitation for her to continue caused her to flush pink, as he knew it would.

She licked her lips and lowered her gaze. "Sorry."

"No, you're not."

Her head snapped up, and she gulped. "I'm just curious."

"Is that what you call it?" He gave her a mocking smile. "I find your interest in Sylvia quite strange."

"It was a simple question. I was just trying to make conversation."

"If you say so." He focused on the unfinished P-51D Red Tail.

After a bit, he cleaned his brush, then wrapped it in a paper towel. "Come take a ride with me. I'd like to show you something."

Her face lit up like Christmas morning. "Okay." She cleaned her area, then joined him at the door. "Where are we going?"

"You'll see."

When he later swung the Chevy onto a gravel driveway and slowed to a stop, Rylee scooted closer to the windshield, her eyes bright. "Is this some kind of airport?"

"It's a private airstrip." He opened the door and motioned for her to follow.

"I didn't know you had this."

Now *that* was a strange thing to say. He cocked his head at her. "How could you?"

They made their way to the small hanger's entrance.

"I heard you liked airplanes." With a wink, he inserted a key into a large brass lock.

"You know I do."

"Then you'll love this." He moved left. "Grab that side."

Together they pushed open the tall sliding doors.

* * *

Rylee stepped into the warm building as if in slow motion. Her heartbeat seemed to slow, and she reached for the side of the door to steady herself. Parked in front of her was her grandfather's Cessna —*her* Cessna.

"Wow." Heat burned her eyelids. Her breath caught. "It's beautiful."

"She is. I thought you'd enjoy seeing an actual aircraft instead of the models."

"You thought right." Still clinging to the door for support with her legs wobbly, she ran her gaze over the glossy paint. "It looks brand new."

"That's because she is. Well, new to me, anyway. It belongs to a friend of mine." He moved forward. "She's Dolly, a one—"

"Seventy-two Cessna," she finished. Dolly. The word wove in and around her heart, and she blinked back the heat rising to her eyes. Of course, Jaxon Scott had named his baby.

"Man, you do know your aircraft."

Somehow, she pried her grip loose from the door and managed to enter the building fully. Her steps shuffled across the concrete floor, the scent of old wood and hot tires drawing her in. He ran a hand along the right wing, around the tip, then down the side of the fuselage. Much like she did when her grandmother surprised her with it. Then he stepped back and surveyed the body.

Breathe. She had to remember to breathe. But a moment like this—suspended in time, *literally*—made it hard to believe she even needed air.

Enthralled, she hugged her arms across her chest. The light in his eyes said it all. Her spirit soared. Man, she identified with Jaxon Scott! Each moment here, she fell more in love with him—the *real* Jaxon Scott, not a phantom she'd heard stories about.

"Well, what do you think?" he asked.

"She's sweet."

"Sweet, huh?" He nodded. "I like that."

Then he cocked his head toward her, and his lips quirked in the half smile she was coming to know. "You want to get in?"

Ooooh! The air she'd fought into her lungs slid out in a rush. "Can I?"

"After you." He waved toward the plane. "I'll join you in a sec."

She scrambled in, gripped the yoke, and breathed in the scent of eucalyptus and leather. Closing her eyes, she savored the moment. When she opened them, half afraid, half hopeful this was all a dream, and after her excitement died down, she noticed the compass dial. While he checked the prop, she slipped her phone from her pocket, but before she could turn it on and snap the picture, he'd returned.

"Finished. Ready?"

As she hid the phone from his line of sight, he rested his hand on the side of the pilot's seat. "Is it everything you thought it would be?"

"More." The word gushed from somewhere deep inside her.

"Maybe I'll take you up in a day or so."

She nearly choked trying to hold in a gasp. "Seriously?"

"I'm always serious when it comes to flying. I wouldn't suggest it if I didn't mean it."

"But why? You don't even know me."

"I know you love planes, and that's enough for me."

"You're allowed to fly it?"

"I'd better be." He patted the dashboard. "She's almost mine. I'm making payments on her. I only have one left."

Jaxon Scott was incredible, and he was *her* grandfather. "Then yes, I'd love to go up sometime."

"You remind me of me," he said. "I was twelve the first time I got to fly, and crop-dusting by the time I was—"

"Thirteen."

His head jerked up, and his hand slid from the dashboard as he gawked. "How did you know that?"

"Um, Doris mentioned it?"

"Anyway, I swear I was airborne before the plane left the ground."

"I know the feeling."

As she ran her hand along the dashboard, he climbed in beside her and began telling her about the different instruments on the control panel. She knew what all of them were for, but she let him talk. Hearing him go over the key ones was heaven. If only she could document this moment with her iPhone—document *him* this very second—so she could remember this and him forever.

She tore her gaze away from his profile and focused on one particular instrument. She pointed to the dial. "This is different."

"It's an invention of mine. I'm not sure it works, yet."

Oh, it works.

"What's it for?"

"I'm afraid that's top secret."

"Come on. You can tell me."

He slanted her a sideways look. "You're persistent. I'll say that for you."

Although the peculiar light in his eyes warned her to be careful, she couldn't resist one more push. She gave him the most innocent look she could muster. "Please?"

"Careful or you'll have me thinking you work for one of our competitors to Lockley Aeronautics."

Although he'd said it in a teasing manner, she got the impression he was serious.

"Lockley Aeronautics. As in Sylvia Lockley?"

"That's the one," he said.

She gazed at the special instrument—he hadn't touched it once during his little talk. But it had to be the link, the connection to how she'd traveled through time.

Tears rushed to her eyes. His attention to detail, his confidence, his expertise—it was all on display with every precise flip of a switch and verbal explanation. Each step in the process was second nature, not a single pause or hesitation.

Jaxon Scott was everything she'd imagined and more. And somehow, a cosmic event had brought her to the past and to him. How could this bigger-than-life person simply disappear? She fisted her hands and tightened her jaw. This could not happen. Why else had she been sent here if not to save him?

She was the connection, the link between the past and the future. Whatever she had to do, she'd have to do it quickly. Time was not on her side.

"Are you crying?"

She shook her head and grinned. "Tears of joy."

His pager went off as he reached for the door handle. "Looks like there's trouble in River City."

"Where?"

He winked. "It means something needs my attention and I have to make a call." They exited the aircraft, and she stayed with the plane as he hurried over to the wall phone. Once he'd hung up, he made his way back to her side. "Sorry to cut this short."

"That's okay. It was wonderful sitting in the Cessna. . . ." *Next to you.*

At the hanger doors, they each took a side and pushed. Once done, he locked the massive panels.

"Next time we'll go up."

Would she be here long enough for a next time? "I'd love that."

They walked side by side, then separated at the car. As she got in, she thought about the special dial. He'd installed it. If only he trusted her enough to give her the details.

He'd sidestepped her questions, practically accusing her of spying. In the next day or so, she'd have to figure out a way to get back inside and take some pictures. She'd have to watch where he kept his keys.

CHAPTER 12

Jax slipped the key into the ignition and revved the Chevy to life. As he put the car in drive, he contemplated the girl's identity. She'd approached his aircraft with reverence—her eyes bright with anticipation—running her hand along the fuselage and drinking in Dolly's clean lines like an old friend. Who was this minx who gazed at his airplane with such wonder?

In the cockpit, she showed no signs of covert behavior. If she were a plant or a spy, she'd know the Anomaly Detection Device would be somewhere within reach. He'd run through the panel check in an effort to reveal anything unusual about her presence here. Her persistence to learn about the device seemed innocent enough, more from her love of aircraft than espionage. She was much more enamored with the aircraft itself—and *him*—than the controls.

But Rick couldn't find any information on Rylee—anywhere. She didn't exist in any database he had access to.

Jax eyed her profile. She'd pulled her dark hair into a ponytail and wore little makeup. Not that her young peaches-and-cream complexion needed any. She sat in the passenger seat in her blue jeans and a white cotton top, gazing ahead with a slight smile—almost dreamlike.

This wasn't the first time he'd studied her. He'd noticed her coloring the night he'd met her, but without her makeup, she could be his younger sister or even his daughter. His stomach tightened as his mind raced through the math. Eight years. He breathed a sigh. On impulse, he slowed the car and stopped on the roadside bordering the farm.

"Are you dropping me off?"

Filling his lungs with a deep breath scented with a summer-grass and warm-earth smell, he twisted his grip on the steering wheel. "I want to speak with you."

She turned eager, curious eyes toward him.

"Have you tried calling your parents again?"

She bit her lip and ducked her head.

"That's a yes or no question. It requires a yes or no answer."

She fingered the edge of her blouse. "No."

He rested one hand on the steering wheel and shook his head. "So, what . . .? You're planning on staying indefinitely?"

She squirmed in her seat, swallowed, and licked her lips. "Of course not."

"Don't lie to me."

Her head jerked up. "I'm not lying to you."

"Who are your parents?"

"David and Felicity Dean."

"Where do they live?"

She glanced down and to the right. "Right now, nowhere."

He sat back and drew in a steadying breath. Whenever she told one of her half-truths, she wouldn't make eye contact.

She lifted her gaze to his. "Something happened, and I don't know why or even how. It's complicated. You wouldn't believe me if I told you." She wrung her hands. "In fact, you'd have me locked up."

He shot her a penetrating look. "So, what . . .? You're telling me I've brought a crazy person home to Mom?" His grip tightened on the steering wheel. He loosened it and flexed his forearms, then tried for another deep calming breath. "You're not helping yourself here. All I'm asking for is a straight answer."

"I know."

He wanted to give her a chance to explain, but her cryptic responses brought more questions than answers. "So, what are you saying—exactly?"

She stared at him with wide, appealing eyes. "The only way I can say this is, well, right now—*today*—they're not alive."

His heart squeezed. He put the Chevy in drive and turned left onto the gravel road to the farm. He parked outside the house and faced her, one arm on the seat backs, one hand on the dashboard. "Are you telling me you're an orphan?"

Those large blue eyes peered out the side window, their reflection on the glass facing him. "Basically."

"Basically?" He pressed his lips together. "What kind of an answer is that? You either are or aren't."

"I've already told you I can't explain it. I just know." She bit her lip.

He ran a hand over his hair. This was getting weirder and weirder. "Your answers are starting to annoy me."

It wasn't unusual for one competitor to infiltrate another to gain their company secrets. But it was unlikely they'd stoop to using a teenage girl. Still, his suspicion seemed more plausible by the second. What better way to ingratiate oneself into the home of a kind elderly woman, known for her hospitality to the less fortunate, than with an adorable orphan needing shelter? The temptation to haul her to Child Services and put an end to the charade grew, but if she were simply a lost and confused girl, his mother would never forgive him.

"Does my mother know?"

"No."

"What are you two doing sitting out in the car on such a hot afternoon?" Doris waved from the side porch. "Come inside for some cold lemonade."

"Saved by the proverbial bell." Jax reached for the door handle. "This conversation is not over."

Rylee didn't look back, but scrambled from the passenger seat, then up the steps.

* * *

Jax took a seat on the screened porch as Doris set a tray of lemonade and warm cookies on the wicker coffee table. Rylee drug over a chair, bouncing it across the plank floor, before dropping into it with a sigh.

"Miss Doris, do you mind if I go to the skating rink tomorrow night? A girl who works at the Baptist church invited me."

"Of course you can go. Who is it? Maybe I know her."

"Tessa Blake."

"I do know her. She works at Billy's—such a sweet girl."

"She is, isn't she?"

"The kind of girl I always wanted for you." His mom patted his knee.

"Don't start, Mom."

She cast a conspiratorial glance at him, then focused on Rylee. "I have a bridge game tomorrow evening, so how about I drop you off on the way?"

"That'd be great." Rylee raised the lemonade glass to her lips.

She hadn't looked at him since they'd sat down. He could sense her mounting anxiety. If she thought her chatter about this Tessa person and her evening out would keep him from addressing their earlier conversation, she was in for a surprise.

To move things along, he asked. "Well, are you going to tell her or am I?"

Rylee's eyes widened, and she gulped another sip.

"Tell me what?" The Dragon reared her head.

"Our little guest has been holding out on us—leading us to think she'd be returning home soon."

His mom's eyes narrowed. "What's he talking about?"

Rylee set the glass down and licked her lips. She darted an anxious glance in his direction. "I'm an orphan."

He folded his arms across his chest. "Keep going."

She swallowed. "And . . . I've been misleading you, letting you think my parents would be coming to get me soon."

The Dragon stalked closer, stopping in front of Rylee. "Why would you lie?"

"I don't want to be put in some institution." She dipped her chin and rubbed at the goose bumps puckering her bare arms.

"I don't hold with lying, young lady. It's not something I tolerate in my house." His mother crouched before Rylee. "And you've done more than your fair share of it around here, but I can understand you being afraid. We need to know the truth, but don't you fret. If you are an orphan, no one here"—she glared at him—"is going to put you in an institution."

Then she pushed to her feet, dropped into her chair, and fumbled with something on the table. "Rylee, I forgot the napkins. Would you get them for me?"

Grabbing her chair arms, Rylee sat up straighter and eyed them both before pushing to her feet. "Of course."

"They're in the top drawer, underneath the counter, next to the fridge."

Once Rylee was out of earshot, Jax shifted in his seat. "Mother, you have a heart of gold, but this child is not a stray cat. You cannot keep her."

She folded her hands over his left one. "I know. Let the child stay while you're on your next test flight or whatever it is you do for the air force and that aeronautics firm. When you return, we'll decide what's to be done with her. In the meantime, she stays with me. I'll call Pat this afternoon and see about getting temporary custody of her. All right?"

"We know nothing about her."

"She's a darling."

"She's been lying to us."

"And she's just told us why."

Of all the . . . His mom was an intelligent woman. He'd never imagined her to defy logic like this. Didn't she understand how much trouble they could get in harboring a runaway or whatever Rylee might be? "Fine." He eased his hand free. "But be warned, something's not right about this whole thing."

He left his mother and Rylee to a second cookie while he dialed headquarters from the living room. "Rick, anything from the database on Rylee?"

"Well, if it isn't the man with the kind eyes."

"Very funny."

A deep chuckle rumbled from the receiver. "Sorry, I couldn't resist."

"I'm sure you couldn't." Rubbing the back of his neck, Jax sank onto the floral couch. At least Mom only had one cat now, so he didn't have to check the seat before he sat. Still, the overly feminine cushion made him squirmy.

"I was just getting ready to call you," Rick said.

Jax sat up straighter. "And?"

"There's absolutely nothing on a Rylee Dean."

"What about the police department?"

"They found nothing."

He sprang to his feet and paced to the planes on the table. "Not even school records?"

"Nope. Nada."

"Birth records?" He picked up the one she had painted. Perfect precise strokes, done with the love he would have.

"There's no one with her age or description. It's as if she doesn't exist."

He nearly dropped the P-51D Red Tail. "That's impossible."

"Tell me something I don't already know."

After tucking the plane safely back in its place, he stood there, ear to the receiver, contemplating his next words.

"Maybe she's a ghost," Rick said.

"That's ridiculous. There's no such thing." So she'd lied about her name too.

"Not that kind." Rick let out a low whistle. "I'm thinking a plant—a spy."

That had occurred to him. "But she's sixteen—way too young."

"What if she's not? Two days ago, Buck, Simpson, and half the men at your party thought she was a stripper."

Jax groaned. "Don't remind me."

"Point is she looks older than sixteen. Maybe she is."

"Or maybe she *is* sixteen and related to one of our competitors and using a fake name." He rubbed his neck again, the tension there getting tighter by the moment. "Think about it. How else would she know my name and where to find me?"

"The same way an older spy would." Rick cleared his throat. "Listen, we're on high alert regarding this project. The last thing we need is a wrench—or wench—in the works. If you're concerned about this girl, then call Child Services, and that'll be that."

"Tempting, but no." Rylee had begged him and his mom not to call them. Sixteen or not, she'd been terrified. Her terror was that of a child. She was sixteen all right—*that* she hadn't lied about. But everything else?

Laughter vibrated from the porch. Hard to tell if it was the Dragon's or the spy's. Eerie how alike they sounded. He couldn't send her away until he figured this out. "If she's a plant, it's important to keep her close. Add the names David and Felicity Dean to your search. See if there's any info on either of them, including death certificates."

"By the way, I checked the anomaly on your property this morning. It's moved about six degrees."

"That's normal." He moved toward the window, but he wouldn't be able to see the porch from here. "Just keep a record of the changes. Anything else?"

"That's it for now."

He replaced the receiver in its cradle. So Rylee Dean didn't exist. Maybe expanding the search to her parents would lead to some answers—*if* they really were her parents. How could he make the kid give her real name?

Her presence might seem harmless. But as he dug deeper, her arrival and knowledge made no sense— *unless* she'd been sent here for a purpose. And if so, by whom?

Her adoration seemed real enough. Obviously, he was important to her. But why? What was he to her? Something didn't add up, but he couldn't believe her entry into his life was for anything devious. Quite the opposite, in fact. And just when he'd thought her being here was benign, she'd evade a simple question or look at him in an odd way, and he'd have to re-think the situation.

Whoever she was, this project was too important to be scrubbed. The anomaly was now moving. He needed answers—and soon.

CHAPTER 13

Rylee finished lacing up her skates and stood. The soft clatter of roller skates echoed off the hardwood floor, laughter reverberated off the high ceiling, and the scent of french fries and onion rings floated with some upbeat music she should have recognized. A food court spanned one end of the oval arena and an arcade the other. Not a bad way to spend a Saturday night.

She hadn't skated since she was eight. If she could pull this off without humiliating herself, she'd be thrilled. But the wobbly sensation beneath her feet had her rethinking her decision to come. Still, if her young grandmother was hanging out here, then here, she needed to be. So where was Tessa? There! Skating alongside two girls Rylee's age.

Here goes. With the wooden bench behind her, Rylee lifted one foot then the other and slid the few feet to the metal railing on her right. She spent the next song skating near the rail. Once she got comfortable, she pushed off, and her feet flew out from underneath her.

She sucked in a breath and groped for the side rail. Ugh. She'd gotten too far away to reach it. Arms flailing and eyes squeezing shut, she waited for the inevitable. But as her skated feet flew into the air, strong arms crushed her to an equally strong chest.

"I've got you."

Air rushed from her lungs at his continued grip on her midsection. The voice belonging to the arms was wonderfully male, and Rylee felt herself go weak. Heart pounding, she glanced upward into a familiar face.

Liam?

With his arms around her, the brown-eyed teenager held her inches from the floor. "Are you okay?"

Pressing a hand to her chest, she tried to catch her breath. Seeing Liam's look-alike surprised her more than the fall.

"I should thank you for saving me from total humiliation," she said as he helped her to an upright position. Wobbling on wheels, she pushed her hair away from her face. As she turned toward him, the skates slid. She squealed and flung her arms around his neck. Their gazes locked, and for an excruciating moment, she simply hung there. Plastered against his firm chest, she couldn't possibly keep her heart steady. That he smelled wonderful didn't help. When he stared down at her with a growing sparkle in his eyes, she found it difficult to swallow. "On second thought, ma–maybe I spoke too s–soon," she stammered.

The sparkle flared into a glow, and the corners of his perfect mouth tilted up. "It was all in the timing. Think nothing of it."

"Huh?"

"I just happened to be behind you when you slipped."

"Oh, right." She loosened her hold while trying to steady her wobbly legs. Making an additional fool of herself was imminently close as her legs refused to right themselves. She gripped his shoulders while her mind groped for a solution that wouldn't add to her current predicament.

As if he could read her thoughts, he asked, "Would you like some help to the railing?"

"Would you?" She knew her eyes pleaded, but if she fell into his arms again, she'd kill herself.

"Of course." He wrapped an arm around her waist and pulled her to his side. "Take my arm." Steadying her, he assisted her to the side rail. "You must be new in town."

"I'm . . . visiting."

As he led her to safety, she peeped at his profile, further unbalanced by the uncanny resemblance to Liam of 2021—the chiseled nose, the honey-brown eyes, the wavy hair falling adorably over his left eye.

Chill out. This is not your Liam.

She almost snorted. As if she had a Liam to start with.

As they reached the side bar, Tessa and the two teenagers swooped up beside them.

"Hey, Rylee. I see you made it," Tessa said. "This is Patricia and Connie. Pat, Connie, this is Rylee."

"Hi," they said in unison.

"And I see you've already met Liam."

Liam? The guy's name was also Liam? Rylee nodded, not trusting herself to speak coherently, then managed a shaky response. "Yes, we, uh, bumped into each other."

"We saw." Patricia laughed good-naturedly.

"It was nice meeting you, Rylee." Liam's smile sent her pulse racing. Then he gave the group a little wave. "See you guys later."

His easygoing manner was so much like Liam 2021, except *this* Liam had paid attention to her. Granted, she'd about knocked him over. But still, being in his arms was a heady experience. She watched him skate across the rink until Connie spoke.

"If you only knew how many girls would love to have been in your place just now," Connie said.

"What do you mean?"

The girl grinned. "You literally fell into Liam's arms."

"Leave it to the new girl to do just that," Patricia added. "Lucky, lucky you."

"Oh no. That's not really, I mean—"

"Love your hair, by the way." Connie skated closer. "Is that wave natural?"

"Yeah." Rylee touched her head.

Connie gave her own hair a fluff. "Both Patricia and I have to perm ours."

She'd noticed. Crazy hair. And it didn't stop there. Both wore loose-fitting jeans belted at their waists. Not a bad look, really, and nothing like the leggings Rylee often wore.

"And I like your jeans," she said. "They look super comfortable."

"They are," Patricia said.

"Can you even breathe in yours? Oh, there's Mick. Gotta run. Nice meeting you." Connie pushed herself forward and disappeared through the crowd.

"Just so you know, Connie wasn't just teasing about Liam. I don't know one girl at Harpeth High who hasn't been mad for him at one time or another. Connie included." Patricia arched a brow at Tessa. "I'm sure Tessa can relate, being twenty-two and all, and bonkers about . . . you-know-who."

Tessa gave Patricia a playful slap on the arm. "Hush! Don't be giving my secrets away. What'll Rylee think?"

"Rylee doesn't need to think," Rylee chimed in. "Rylee witnessed your display of adoration at Billy's Dairy Dip, remember?"

While girls laughed, Tessa rolled her eyes.

"Oh, my mom's here," Patricia said. "I've gotta run. See you guys. Nice meeting you, Rylee."

"Same."

After Patricia left, Tessa glided over to the bench and sat. While Rylee followed and perched beside her, Tessa reached forward and began to unlace her right skate. "Was I so obvious?"

"At the Dip?" Rylee couldn't help it. She rolled her eyes.

Tessa rolled hers back. "Oh brother. Please tell me *he* didn't notice?"

"I doubt it." Rylee deflated, bracing an elbow on her knee and plunking her chin into her upraised hand. "He was way too busy drooling over that Sylvia person."

"Jaxon was the Liam of my high school years," Tessa said. "Two years older and the most gorgeous thing I ever saw. He had a thing for airplanes—still does. I heard he flew the most dangerous missions while in the air force."

"Is he still in the air force?"

"I'm not sure, but he does *something* for them or is connected in some way. Subcontracts with them or something." She shook her head, sending those Farrah Fawcett locks dancing. "Look at me prattling on like I know stuff."

They sat in silence unlacing their skates.

"What do you think he does with the air force?" Rylee asked.

Tessa shrugged. "From what I hear it's hush-hush and definitely military." She glanced right, then left. "But if anyone asks, you didn't hear it from me."

"Do you know this Sylvia Lockley person?"

"Not personally, although most everyone in town knows everyone else in one way or another."

Tessa yanked off the left boot and sat up straighter. "I'm so glad you came tonight. Did you have a good time?"

"Yeah, it was fun."

"Where do you live?"

"Um, I'm staying with . . . the Scotts."

"What?" Tessa's face went white, and she wobbled like Rylee wobbled on her skates. "And you let me babble on about him?"

"I'm sorry. I wasn't thinking—"

"I'm the one who's sorry." Tessa shot to her feet. "I had no idea you knew him or his mother."

"I hardly know them. The sheriff placed me with Miss Doris until I can get home."

"Oh." She pushed her hand to her chest, wrinkling up the shiny fabric. "I didn't realize. Are you an orphan?"

"My situation is complicated. My mom and I don't get along, and I . . . well . . ." Rylee shrugged, lifting her hands.

"I understand." Tessa snagged one of Rylee's hands and squeezed it. "No need to explain further."

"Thank you." Just how long could she go on telling half-truths? To her young grandparents no less!

An hour later, she hitched a ride to the Dip with Tessa. It was only a few blocks away and hardly enough time to have a meaningful conversation. Just thinking the word *grandmother* about this pretty blonde behind the wheel did not compute.

As she talked, Rylee tried to spot any resemblance to the sixty-two-year-old Tessa. The nuances of familiarity were there in her sudden smile and the tilt of her head when she focused on you. When Tessa mentioned her love of baking, Rylee couldn't resist saying, "My grandmother makes the best peach turnovers."

"I make them, too, but I can't figure out why the crust is so bland?"

"Um, have you tried adding mace to the dough?"

"The spice?"

"Yeah, after my grandmother put it in her pastries, she won the county fair four years in a row."

"I'll have to try that."

"Tell me about your family—your parents," Rylee said.

"My mom's the absolute best, always encouraging me to trust my instincts and follow my heart. There's a bit of a wandering spirit in her. My dad, well, he's just the opposite. 'Dreams are fine, but just remember they won't pay the bills.' " She wagged a finger and mimicked a man's grouchy voice.

"So he's the practical side of the family. Opposites attract."

"They're opposites, all right."

"And you wouldn't have it any other way."

Tessa gave Rylee a sidelong glance. "You're absolutely right. My parents are great." She turned the left into Billy's parking lot.

"I'd love to meet them."

"Sure thing."

Rylee spotted Jaxon and Sylvia as she and Tessa pushed through the glass doors. From Tessa's dazed-in-the-headlights look, she noticed them, too. The gorgeous Sylvia flicked her hands in the air as she chatted. The flirtatious goings-on didn't bode well for her grandmother's chances.

"Let's grab those two seats at the counter," Tessa said.

Poor Tess, if only Rylee could say something to encourage her. "Sylvia's in her element tonight."

"I noticed." Tessa huffed. "But no gawking from you, okay?"

Rylee smothered a laugh.

"What's so funny?"

"When I first met you, that's what you were doing —gawking."

Red highlighted Tessa's pale apple-round cheeks. "I . . . no, I was not. I was *swooning!*"

The burly man from her first visit set a water glass before each of them. "Hey, Tess, enjoying your night off?"

"That I am, boss." She hoisted the glass in a salute.

He slapped the weekly flyer down in front of her.

Her smile faded. "Don't tell me. I did it again?"

"How many times do I have to remind you to stop writing dates—"

"Like the English do?" Tessa finished his sentence.

He glanced at Rylee. "The English write their dates backward."

"Not according to the English." Tessa wagged a finger, reminding Rylee of Grandma again.

"They also drive on the wrong side of the road."

"Touché." She slapped the countertop. "Billy, this is Rylee. Rylee—Billy. He owns the place."

"Hey, Billy."

"What'll it be, ladies?"

"Large iced tea, hamburger, and fries," Tessa said. "And hold the onions."

"And I'll have a grilled cheese with fries and a Coke."

"So, that's Billy," Rylee said as he walked away. "I can't believe I'm meeting the famous Billy."

"Famous?" Tessa grinned. "What planet are you from?"

Oops. Still, Rylee couldn't help but add, "You wouldn't believe the stories I've heard about the people in this town."

"That's hard to believe, but I'll take your word for it." Tessa's sweet chuckle hadn't changed over the years. Rylee's heart squeezed at the familiarity. She gazed at her young grandmother—her perfect, youthful complexion and her sparkling eyes touched Rylee deeply. What a gift to be sitting next to her, seeing her as a young woman with her whole life in front of her. Rylee better not have messed it up by showing up here.

"Hey, what's wrong?" Tessa nudged her with an elbow. "Your eyes are all misty."

Rylee blinked and waved a hand. "It's nothing—just allergies. So how do the English write their dates?"

"They put the day first, then the month, then the year. And we write the month first, then the day followed by the year."

"Cool. I didn't realize that."

Their small talk continued until Billy set their meals in front of them.

"Hey, Tess, Karen went home sick, and I could use your help tonight," Billy said. "Any chance you could finish her shift?"

"Of course. I hope it's nothing serious."

"Sore throat. Don't rush through dinner, and thanks."

Tessa shoved a fry into her mouth and swiveled on her barstool. Each time she did, she darted a glance at Jaxon and Sylvia in the corner booth.

Rylee leaned in and whispered, "You know, if you change places with me, you can get a much better view."

Tessa groaned and positioned her seat forward. "I can't seem to help it. I hope he hasn't noticed."

"You're crazy about him, aren't you?"

"Pathetic, I know."

"Nothing pathetic about love. Why don't you do something about it instead of mooning over him?"

"Are you kidding? Look at him—he's smitten. Besides, I missed my chance." She twirled a fry on the edge of her plate.

"What do you mean?"

"Wednesday night, he was scheduled to be one of the chaperones for the student lock-in at the church, and he canceled last minute."

Lock-in. Doris mentioned that two nights ago.

"What's a lock-in?"

"The kids in the youth group stay up all night in the gym. It's tons of fun. There's skating, basketball—we even have two bowling lanes upstairs. And we set up all-night movies in a classroom with popcorn and the works."

Rylee's heart stopped. *That* was the night she'd showed up. And Jax canceled because he had to deal with her. That's when he should have met and gotten to know Tess. *That* was their moment in time, and *she* messed it up!

"You okay? You don't look so good."

Rylee fanned her face with her hand. "I feel a little sick."

"Hope you're not getting Karen's sore throat."

"It's nothing. I'll be all right."

"If you're sure you're okay, I need to get going. Billy keeps eyeing me."

"I'm fine, I promise. You go on."

Tessa excused herself and untangled her apron from a hook behind the counter. "Will you be able to get home all right?" she asked as she tied the pink fabric at her waist. "If not—"

"I'll ask Jax to take me back. If he can't, I'll call Doris."

Tessa nodded and approached a customer at the far end.

Rylee slid a fry between her lips and eyed Jax and Sylvia. Frowning, she munched on the crisped potato. She would have to break those two up—starting right now.

Without another thought, she jumped off the stool and walked to their table.

The man in question stopped talking to Sylvia and turned a somewhat irate glance in her direction.

"Hi." Okay, that wave was a bit more animation than necessary, but the mute regard on his face boded ill for her intrusion.

She should go back to her seat—really, she should. But time was not on her side, so she continued to hover, hoping he'd say something. When it looked like he was more stubborn than she was, she focused on Sylvia.

"It seems our Jaxon has forgotten his manners. I'm Rylee. I'm staying with the Scotts for a few days. I came over to say hi to Jax and to meet his friend."

Sylvia darted a questioning glance in Jaxon's direction. "I'm Sylvia. Nice to meet you."

"And you."

Jax, eyeing her with amused intolerance, grumbled, "Sylvia and I are on a date. You know, where two people would like to be *alone*?"

His emphasis on the word *alone* said get lost. Although tempted to stand there longer, she couldn't ignore the message in his eyes. Fine, she'd have to dismantle their relationship piece by piece, anyway.

"Right. I'm sorry." She shot them both a bright smile. "I'll go back to my grilled cheese." She turned slightly, then stopped. "One more thing. I'm going to need a ride home. Bye."

She spun on her heels and hurried back to the counter. Once seated, she brought the straw to her lips and sucked.

An eternity passed before they finished their meal. But eventually, Jax walked Sylvia out of the restaurant. So much for her ride home. She'd have to call Doris after all. Rylee rummaged through her pocket for a ten-dollar bill and placed it next to her empty plate.

"You finished?" Jax took the seat next to hers.

Rylee jumped. "Just about." She hadn't realized he'd come back in. "I saw you leave. I thought you'd forgotten about me."

"Hardly. So what was all that storming the castle about?"

"What castle?"

"Appearing at our table?" He drummed his hands on the countertop, rocking the stool a bit. "Couldn't you see I was *busy*?"

"Oh, yeah, that. I don't like her."

He barked a laugh. "You've just met."

"And what I met—I don't like."

"So, the kitten has claws. I thought you were nice."

"I am nice. And speaking of nice, that's who you should want—someone nice."

"There you go again, sounding just like my mother."

She swiveled in her seat. "Take that waitress at the other end of the counter, Tess. She's very nice. You should sit in her section sometime and get to know her."

"When I need advice with my love life, I'll ask. Until then—"

"How come your mother doesn't like Sylvia?" Rylee hopped off the stool and followed him to the entrance. "You never did say."

As he held the door for her to go through, he groaned. "That's in the none-of-your-business category."

CHAPTER 14

Jax didn't often work on Saturdays, but due to the anomaly's movement, he and Rick and a small crew spent the entire day working on the patent. He'd taken a break to go out for dinner with Sylvia. But once he brought Rylee home, he'd headed straight back to the base. When he got home later, his mom and Rylee had already retired for the evening.

As he lay in bed, he stared at the ceiling, finding it difficult to sleep. He usually blamed a sleepless night on Sylvia, but not this time. Over the past year, the project had become more than a moneymaking endeavor. Everything he'd discovered about Earth's anomalies had refocused their research toward national security.

He turned to his side, punched the edge of his pillow, and blew out a breath. But the project wasn't the only thing keeping him up. What was with Rylee Dean—*if* Rylee Dean she be? She'd lied about other things, so maybe she'd lied about that, too.

She had to be lying about her name. Otherwise, how could a living, breathing young woman not exist when she plainly did? *Who* was this girl who from day one displayed a comfort level in and around the house as if she'd been there before? Not once had she asked where anything was. She just knew. Her presence irritated Sylvia and caused more questions than answers.

He pressed his fingers to his forehead. It was no use. He threw off the covers and padded to the kitchen. When he flipped on the light, Redo popped her head up, then eyed him with unblinking, watchful green slits, before retucking her nose into her shoulder.

He crossed the wide plank floor to the freezer and settled on ice cream. Hearing a noise, he closed the door and turned.

And there she is.

"Sorry, I didn't know anyone else was up," Rylee said.

"I'm a bit of a night owl, myself." He gestured with the ice cream bucket. "Hungry?"

Scuffling her feet where she stood, she hugged her arms around herself. Was that a nod or a head-shake? Had to be a nod.

"Ice cream all right?"

"Perfect." She plunked down at the table, picking the chair she always picked as if it had been hers all her life, while he grabbed another spoon and bowl.

"You seem to have settled in rather quickly."

"Oh yes. The house is inviting and your mother so welcoming."

"So, why can't you sleep?"

"I have a lot on my mind."

"You, too, huh?" He finished scooping and pushed her bowl across the table. "Here you go."

She slid the spoon into the pink creamy goodness and lifted it to her mouth. "Mmm, strawberry. My favorite."

"Mine, too."

Those deep blue eyes so mirroring his own widened. As something secretive curved her lips, an adoring twinkle lit their depths. "Something else we have in common."

"Something else?"

"Strawberry ice cream *and* aircraft."

He planted his elbows on the table. "That seems important to you."

"What do you mean?" She scooped a large bite and flattened her lips together, pouting at the scoop midair.

"Look, if you're going to be staying here a while, this . . . *thing* you seem to have for me . . . needs to go back a notch."

"What thing?" She licked her lips and dipped another spoonful.

"Some might call it a crush."

Her eyes grew to the ice cream bowl's size. Her face flushed a pretty pink, almost matching the strawberry cream. "Is that what you think?"

He gave a slight smile.

"I . . . I don't have a crush."

Yeah right. He rested his chin in his right hand and arched a brow. "Really?"

"No, it's much more."

Whoa. He blinked and sat back.

"What I feel for you is love and admiration."

Her declaration was so sincere—so matter of fact —as if what she'd said made all the sense in the world.

"I've traveled a long way to see you."

"Then your coming here was deliberate?"

She shook her head. "More like an accident."

He gaped at her. Now, what was a guy supposed to make of *that*? "Where did you come from?" He shoved a heaping spoonful between his lips.

She latched him with a long and thoughtful stare. "Across time."

Of all the giddy comments! "Now see"—he shook his spoon in the air—"that comment has all the elements of romance. Isn't that the same thing as a crush?"

She tilted her head to one side as though pondering his question.

"Back home, there's this guy. . . . I have a crush on him, but what I feel for him is nothing like what I feel for you."

Her frank forthrightness was adorable, and somehow, her words touched him deeply. "Well, thank you."

"You're welcome."

She put all of her attention on the sweet dish. He'd embarrassed her and shouldn't have. He focused on his own melty bowl. "So, what's on your mind, Kitten, that keeps you from sleep?"

She kept her eyes lowered and spooned another bite. "I don't know, just stuff."

"Stuff, huh?"

A half nod, half headshake somehow rolled her head. "It's all so confusing."

Hadn't she used that word in his car? He shoved his ice cream bowl aside, braced his forearms on the table, and leaned on them. "Maybe I can help."

She scowled at the soupy stuff left in her bowl. "There are things I want to say—*need* to say—and I'm trying to make sense of it all. But I can't quite find the right words."

Such seriousness squinched up her young face.

"Because it's confusing."

"Exactly."

"I'm sorry if I embarrassed you."

"Oh." She waved her spoon. "No worries. I'm sure it's strange having me here. It's strange for me, too—more than you can imagine."

He tugged his bowl back again and spooned another portion into his mouth, savoring the strawberry essence. "I'll admit . . . your entrance into my life does seem unusual."

"May I ask you something?"

He couldn't help but laugh inside, given all the questions she'd bombarded him with these last days. "Of course."

"If you could go back in time to save someone's life, would you do it?"

"Wow." He sat back. "That's some question."

"It's loaded, I know. But would you?" Strawberry ice cream dripping off her spoon, she held him with an intense stare.

"First of all, it would depend on who I was supposed to save. I imagine there would be great risk in traveling through time. I'd have to weigh those risks."

"And if the person were worth the risks?"

"Then yes . . . yes, I would."

She breathed out, seeming inordinately pleased.

"I take it that was the correct answer?"

Nodding, she used her finger to lick up the ice cream dribbles she'd let hit the table.

"And you?" he said. "Would you travel through time to save someone's life?"

"Most definitely."

He gave her his forthright stare. "That didn't take you long."

She shrugged. "I've already . . . given it some thought." She finished off her ice cream, then pushed the bowl aside.

"I see," he said.

"So." She folded her hands, somewhat like his mother would do, and rested them on the table. "What's keeping *you* up?"

"Things you wouldn't understand."

"Things about your work?"

It was his turn to nod. "I'm a subcontractor of sorts. I work with an aeronautics company and the air force. I guess you could call me the middleman. Sometimes the work's . . . complicated."

"And dangerous?" She breathed the question with a low, stealthy inflection like they do in the movies—as if she were playing a part. Her intense blue-eyed gaze stared right through him. Was she trying to communicate something to him?

He paused, spoon midair. Her comment wasn't a question, but a statement—as if she knew. How could a sixteen-year-old know about his work? As to any danger . . . "There're always risks in flight." He shoved his chair back, stacked her bowl and his, and walked to the sink.

"I'm sorry." Rylee pushed her chair back too. "Was that too personal? Sometimes I can be nosy."

"It's all right." He sloshed water in the bowls so they didn't attract flies. "I'd expect you to ask questions at your age. Questions are a good thing—most of the time." He pinned her with one of his *looks*, the kind he reserved for the men in his squadron. "What I most appreciate about them is what they reveal about the person asking."

* * *

Sunday morning, Rylee sat on her bed, unable to make herself venture into the kitchen. She kicked one leg then the other, the yellow-and-green floral bedspread crinkling up beneath her. Just what *had* last night's questions revealed to Jax? Had they clued him in on her identity? She hoped so.

She stopped kicking her legs, every bit of her going still as his heavy footsteps passed through the hall.

Her unplanned arrival hadn't allowed her to pre-pare—ha, as if preparing for something like this was possible! Being forced to wing it, she'd best ease him into the truth, give him clues, and hope he'd figure it out.

Everything had been going fine until she'd men-tioned how dangerous his work might be. His work had to be dangerous, or he wouldn't have disap-peared. Whatever. She'd hit a nerve, and he'd ended their evening.

Last night, it would've been so easy to confess ev-erything in that setting—the late hour, the familiar kitchen, the camaraderie, the ice cream. As if they'd been family. Despite her connection to him, it was too early to gauge his reaction.

I'm your granddaughter—from the future. You disap-pear this month.

Even thinking those words made her feel crazy, but saying them out loud? Yeah right. Call the police. Maybe it was *her* who wasn't ready to voice it. Some instinct warned her the timing was critical to everyone's future.

She blew out a breath and slipped her phone from underneath the mattress. She flipped it over in her hand, wishing she had enough battery power to leave it on.

She'd found comfort in the occasional sneak peek of her photos and a sweet reminder of those she left behind, but draining the battery wouldn't get her any closer to saving Jax or finding her way home.

But she could take care of one thing now. She pressed the power button, then brushed her thumb across the screen to Settings. She needed to delete the lock screen code. If something happened to her, Jax or Doris needed access to her true identity.

The display on the screen hadn't changed—9:30 Thursday, June 3. She hadn't thought about the year being recorded until she'd clicked on the calendar app, and 2021 had stared back at her. The date had puzzled her, but then there weren't cellular phone towers in 1981 for the phone to connect with, so the date had no ability to realign itself.

An odd comfort came from checking the date. The first night of her arrival, she'd checked it several times to make sure she hadn't lost her mind, letting it remind her of reality, that what happened to her hadn't been a dream—or a fantasy—but real.

She scrolled through the photos, stopping at one with her mom and some of her friends. Balloons, colorful wrapped gifts, and a three-tiered cake decorated the kitchen table. Frankie had snapped the picture capturing the happy moment from her sixteenth birthday. Was that really just three weeks ago? And would she ever see them again?

She thumbed across the screen to a picture with her grandmother. It was the same party, and they were hugging each other. A raw ache hollowed out her midsection. She must be worried about her disappearance—her mom, too. Were they even alive *to* worry? Had she done something in 1981 to forever change their future, their existence—and hers? She blinked away the heat building behind her eyes.

Except for the Cessna, her phone was the only link to her life in the future. She eyed the green power bar—a constant reminder to keep the visits here brief. The battery showed less than half. She pressed the sides until the phone powered off. Getting lost on memory lane wouldn't conserve the battery much less get her back home. It was only a matter of time before the phone died, and if she didn't get back or figure out a way to charge it, all she'd have would be memories.

She glanced at the bedside clock—7:17. She threw back the covers and tucked the phone back underneath the mattress. The house was quiet. Had Doris and Jax gone to church? Surely, Doris wouldn't have let her miss church. She didn't have any Sunday clothes, but they wouldn't have left her behind because of it.

She dressed in her jeans and top and shuffled to the kitchen.

Fifteen minutes later, she flipped the last pancake on the griddle, lowered the flame, then continued scrambling a half dozen eggs in the pan on the right. That done, she swiveled left to grab three plates from the side cabinet. She set the table, keeping a sharp eye on the pancakes.

"What's all this?" Doris entered the kitchen, dressed in her floral robe, with her hair in some odd-looking pink rollers.

Rylee couldn't help but stare. "Speaking of questions, what's in your hair?"

"Sponge rollers." Doris patted the top of her head. "Don't tell me you've never seen them. I'm sure your mother and grandmother have a set. They're soft, so you can sleep on them."

"Oh." Rylee scooped up the pancakes and eggs, then proceeded to divide the food onto three plates. "And to answer your question, *this* is breakfast. I wanted to surprise you and Jax."

"Not much of a surprise with all the noise you're making in here." Jax entered the room in basketball shorts and a crumpled T-shirt. He rubbed his hand back and forth over the top of his head and made for the coffee.

"I didn't know if you guys went to church or not, but wanted to fix breakfast as a thank you."

"Yes, we go to church and would love for you to join us."

Rylee glanced down at her outfit. "This is all I have to wear, I'm afraid."

"Don't you worry, sugar. No one in this town will mind."

Jax leaned in close to Rylee's ear. "Especially if you're with the *Dragon*."

"Hush, you," Doris reprimanded. "What will Rylee think with such comments?"

"You know"—he eyed Rylee over the rim of his mug—"I've been wondering the same thing."

She caught her breath and ducked her head from his all-knowing stare. So he'd heard her say that the night she'd arrived. He had to have found it odd. Why had it taken him so long to bring it up?

She forked a bit of pancake and shoved it into her mouth. Maybe if she were chewing, she wouldn't have to answer.

"Speaking of clothes," Doris said. "Since you'll be staying with us for a while, maybe you and I could go shopping tomorrow."

"Um . . ."

"And if it's money you're worried about, we have plenty. And, while you're here, we'll get you a library card, too. In the meantime, you're welcome to use my card. It's in the hall drawer. I'll let Ethel know you might be using it."

"I would so love to have something other than jeans to wear."

"That settles it, then."

When Doris fetched cream from the fridge, Jax whispered to Rylee. "You may have my mother wrapped around your little finger, but I'm wise to you, Kitten."

His gaze still on her, he grabbed his plate, stood, and crossed to the counter. "I won't be joining you two ladies this morning. Work calls, I'm afraid."

"Again?" Doris joined him at the sink. "Can't you at least take the occasional Sunday off?"

"You know how important my job is." Jax spoke softly as if trying to reassure his mother. "Not much longer now. I promise."

As Doris placed her dishes in the sink, a sudden feeling of doom weighed down on Rylee's shoulders. She bowed her head. Was this the moment all of their lives would change? It couldn't be. It was too soon. He was supposed to be married to Tessa first. She was supposed to be carrying their child.

Rylee sat in her chair watching them—communicating with their eyes. It should've been a private moment between mother and son except she was here, intruding, in the way, not needed or wanted. To them, she was a stranger. Because of her, they had to stand with their backs to her—one whispering her concerns, the other his assurances.

She shouldn't be here. Her arrival had messed up the timeline. What had she done? Overcome with an urgent desire to get back home, she made her way to the bedroom. The answer had to lie with her plane.

A few minutes later, Doris stood in her doorway, arms crossed, head cocked, looking every bit the Dragon. "Are you all right?"

"I'm not feeling all that well. I . . . I ate too much. Do you mind if I stay here this morning?"

"Of course not. I'll stay with you."

"Oh, please don't. I'll feel worse if I keep you from going."

"Well, if you're sure."

"I'm sure." Rylee laid down on the bed, hoping Doris would take the hint. Once she was certain they'd left, Rylee retrieved her phone and the jumpsuit she'd worn over her clothes. In the living room, she turned on her phone and tapped the camera icon. She took several shots of the mantel photos, including one of the model airplanes, then ran from the house, down the steps, and across the field to her airplane.

* * *

"Where is it?" Blood rushing through her ears, Rylee tromped along the area where she thought she'd left the Cessna, stopping only to brush the sweat from her brow. This was where she'd parked it. She kept pushing along the dense tree line. Could it have disappeared? Had it been swallowed up in some time-warp thing?

Her heart thudded, and chills coursed down her spine. For the first time, she was afraid—as in really afraid. The airplane was her security, her link to her home, her way back, even if she didn't know how yet.

Fighting off dread, she made her way back over the area. About to give up, she spotted it.

"Thank goodness." Her heart rate soared, leaving her dizzy. She must have taxied deeper into the trees than she'd thought. But next time, she might not be so lucky. She needed help, information. But where does one go to find out about time travel?

The library.

CHAPTER 15

Rylee held the stack of books to her chest and pushed through the library door onto the sidewalk. Squinting against the noonday sun, she collided with someone at the entrance. A pair of strong hands gripped her arms as the books tumbled.

"I'm so sorry," she said.

They both bent down to gather the books. Crouched beside him, she glanced up into the young man's face.

Oh, for crying out loud! "Liam."

"And you're Rylee, right?"

"Right."

He held two of her books as they both stood. "I see you like science fiction. And . . . some heavy reading."

"Huh?"

Liam handed her *Quantum Physics for Beginners.*

"Oh, right."

"And here's one I could enjoy, Ray Bradbury's *The Sound of Thunder.*" Grinning, he peered over the stack of books she'd snugged against her chest. "What else you got there?"

"Um, *The Time Machine.*"

"I haven't read it, but I loved the movie. I didn't figure you for a science nerd. You're waaaay too pretty." The grin still quirking up his lips, he shoved his hands into his pockets.

Liam 1981 just told *her*, Rylee Dean, she was pretty. His honey-brown gaze shone. She caught her breath and hugged the books to her thumping heart. Swooning inwardly, she offered a slight smile. *Stay cool, Ry.* Best not to overdo it until she was sure he'd meant it and wasn't making fun of her. After all, the nerd reference did bother her a little.

"So, you're into time travel. Cool."

"Summer reading."

"Oh, it's a school thing."

"Yeah."

He leaned toward her. "How about we head to Billy's for a Coke float and a burger?"

"Ah, yeah. Sure."

"Here, let me." He lifted the books from her arms and tucked them to one side.

They strolled along Main Street. At the Dip, they took the last booth on the left. The place's retro makeover still surprising her, Rylee slid into the turquoise booth as he laid the books on the table and sat opposite her.

After they placed their food and drink order, Liam glanced at the book on the top of the stack. "*The*

Grandfather Paradox." His eyes narrowed, and he tipped it to read the next one. "*The Theory of Time Travel.* Huh. You're not some genius kid who's already in college are you?"

Rylee stifled a giggle. "No."

"You're new here. So what school is this for?"

"It's for the school I attend back home. I'm just visiting."

"Why time travel? There's got to be less complicated subjects to spend the summer on."

"It's something I'm interested in."

"You're *interested* in time travel?"

"Yes."

A subtle and somewhat doubtful spark lurked in his eyes, and his lips curved upward in a mesmerizing smile. He reached across the Formica top and took her hand and gave her fingers a small squeeze. "Then I'm also interested."

Sure you are.

"What do you say we crack these books open at my house? Say tonight—seven o'clock?"

"You mean it? You really want to help?"

His brows scrunched together. "Help?"

She pulled her hand from his and sat back.

"What's wrong? What'd I say?"

"Nothing. It's all right. I thought you were serious."

The waitress who took their order approached. "Here you go—two cheese hamburgers with fries, extra crispy, and two Coke floats. Will there be anything else?"

"Not for me," Liam said.

Shaking her head, Rylee waved with a french fry. "I'm good."

Liam eyed her. "What exactly do you mean by help?"

"The assignment has to do with solving a particular problem."

"That involves time travel."

"Right."

He plopped a fry between his lips. "What's the scenario? What question do you have to solve?"

"I can explain it like this." She propped her elbows on the table. "Let's play what-if. Let's say a girl goes back in time, but she has no idea how she did it. What would be the first thing she should do?"

"See a psychiatrist?" He grinned.

She rolled her eyes. "And if she sees this psychiatrist and gets locked up for her troubles, then how will she get back home?"

"I see your point." He swathed another fry in ketchup and pointed it at her. As he gestured, ketchup plopped onto the Formica. "Would she try to find someone she could trust and tell that person?"

"She would work on that, yes."

"But it would take time to find such a person."

"Most likely," she said.

"Until then, she'd go to the local library and check out all the books she could find on time travel."

"She would."

When he burst out laughing, Rylee lowered her gaze to her plate. *That* was not the reaction she'd been hoping for.

He sobered, wiped his mouth, and crumpled his napkin aside. "Look. Rylee. I didn't mean to laugh at you."

He thinks I'm nuts. It lurked there in his gorgeous eyes—eyes no longer holding their subtle, teasing sparkle. *He's sorry he's here with me and wondering how he can politely leave.*

"It sounds crazy, but I believe time travel is possible. And for this assignment, I'm trying to prove it." She bit into her burger.

"Okay, fine. I'll play." He sat up straighter and took on a serious expression. "Let's see, the scenario is a girl has traveled back in time and doesn't know how to get home?"

She didn't answer right away, just stared at him, assessing. With his eyes narrowed like that, he still didn't believe it possible, but he didn't have to in order to help. "Theoretically, yes."

"I like you, Rylee. But you do realize how crazy this sounds. Time travel is fantasy. It makes for great science fiction, but to prove it or say it's true—"

It is true! I'm living proof.

She'd misread him. She was in a hurry—that was all. Because he looked like her Liam, she'd taken it as some sort of cosmic sign.

"I know." She shrugged. "I just find it fascinating, and if you don't want to study it with me, then that's okay."

He glopped ketchup on another fry. "I mean, if it were more than a theory, some brilliant scientist would have proven it by now."

"Right." She braved a smile, feeling far from happy. Time travel was no longer in the fantasy category. Sure, it made for great fiction, but what had happened was real. Maybe something in these books could help her figure out what to do.

But she needed help, and the most likely person to ask was Jax. She just didn't know how to tell him. He'd ask too many questions, and the answers would disrupt his life in more ways than she could count.

Time was running out, and as nice as it was to have Liam '81's attention, she couldn't sit here another minute. She took another bite of her burger, then washed it down with her Coke float.

"I have to go." She placed money on the table and gathered up her books.

"But you're not finished."

"Actually, I am. I'm sorry."

Once outside the Dip, she stored the books in the bike basket. Disappointed with Liam's response, she climbed onto the seat and pedaled back to the farm. She was still on her own.

CHAPTER 16

Rylee entered the farmhouse through the back door so as not to disturb Doris. Once securely in her bedroom, she unloaded her haul on the bed and sat. She slipped the phone from her pocket. She'd left it on earlier and forgotten to turn it off. As she'd feared, the battery power had now lowered. She blew out a breath. Dang, almost half of what she'd had was now gone.

"Is that you, Rylee?"

She shut down the phone and had it tucked in her back pocket as Doris entered the room. "Yes."

"Feeling better, I see."

"I am. I went for a bike ride and meant to be back before you got home. Sorry if I worried you."

"Not at all. Just glad you're feeling better. You have a visitor."

"Who is it?"

One side of her mouth quirked the way Jax's did, and a subtle twinkled lurked in her eyes. "A gentleman caller."

Rylee slipped off the bed and followed Doris down the hallway. Liam stood from the sofa as they entered the living room.

"I'm on my way to the grocery store." Doris paused by the living room doorway. "You two help yourselves to anything in the fridge while I'm gone."

"Thanks, Miss Doris." Rylee laced her fingers together behind her back as Doris's footsteps retreated, then braved a look at Liam.

"Hi."

"Hi."

They stood staring at each other until the back door slammed shut. "Please, sit down." She loosened her tight grip on her hands and dropped onto the floral sofa cushion next to him. "What's up?"

"We didn't finish the what-if game."

"No, we didn't, did we?" Something fluttered in her chest. She tucked strands of hair behind her ear.

He clasped his hands together and angled his body toward hers. "I feel like I've offended you and I ought to apologize."

"You didn't offend me. That you want to continue with the game is apology enough." She offered him her best smile to end the matter.

"It means that much to you?"

"The game?" she asked.

"Time travel."

"Yes," she said.

"Okay." He clapped. "So, to continue . . . After this girl checks the books out of the library, she would need someone to help her go through those books."

"She would."

"No time like the present." He grinned.

What a way to put it! She stifled a comment on how she'd much rather be in *her* time, then shot off the sofa. "I'll get the books and meet you at the kitchen table."

A few minutes later, they sat poring over the stack.

"You take *The Grandfather Paradox*," she said. "I'll look through *The Theory of Time Travel*."

Taking their respective book, they perused the pages. Every few seconds, Liam glanced her way, so much so, she began to feel his gaze on her and found it hard not to stare back. Somehow, she focused on the book.

"I never knew there were so many paradoxes." He broke the silence. "There's the temporal paradox, the Fermi paradox, which asks the question: If time travel were possible, then where are all the travelers from the future?"

Here's one right here. Pressing her lips tight to hold in the quip, she scanned a page. "What other paradoxes have you found?"

"Newcomb's and another one called the causal loop where something in the future causes a past event—that is then the cause of the future one." He gave a quick headshake, ruffling his shag haircut. "That's a mouthful."

"What about a person?"

"It says it can also happen with a person."

She sat back, her heart rate picking up and her breath coming fast. Her hands shook so much the page she was holding nearly ripped. She let the page flutter back into place. What did that mean? Was it saying . . .? "A person can be in the past and in the future—at the same time?"

"I guess." He flicked dark hair away from his eyes.

And if that's the case, then no one is looking for me or worried about me because I'm still there. Her temples throbbed, but she resisted the urge to press at them. "No. That's impossible." She slapped the table. "I refuse to believe it."

"Hey, don't shoot the messenger." He slanted his honey-brown eyes her way. "It's all conjecture, anyway."

More silence as they continued to read.

"Here's something. The butterfly effect doesn't exist. There, see?" He snapped the book closed. "Now, let's go take a walk."

"This is serious."

"Fine." With an exaggerating groan, he reopened the book.

"What else does it say?"

"Any changes that might occur from going back in time would be insignificant on the future. It has something to do with quantum mechanics. Whatever that is."

Rylee slumped forward and rested her chin in her hands. "This is going nowhere. It's all so complicated. I'll never understand any of it, much less be able to use it to get—"

"Get what?"

"Um, clarity for my assignment."

"You seriously want an A, don't you?" He closed his book. "What do we do now?"

Giving in, she rubbed the throbbing pulse at her temple. Didn't do any good, of course. Her shoulders slumped forward, and she smudged a toe across the creamy linoleum. "Why are you really helping me?"

His mouth spread into an irresistibly devastating grin. "Okay, I admit to wanting to see you—to spend time with you. And I'd use any excuse to be here. I mean, have you looked in the mirror?"

She couldn't help but smile. What she wouldn't give to have Liam 2021 look at her the same way, say the same things. "At least you're honest."

"You're into this time-travel stuff, aren't you? Not only that—you believe it."

"And if I do?"

He leaned toward her. "Are you from the future?" A playful spark lit those warm brown eyes as he gazed at her from across the table, and that devastating grin took her breath away.

Okay, so it wasn't a serious question. But did some small part in him actually want to know, or was he simply flirting?

"And if I am?" She clasped her hands together and rocked back in her seat. "Do you have any idea what it's like to go on the most incredible journey and have no one believe you?"

"I can't say I do." He propped his forearms on the table. "Here's my next question. Does the girl from the future have proof . . . of any kind?"

She fingered the binding on her book. "Maybe."

There. It was spoken out loud. She checked his reaction. A serious regard replaced the playful spark as his brows drew together.

"Can I trust you?" she asked.

He licked his lips. "I'm going to go out on a limb here and say yes, but if you're making a fool out of me—"

"I'm not. I swear. Although, when you hear what I have to say, you may think I am. Even I'm having trouble believing it."

"All right, then. Let's have it."

She slipped her cell phone from her back pocket and pushed it across the table.

He picked up the slender metal and glass rectangle and turned it over in his hand. "Okay, I give up."

"It's called a cell phone."

"I know what a phone is, and this is not it."

"Oh, but it is."

"You're yanking my chain, right?"

"I've never paid much attention to the science behind it, but in my time, these work off cellular towers. Companies like Bell South and AT&T developed it."

He lifted a skeptical brow. "Your time?"

"Here, let me turn it on." She pressed the power button and turned the face of it to him so he could see. It was a picture of her standing next to the Cessna. "That's my cover photo."

"You have an airplane?"

"Yes, it belonged to my grandfather. But look at the date."

"June third. That's not today's date, but so what?"

"It's the day I arrived here. The date hasn't been able to change because there are no cellular towers to connect to."

He raised a skeptical brow. "How do I know this isn't some gimmicky gadget thing from RadioShack or Sharper Image?"

"Okay, I've never heard of those stores."

"You're kidding, right?"

"This little *gadget* is not only a phone. It also stores my music and works as a camera. Look, I'll show you." She scooted next to him and leaned her head next to his. "Smile." She snapped the picture. It showed up on the screen. "See?"

He took the phone and scrutinized the photo. "Amazing."

"Watch this." She brushed her thumb from the bottom of the screen resetting it.

"Incredible. What's the story on those little squares?"

"They're called apps, but without the towers, they can't connect to my phone. Plus, they haven't been invented yet. So there is that."

"Watch this." She tapped Photos. "Here are my pictures, and there's the one I just took of us." She continued scrolling across the screen. "These two are my best friends, Lizzy and Frank. And here's my flight instructor, and here's one of me with my grandmother."

"This is unbelievable. There are hundreds."

"And look, I can organize them into photo albums. Cool, huh?"

"How come you don't need the towers for the photos?"

"Because these are in my phone. They're stored here."

He took the phone again. "Like in a microchip?"

"Yes. You know what a computer is, right?"

"Of course."

"That's what this is. It's a tiny computer with lots of little machines inside that do all of these amazing things, and I can keep it in my pocket or my purse."

A low whistle slid from his lips. "This is like spy stuff—like James Bond."

"Do you believe me, now?"

"I guess. I mean . . . I can't think of another explanation." He nodded toward the phone, handing it back. "Are you with some government agency?"

"No." She gazed heavenward. "In my time, everybody has one of these. Plus, look at this picture.

That's my mom's car in the background. You ever see anything like that around here? It's *electric*—well, a hybrid, sometimes gas, sometimes electric. There's so much on here." She shook the phone in his face. "This is the link to my life." She pushed the power button. "I need to conserve the battery."

And he stared at her in stunned silence.

"You're looking at me as if I'm from another planet."

"You may as well be." He sat up straighter and smoothed a hand over his hair. "You say this thing's chargeable?"

"Yes. I never travel without the cord, but in this instance, I had no idea I was going anywhere. I don't know what I'll do if I can't figure out a way to recharge it. This is the only proof I have that I'm not from around here. When this battery goes dead, so does my past."

"You mean your future." He held out his hand. "May I?"

She handed it to him.

"I have to say, this is one amazing piece of equipment. And you say everybody owns one?" One of his brows arched again, and he shook his shaggy hair away from his eyes. Liam's killer grin flashed before he let out another low whistle. "I'm pretty good with electronics. Maybe I can figure out a way to charge it."

Seriously? Was there a chance . . .? "If you could do that, I'd love you forever."

"Then I'd better get right to work." With a wink, he flipped the phone over. "First, I need to take a gander at the battery. I need a knife."

"Gander?"

"What? They don't use that word where you're from?"

She rolled her eyes. "Hold on. I'll get one." She jumped up, grabbed a paring knife from the kitchen drawer, and then spun toward him. "Will this work?"

"It should."

Within minutes, he'd maneuvered the back off. With their heads together, she watched him ease the blade along each end, prying the metal apart.

"You've got it. That's it," she told him. "That's the battery."

He slid it out and held it up between them. "Interesting. It has a positive and a negative input on one end."

"Like a car battery."

"Right." He snapped it back in place.

"What year did you travel from?" He blinked and stared. "Now there's a question I never thought I'd ask."

"I'll show you." She turned the phone back on and brought up the calendar app. "Look, 2021."

"That's"—he squinted at the ceiling—"forty years from now."

"Right."

"So, technically you haven't been born yet."

"Correct."

"Unbelievable. And you have no idea how you got here?"

She hesitated, not certain if she should mention the strange instrument. "No, I don't."

"*And* the reason for all of these books." He ran a hand over his chin. "Sooo, you don't know how you got here, and you don't know how to get back?"

"That's why I need help."

"You think the answer's in these books?"

"Maybe. But if I don't know how to interpret what I'm reading or how to apply any of it, then what use are they?"

He rocked back on the rear chair legs and clasped his hands behind his head. "What we need is a scientist."

"Or someone from the military."

"Where are you from?" he asked.

She spread her arms. "Right here."

"As in, Harpeth? Do you know me . . . in the future?"

She shook her head. "Sorry."

"It's okay. Makes sense, really. Why would a sixteen-year-old know some guy in his fifties?"

"I should put these books away before Miss Doris gets home. The last thing I need is more questions about time travel."

The chair resettled on its legs. "They don't know?"

"You're the only one I've told."

Liam stacked the books as they stood. "Where do you want these?"

"In my bedroom. This way."

Rylee waited in the doorway while Liam placed the books on the dresser. Then he followed her out to the front porch.

"Thanks for coming." She paused at the railing and tucked some hair behind her ear. "And for listening."

"Sure. Anytime."

She followed him down the steps to his red Datsun Coupe, hot humid air striking her as she exited the house. Sunlight filtered through the trees, and birds swooped across the yard, a sparrow at the feeder making a mess. Seemed so normal, but nothing was.

As they stood staring at each other, an awkward silence filled the space between them. "Listen, I want you to know I'm here for you and your secret is safe with me."

Rylee breathed out long and low. "You have no idea how good that sounds. Just knowing someone else knows makes me feel less alone."

"I'm glad." He opened the car door and pulled a pen and a piece of scrap paper from the console. "Call me tomorrow." He jotted down his home phone number. "I should know something by then."

She took the paper. "Thanks." The sincerity in his warm brown eyes touched her deeply. "I will."

As Liam drove away, Jax passed him in the driveway. Sylvia was with him.

Rylee ran up the steps and entered the house. She kneeled on the chair behind the blinds and flicked one slat down for a better view.

After he parked and got out, he walked around the car and opened the door for Sylvia. With her hand in his, they strolled across the side yard to the swing overlooking the meadow beyond.

Rylee drummed her fingers on the windowsill. She might have another opportunity to disrupt Sylvia and Jax. Seeing them cozied up on the swing gave her an idea.

She ran through the house and entered the backyard through a screened door. Turning left, she walked a few feet to the control box for the sprinkler system. She opened the box and flipped the switch from auto to on. Having no idea which zone number corresponded with the area around the swing, she stood by the controls and waited. About ten minutes later, she heard a yelp, then an all-out female squeal.

She hurried over to the corner of the house and peeked around the edge. Sylvia screeched again, then trounced across the front yard spitting not-so-nice words at the equally soaked Jax trailing her. Didn't matter what they were saying. The wet matted hair and tossing arms spoke plenty.

After hustling back to the sprinkler panel, she switched it to auto, then slinked inside. Seconds later, she met Jax coming down the hallway.

She mustered every ounce of innocence. "What happened to you?"

He slung his wet hair to one side. "Stupid sprinkler system. That's what." He entered the hall bathroom and slammed the door.

Rylee slapped her hand to her mouth as Doris entered with a bag of groceries.

"Here, let me help with that." Taking the bag from her great-grandmother, Rylee offered her help with Sunday dinner.

Chapter 17

After dinner, the weather turned nasty—pelting rain sounded like pebbles hitting the metal roof. Rylee shuffled to the kitchen for a drink and noticed the light blinking from the answering machine. She pressed the button.

"Jax, darling," the recording grated out Sylvia's voice. "Call me. It's important."

Rylee gnawed her lower lip. Keeping her eye on the doorway, she placed her finger on the delete button, took a deep breath, and pushed it. Then she sauntered into the living room. Weren't certain actions acceptable in life-and-death situations? In this case, hers and her mom's. She selected a book from the shelf and sat on the sofa.

She'd only flipped a few pages before Jax brought over two small boxes. "I have a surprise," he said. "I've been saving them for such a night as this. Come on over."

At the game table, he handed her one of the boxes —a model airplane kit. The aircraft on the cover looked like one from her grandmother's living room. Her heart pounded in her ears. Had *she* built this one? She'd always assumed Jax built them all. All she could do was stare. Maybe her future had proof of time travel before she'd experienced it.

"You okay over there?"

Somewhat dizzy, she sucked in a quick breath—something it seemed she kept forgetting how to do around him. "Yeah, yeah, I'm fine."

"That particular model takes smaller hands. I'd bought it for Sylvia, thinking she might enjoy building one with me. But she hasn't called, so I guess she's not interested."

"Have you checked the answering machine?"

"I did." He shrugged. "But she hasn't left a message."

"Her loss," Rylee said.

They opened their respective boxes and organized the paints and plastic pieces. Rylee set out her parts in an orderly manner, placing the pieces in straight little rows until her hand stilled on the tiny control panel. She lifted it up for inspection.

"Looking for anything in particular?" he asked.

She met his questioning gaze. "Um, nothing really. I was just checking to see if the control panel was authentic."

* * *

After the way she'd hounded him about the Anomaly Detection Device, he wondered if her inspection of the model had been more than curiosity. She must be more knowledgeable than he'd first thought.

The rain continued pelting the roof, the night cooler, but the humidity cloying as they worked. While he glued the first pieces together, he studied her bent head. Holding a small tube of glue, she sat perfectly still, hovering over the plastic fuselage as if she were performing heart surgery.

"You're taking this seriously."

"Of course I am." Her head angled in a haughty tilt as though his remark affronted her.

He couldn't help but laugh. "That was a compliment, Kitten."

"Oh." Loosening her shoulders, she gave a rueful smile.

"If you think you can talk and glue at the same time, tell me more about your grandfather."

She ran a thin layer of glue across one edge of the fuselage, then pressed the sides together while they set. "My grandfather loved flying—loved everything about it."

"Which explains your passion for it." This time, his remark brought forth one of her dimpled smiles.

"He was young and handsome and very brave. He was a pilot serving his country. He was a lot like you in that respect."

This humidity . . . Man, nights like this were miserable. He tugged at his collar, aching to go for a spin in the Cessna. "If he died so young, how do you know so much about him?"

"From my grandmother. We'd sit together for hours poring over the family photo albums. I loved listening to her stories, and I fell more in love with him with each telling."

"He was obviously a favorite subject of hers. Sounds like they were very much in love."

"They were." Those eyes—so much like his—looked more violet with tears gleaming in them.

He contemplated Sylvia. He couldn't picture her sharing stories about him if he were no longer in the picture. His lips pressed tight, and he swallowed down something stronger than irritation. Sylvia was all about Sylvia. Why hadn't he noticed sooner? He jerked at his collar again, unable to concentrate on the model. "Sounds like they were very lucky. A love like theirs is hard to come by."

The girl's fingertips went red, her fingers turning white as she pinched a piece together. "I grieve his loss more today than I ever have before."

"What about your mother? Did she have any stories for you?"

Her shoulders slumped, her forehead crinkled, and her lips flattened together as if holding in pain. "She never knew him."

"Wow. So everything you know about him came from your grandmother."

"On our farm back home, we have this large shed-like structure. We call it the barn even though it wasn't built for animals."

"Much like the one I have here."

Her eyes widened and she blinked. "Yeah. Anyway, it served as his hanger. He had a single-engine airplane like yours. My grandmother told me he used to spend hours working on it, which she never understood because at the time it was only a few years old."

"And when he wasn't tinkering with it, he was flying it?"

"Exactly."

"Sounds like he loved the mechanics of flight as much as flying." He held the glued wing in place and blew on it. "I would've liked your grandfather."

He glanced up, catching her in one of her usual stares. He'd gotten used to them. They were some of the few times she'd let her guard down. No cryptic messages lurked in them as in many of her answers. This particular stare was winsome and sweet as if he'd said something she'd treasure for the rest of her life.

His chest warmed when she nearly dropped the piece in her hands, flustered at having been caught.

"Back home, I've been working on getting my pilot's license."

"And I'm just now hearing about it?" he teased. "You should've mentioned this the other day when I was waxing on about the instrument panel."

"Oh no. I enjoyed it. It was a good review for me."

"Where are you in the process?"

She sat forward. "I'm finally all ready to advance to my solo flight. It took a while because I missed a few things during my preflight check."

"That doesn't sound good. What were they?"

"I missed the fact that a tire was low. Then I forgot to double-check the fuel filler caps."

He shook his head. "No, no, you can't do that. You're using your eyes in place of your hands. The visual check is part of the physical. Takes both. If the filler caps aren't properly attached, the fuel could leak from the top of the wing, which could make for a very bad day. There's a reason for the preflight check. Doesn't matter who else has checked it—it's your responsibility as the pilot to do your own checking."

"I know. Believe me, I know."

He grinned. "I take it you've got a tough instructor."

"You have no idea."

"Sounds like he's trying to keep you safe. And if it makes you feel any better, I had one like that, too. Their job isn't easy, you know."

She gazed at his profile. "You're right. Safety is very important." She licked her lips. "So, in all your years flying, have you ever forgotten something or screwed up anything?"

He rested his forearms on the table, the edge cutting into them. "Not that often. But even when you make sure your craft is serviced regularly and check the basics before taking off, there's still the possibility something unforeseen can go wrong. That's just a given. When that happens, you keep your head and do your best to solve the issue."

"Have you ever experienced the unforeseen?"

"Thankfully, no. At least not yet anyway." He dipped his paintbrush in water and swished. "You mentioned your grandfather served as a pilot. Air force or navy?"

"The air force."

"World War II?"

She exhaled a loud breath, "Post Vietnam. He flew special missions and stuff like that."

"Wow, that's more recent than I thought." He finished cleaning the brush, then wiped the tip with a cloth. "What division? Maybe I knew him."

"I don't know."

"What was his name?"

When she didn't answer, he glanced at her. She was staring at him as if he'd asked her to explain quantum physics. She opened her mouth to speak, but not a word came out. The wall phone's shrill ring broke the silence. Something like relief slackened her jaw. She lowered her head and focused on adding a stroke to her wing. The phone rang again. Keeping an eye on her, he stepped across the wide hallway into the kitchen and lifted the receiver.

"It's Rick," his friend said as soon as Jax answered. "We're having trouble with the ADD simulator. We could use your help. I know it's late, but—"

"It's okay. I'll be right there." He hung up. "I have to go. This may be an all-nighter. Feel free to finish up your model, but leave mine for now."

She smiled and nodded, stammering something about leaving it to her, obviously rattled. He returned her nod and left her staring after him from the table.

Once outside, he started the car ignition, but didn't press his foot to the accelerator. Why had she gone pale when he asked her grandfather's name? Why not just tell him? She adored the man and loved talking about him, so why all the secrecy about his identity?

CHAPTER 18

Rylee picked up the brush and slid a finishing touch to the yellow stripe on the wing, then set it aside to dry. Cleaning everything took about five minutes, giving her plenty of time to get back to the book she'd been reading. She settled herself on the floral sofa near Doris, who sat nearby focused on her knitting.

Attempting to appear peaceful, Rylee was anything but. How come she'd balked like that? What kind of person doesn't know her grandfather's name?

She cringed. He'd eyeballed her as if she were some kind of idiot. Couldn't she have made up a name?

"I'm for bed," Doris said. "Don't stay up too late. Good night."

"G'nite."

Except for Doris's occasional light snoring, the house was quiet. Jax's all-nighter at the base was the perfect opening for her to take those photos of the strange compass.

Earlier today, when they'd worked on the model, the tiny control panel reminded her of the dial and the need to get into his Cessna to photograph it. Who knew what comparing the two would accomplish, but she had to start somewhere.

She padded down the hall to his bedroom, edged inside, and closed the door. Holding her breath for the coming *cliiick*, she flipped on the light. She approached his desk and put her hand on the drawer pull and stopped. Her actions invaded his privacy. Instead of searching each drawer for the key, she'd keep her search on the surface level.

At his chest of drawers, she checked the top. Not there, either. She gnawed her lower lip. Spotting a wooden box on the bedside table, she crossed the room. Her hand hovered over the closed box. She squeezed her eyes tightly together. So much for her vow. She flipped open the lid. The large key gleamed at the bottom. She stuffed it into her pocket.

Twenty minutes later, she dismounted Doris's bike and leaned it against the hanger. Rylee glanced right and then left to ensure she was alone, then unlocked the massive doors. She opened one side just enough to slip through.

Heart thumping, she hurried to the Cessna and climbed in. Careful not to touch the instrument, she turned on her phone and pressed Camera. She took several photos of the odd-looking dial, zooming in for detailed close-ups, then snapped the entire panel, for good measure. She'd compare them with the panel on her Cessna for any differences as well as similarities.

It took some time to get the heavy sliding door to close. Once she'd locked it, she headed to the bike.

An hour later, with the key back in its box, she sat against her headboard examining the photos. She spread her fingers across the screen, enlarging the picture. She counted seven strands of copper wire. Five symbols were housed in between each strand on the dial's perimeter. In the center sat the compass needle.

Was something important about the ratio between five and seven? The symbols could likely be positioned in a multitude of ways, allowing even more destination possibilities.

"Seven copper strands and five symbols." She scowled at the circular pin in the center. "What made you spin like you did? How did you trigger time travel? And why back here? Why not somewhere in the future?"

She tapped her head against the headboard. Tampering with this was out of the question. There were way too many variables. She could end up in another time altogether.

Tomorrow she would go to her plane and compare these photos with the dial on her aircraft.

For now, she replaced the original cover photo with the compass picture so she could examine it without using up more battery power.

She powered off the phone and scooted under the covers. Today she'd discovered a connection and most likely the link to getting back home. The symbols had to be a part of that equation.

As she lay there, sleep wouldn't come. She'd never figure it out on her own. Only Jax had the knowledge and the understanding of the compass dial. She'd have to tell him where she'd come from while keeping her relationship to him a secret. He could not know. It could taint his future decisions. So much was still uncertain, but one thing was clear—Jaxon C. Scott had invented a way to travel through time.

* * *

Jax slept in Monday morning until around noon. After a quick lunch, he joined Rylee on the yard swing. "Let's take a ride."

She slid off the seat and followed him to his car. "Where are we going?"

"You'll see."

Five minutes later, he turned right off the main road and approached his hanger. When her face lit up as he parked, he got out and motioned for her to follow.

"Are you taking me up?" She hurried after him. "Is that why we're here?"

"Not today, I'm afraid." He unlocked the massive doors. "Help me get these open."

They each took a side and pushed, hot air rolling out to greet them. Inside, he flipped on the lights. In less than a month, Dolly, the aircraft in the center of the building would be his.

Rylee's laughter rushed toward him on the warm air. "You're all dreamy eyed."

He raised a brow. "I am?"

"You see it, too."

"See what?"

"How the aircraft commands the space, you know, like when an important person walks into a room and everyone turns at his entrance."

"You're right. Dolly does command this space. She owns it." He ran an admiring hand along her belly. "She's a star."

"Thank you for letting me see her again."

"Oh, you're going to do more than see her."

"What do you mean?" she asked.

"I want you to take me through your preflight check."

Her mouth dropped open.

He stifled a laugh. Talk about dreamy eyed. All big eyed and flushed, she was such a cute kid. "I want to see what's tripping you up. Come on. Show me what you got."

"Seriously?"

"I'm always serious—"

"When it comes to flying," she finished for him.

"Before you start, I want to show you a trick." He strolled around the plane, tapping the aircraft as he went. "Do this each time and listen for any loose rivets rattling. You already know the importance of looking and touching in your preflight check, but you must listen as well. This trick enables you to check the things you might not ordinarily see."

"Cool," she said.

"You ready?"

She approached the Cessna with respect, becoming serious. After checking the door hinges, she stepped to the front of the plane and checked the propellers.

"It's okay to talk while you check," he told her. "Why are you checking the door hinges?"

"To make sure they're secure."

He stepped out of her way, folding his arms across his chest. "And the props?"

"To make sure there are no significant dents."

"Good, go on."

"The screws on the spinner are secure. The fuel tanks in all three areas are free of water and debris."

"Excellent."

Her smile dimpled up her cheek. "I'm now checking the right-side magneto, making sure all the wires are securely attached."

She continued her check by opening the engine compartment. She reached inside and checked levers and tugged on wires. "No bird's nests or oil leaks, and the spark plugs are properly connected to the magneto." Rubbing her hands together, she spun to him with an I-did-it bravado.

"Great job," he said.

She clasped her hands to her chest and beamed. "If Coop could see me now."

"You didn't miss a thing. Your flight instructor should be very proud of you. Ready to continue?" Jax opened the pilot's door.

"Yes." She turned on the beacon switch and climbed into the pilot's seat.

"What's next?" He leaned in after her, bracing one hand along the side of the door.

Rylee methodically went over each step, checking the fuel pump, the airspeed, and all instruments. As she did so, he nodded his approval to encourage her.

Once she finished, her blue eyes glowed as if she'd won the lottery.

He held up his hand for a high five. When she slapped his palm, he caught her hand and held it there. "You got this, Rylee. You were precise, concise, and focused. You keep doing that, and you won't miss a thing. When you get back home, I expect you to sail through the preflight check with this Coop guy."

"Thanks. I will." She squeezed his hand back, then slid hers free. "I tried to explain to Coop that my lack of thought was due to my excitement about going up solo, but he said that was no excuse."

Jax lifted a shoulder. "Your instructor's right. There really isn't any excuse. What you do on the ground is important to your safety in the air."

As they exited the Cessna, she glanced again at the aircraft, her face glowing, her lips parting as air rushed past them, and then her chest swelled. Her interest and love for aircraft and all things related to flight were real. This bright, eager girl touched him. As she stood, caught up in the moment, he couldn't help being caught up with her.

"What is it that touches you, so?"

"Flight and the fact that someone figured it out." She swung toward him, her bright eyes all sparkly. "When I'm up there, nothing else matters. This metal bird lifts me way up in the sky, through the clouds, high above the earth, defying gravity and allowing me to see the world from another perspective. Everything comes into focus."

"Love at first sight." His chest tightened. Sometimes he wondered if he could ever feel that for a woman. "I know how you feel. The world with all of its problems simply falls away. I felt it, too, when I was your age."

"You're one of the few who gets it. Mom hates that I love it. Says it's too dangerous and no place for a girl my age."

He tilted his head and rubbed his chin. She'd just spoken of her mother as if she were still alive. "Mothers can be like that," he said slowly.

"Yours isn't."

"I'm one of the lucky ones. I love the feeling of being one with my F-16." As she gave him her rapt attention, he rocked back on his heels. "I know her every move and every nuance of what she's capable of. I speak words of love to her during flight and even more so when she safely brings me home."

"Wow." She clamped her hands over her chest. "That was beautiful."

He smothered a smile. This kid was a knockout at sixteen. He could only imagine her at twenty-five. Heaven help her future boyfriends.

"I want you to know, being here with you and your Cessna has been one of the happiest experiences of my life." She let out a contented sigh. "Thank you."

CHAPTER 19

After work, Jax passed Rylee on the couch, struggling with two long needles and a wad of blue yarn. He doubled back. "You're knitting now?"

She rolled the ball of wool in her lap, her lips twisting to one side. "Doris is teaching me. She told me to practice while she was at her bridge game."

"Sylvia is coming over tonight to fix me dinner." He stuffed his hands in his pockets. "I thought you were going to be out tonight, as well."

"Oh." Rylee waved a hand in the air and lifted a sparkling smile. "I'll fix a ham sandwich and work on this mess in my room. You won't even know I'm here."

He doubted that.

* * *

Rylee sat on her bed, holding the long needles. "Knit once, purl twice." She paused and stared ahead. "Or is knit twice and purl once?"

She slumped against the headboard and huffed. She'd have to wait for Doris to explain it again.

Sitting up, she threw her legs over the side of the bed and stood. She stepped into the hallway to absolute deliciousness. Whatever Sylvia was cooking smelled wonderful.

Rylee slipped out the back door so as not to disturb them. Once outside, she sauntered to the back of the house, stopping when she heard voices.

"What do you mean she's in the house? I thought we'd be alone tonight?"

"Quit worrying. She promised to stay out of our way."

"It's time you found another family for that girl. How many days has it been now? Six—seven?"

Another home? Of course, Sylvia would want that. Rylee tiptoed to the edge of the house and peeked around the side.

"And I feel a bit bad for her," he said. "We'll be eating your wonderful meal, and she'll be in her room having a ham sandwich." He scooped Sylvia in his arms. "The least I can do is bring her a plate of your beef Wellington."

"You will not—"

As he silenced her with a kiss, Rylee snapped back and hurried indoors. The instant she stepped inside, her mouth watered from that delicious aroma. The buttery beef fragrance lulled her into the kitchen like a mouse to cheese. She opened the oven door and looked inside.

With Sylvia's words ruminating in her brain, Rylee turned the temperature from 350 degrees to 400 degrees. For extra good measure, she added ten minutes to the timer. There! She brushed her hands together, marched back to her room, and put aside her ham and Swiss on rye.

Sometime later, the smoke alarm screeched. Then another alarm shrieked—*Sylvia*. Rylee plugged her ears with her fingers. As she plopped on the edge of the bed, she realized it would seem odd if she didn't investigate. Holding the second half of her sandwich, she ran from her bedroom to the kitchen.

She skidded to a halt as the black smoke billowed from the room. "What happened?" she hollered.

Jax stepped through the kitchen door, fanning the billowing black cloud with a tea towel, squinting against the smoke. Sylvia followed in a coughing fit.

"I'm positive I set that to three fifty."

For a minute, Rylee felt sorry for her—but only for a minute.

"Now what do we do?" Sylvia wailed.

"There's ham." Rylee held up her sandwich.

Jax caught her eye and shook his head. "I'll take you out, sweetheart."

"Fine. I'll grab my purse."

As Sylvia turned down the hallway, Jax gave Rylee his full attention. "I don't suppose you have any idea how the temperature on the oven got turned up?"

Rylee caught her breath. "No." With a quick head-shake, she bit down on her sandwich. His gaze heated her as she chewed.

"Come with me." He motioned for her to follow, then strode down the hallway toward the back door.

Rylee's heart fluttered—not in a good way. She swallowed hard and trailed him. When she stepped outside, he was nowhere to be seen.

"Rylee." His voice sounded from the other side of the house.

She turned the corner and froze—he held the hose, spray-nozzle in one hand, pointed straight at her. She sucked in a sharp breath right as the water doused her face and upper body. She squealed, dropped her sandwich, threw up her hands, and squeezed her eyes against the drenching, then coughed and sputtered as he released his hold on the nozzle.

He didn't say a word. He didn't have to. This was payback, pure and simple. With cool deliberation, he turned off the spigot and went back inside.

Rylee wiped her face, then flung her wet arms and hands outward to shake off some water. She sucked in a deep breath, blew it out, and edged in through the back door.

Jax stood in the hallway—his lips quirking and eyes gleaming. He tossed her a towel.

She caught it and pressed the cotton mass to her face as Sylvia entered the hallway.

"Ready, darling—what happened to *you*?"

"Faulty sprinkler system," Rylee choked out. If Sylvia looked so appalled, Rylee must really be a mess.

"You must get that thing checked." Sylvia placed her hand on Jaxon's arm. "But what about the kitchen? I feel terrible leaving it in such a mess. What'll your mother think?"

"Don't worry. Rylee will be happy to clean everything up before Mom gets home." He leveled her a look—something like she'd expected him to reserve for his men.

"Absolutely." She slopped wet hair from her forehead.

* * *

The following morning, Rylee stayed in her room until she was sure Jax had left. Embarrassed by her prank, she had no desire to see him. It was now Tuesday. Plenty of time had passed for Liam to come up with a solution to her dying phone. At least she hoped so. After a quick bite, she dialed his number and waited.

"Hello?"

"Liam?"

"Yeah."

"It's Rylee."

"Hey, I've been—"

"Have you figured out how to charge my phone, yet?"

"Yeah, I have. Can you bring it to my house later today? I have some ideas that might work."

"I'd love to."

Today of all days she was glad Doris had suggested their shopping spree. She'd tired of dressing in the same pair of jeans and shirt. Despite Doris washing them, they were getting grungy. She dressed in a bright purple ribbed tank top, then layered it with a neon yellow one. She finished up with a pair of high-waisted star-patterned shorts, then completed the look with a white, ripped-up sleeveless vest.

She arrived at Liam's within the hour. Doris was happy to drive her to a friend's home, saying it would be good for Rylee to have some fun.

Doris waited in the driveway until Liam's mother opened the door. The ladies waved as Rylee stepped over the threshold of the two-story brick home.

Liam bounded down the stairs while his mother closed the front door. "I see you've met my mom."

Smiling, Rylee tucked her hair behind her ears. "I have. Thanks for having me over."

"Of course. Liam says you have a cool piece of electronics he wants to examine."

"Yes, ma'am."

"Come on, Rylee. My shop's in the basement."

The smell of old metal and plastic greeted her downstairs. Two rectangular tables ran along one wall filled with TVs, speakers, old radios, video recorders, and other pieces of electronic equipment she'd have a hard time identifying.

Several square tables in the center of the room held smaller pieces with names like Emerson, Sharp, and Philips. Wires and cords of all types spilled over boxes stacked on the floor to her left. A worn upholstered sofa was somehow wedged in between it all.

Liam spread his arms and spun in a tight circle. "What do you think?"

"It's incredible."

"I'm sure it looks like a mess to you, but I know where everything is."

She laughed. "There's a method to your madness."

"Exactly." He motioned to one of the tables. "The stuff I'm working on for you is over here. Yesterday, I found a couple of old cords that charged my mom's old transistor radio. Unfortunately, they don't still work. I found a smaller one we can try today."

"What's a transistor?"

"In the dark ages when my parents were kids, they replaced the tubes used in TVs and large radios. They're obsolete now. Anyway, that cord would be too big, so I'm going to try one used to charge that small voice recorder."

She picked up the miniature radio. "I've never seen anything like this."

"Obsolete, but pretty clever stuff in its day."

"You really are into this, aren't you?"

He shook his hair away from his eyes and grinned Liam's killer grin. "Like you and airplanes."

"And you called me a nerd." She set down the recorder. "What's next?"

"I need to remove the battery."

They sat close together, her head almost touching his as he pried the back off the phone.

"Now, from my expert experience on small electrical equipment"—he lifted a finger dramatically in the air and held a pause—"I think I've figured out how to charge your phone."

Playing along with his overt dramatization, she clasped her hands to her heart.

"I began by stripping off the end of this electrical cord exposing the wires. See? This one has red, black, and white wires. But we'll only need the red and black ones."

"Why not the white?"

"Because like a car battery, red is positive while black is negative—like these little icons on *your* battery."

Good looking and smart. So not fair. She sighed out the emotions clogging her throat.

He inserted the red wire in between the positive notches, then repeated the action for the negative side. "Now for the tricky part."

His brows pinched together, the tip of his tongue snaked between his lips, and a bit of sweat slithered down his left temple. Her fingers twitched to reach up and brush it away—merely so it didn't distract him, of course.

"Done." He snapped the battery back in the phone, then held up the end with the plug. "Ready for the verdict?"

She nodded.

"Fingers crossed." He inserted the plug into the wall outlet, then held the power button down.

"The green light is on." She squealed and flung her arms around his neck. "You did it!"

Easing away, she dropped her arms and stepped back. Heat tingled up her neck and scorched her ears. Seriously? Had she just done that? "Sorry about that. I got carried away."

"No need to apologize." He grinned and stuffed his hands in his pockets. "How long does it take to charge that thing?"

"An hour or so."

"In the meantime . . ." He took her right hand in his and led her to the sofa. They sat side by side. "Tell me about the future. Do I have any kids or grandkids?"

"Oh, I see—what you're really asking is about *your* future?"

He shrugged and flushed an adorable peachy color, then grabbed a piece of candy and held it up. "Hershey's Kiss?"

She plucked it from his fingers and unwrapped it. "If you must know, I have a terrible crush on your grandson." She popped the chocolate in her mouth.

"You're kidding."

She scrunched up her nose and swallowed. "By the way, he's named after you."

Liam gulped and went all goggle-eyed. "He is?"

"Uh-huh. He's supercool, not a nerd like his grandfather."

"Hey."

She giggled.

"And how does he feel about you?" He selected another chocolate Kiss and handed it to her.

"Sadly, not a thing. He hardly even notices me." She unwrapped the silver-wrapped candy and plopped it between her lips.

"More fool him. I'll have to give him a good talking to when he's about twelve—*if* I'm still around." He scratched at his jaw, one brow rising. "Am I? Still around?"

"I don't know." She wiped the sides of her mouth with her index finger. "Should I look you up when I get back?"

"Do you think I'll remember? I mean, when you get back, will it be as if you never existed here, or will I have memory of you?"

"Good question. I'll look you up when I get back, and then we'll see."

"Okay. In the meantime"—he leaned toward her—"I'm a teenager. . . . You're a teenager. . . ."

"And we must make use of the time we have," she filled in.

"Right here . . . right now."

She was no expert on boys, but what guy could resist saying he kissed a girl from the future? Come fall, he could tell all the jocks in the locker room. Talk about bragging rights.

Her heart skipped a beat as Liam's mouth hovered near hers. His eyes held an intense gaze, more curiosity than longing. Whatever it was squeezed the breath right out of her. "I–I totally agree," she stammered as his flawless, beautiful mouth covered hers.

Her heart raced, and she held herself absolutely still, not at all sure if she was doing it right. Never having been kissed before, she tried to relax and go with it. She found herself responding, so that had to be a plus. As far as first kisses went, this one was perfect, although that could be attributed to the chocolate. Sure, she had nothing to compare it to, but so what? She'd dreamed of kissing Liam her entire tenth-grade year. So what if it was the grandfather instead—a girl had to start somewhere, right? And if the grandfather was a complete and total hottie, who was she to complain?

Liam lifted his head, breaking the spell, and the kiss ended all too soon. Feeling a bit drugged, she opened her eyes to a blurred Liam, then blinked twice to clear up his image. His lips parted, and his eyes sparkled.

"You're laughing at me." Heat flushed her cheeks. "Is it that obvious?"

"What?" His brow furrowed.

"That it was my first kiss. Yours was so . . . so . . ."

He placed a finger to her lips. "Don't sell yourself short. You kiss just fine."

CHAPTER 20

As Rylee perused the oak bookcase hours later, her mind drifted to the afternoon. Liam had been wonderful creating a way to charge her phone and promising to fine-tune the device to make it easier for her to use. She sighed as she recalled that perfect kiss. She still had no clue if she'd done it right, but Liam didn't seem to mind either way.

"Searching for anything in particular?" Doris asked.

"Actually, yes. I wondered if you had any family photo albums?"

"Look left—should be on the bottom shelf."

Rylee spotted a thick green leather album, bent to retrieve it, then joined Doris on the sofa. Rylee lifted the cover and flipped it aside. Most of the photos here were black and white, and some were faded and frail.

They were halfway through the album when Jax hollered from the foyer. Then he and Sylvia entered the living room.

"Hey, you two." He braced a hip against the door-jamb, Hollywood-poster cool.

Rylee shut the album and stood along with Doris.

"Good evening, Sylvia." Doris smoothed her cotton dress where the album had wrinkled it.

"Evening, Miss Doris." Sylvia grinned, held up her left hand, and wiggled her fingers. She linked her arm through Jax's and flashed a superior smile. "I finally got the ring back and—"

"You're engaged!" Rylee hadn't meant to shriek, but the others' stunned reaction indicated she had. With the album clutched to her chest, she gawked at them. "Sorry. I, um, congratulations."

Lame, but what was a granddaughter supposed to say? Please don't kill me and my mom with such a mistake?

"Rylee, why don't you put the album away for now?" Doris clamped a warm hand on Rylee's shoulder. "We'll finish looking at it later."

Thankful for the reprieve, Rylee stepped over to the bookcase. When she turned back, Doris held Sylvia's outstretched hand, oohing and ahhing over the diamond ring. Jaxon stood with his arm around his bride-to-be, clearly enamored.

Rylee squeezed her eyelids shut. This could not be happening. Her plight was bad enough, but having to stand here and witness her possible demise was too much.

She stood, invisible to the others while Sylvia basked in all the attention. She was a beautiful woman—tall and sophisticated compared to the petite Tessa, who, when it came to cosmetics, believed less was more. As much as it pained her, Rylee conceded how a gorgeous guy like Jax would choose someone like Sylvia over her sweet grandmother.

Unable to watch, she slipped past them to the kitchen. What had happened between Jax and Sylvia to get him to fall for Tessa? Their relationship couldn't have been stable if meeting Tessa were the only reason for the breakup. You don't meet a girl one night, then break up with your fiancée the next day. There had to be something more to this. She gripped the back of a chair. Like she'd ever find out what.

Her lame attempts to spoil their relationship had come to nothing. She tried to push away the mounting ache in her heart, but how could she? If only her arrival hadn't kept him from meeting Tessa at the church lock-in!

She grabbed a pitcher of iced tea from the fridge and set it on the table. She was reaching for a glass from the cabinet when Jax entered the room.

"We miss you in there."

Refusing to look at him, she muttered under her breath, "Somehow I doubt that."

He gripped her arm, took the glass, and set it on the counter. "That was some reaction."

Heat stole up her neck, scorching her cheeks, and a quivering started in her legs. "I know. I'm sorry. I was . . . surprised. That's all."

"More like shocked. You didn't see your face."

She sucked in a calming breath. "That night at the base—that was your bachelor party, wasn't it? You were already engaged?"

"True on both counts."

She plopped into a kitchen chair. "Your mother seems to be taking it well, considering she doesn't like her."

"My mother is a gracious woman who will come to love any girl I chose to marry. If you're going to stay with us, I hope you can show Sylvia the same courtesy."

She raised her gaze to his. "What do you mean—stay with you?"

He sat in the chair next to hers, reached into his jacket, and pulled out a folded piece of paper. "I mean this."

She accepted the paper and scanned it. "I don't understand."

"It's a document giving my mother temporary custody of you."

"For how long?"

"Until Child Services can place you with another family."

"Oh. Did you do this?"

"No, this is my mother's doing."

"I see." The Dragon's doing. She almost smiled, but her heart hurt too much. She refolded the paper and handed it to him. "But you don't want me here."

"It's not that." He closed his eyes and rubbed them.

"You don't trust me. I understand. Really."

He ran his hand around the back of his neck. "It's a little more complicated."

"I know."

"By the way, good job on the kitchen. It's spotless."

As his lips quirked to one side in that way of his, she guessed he was trying to lighten the mood.

"No more tricks, okay?"

Easy enough to agree to since they hadn't worked. "Okay."

He picked up the tray, and as she followed him into the living room, she wondered how her excitement could turn so bleak within hours. After he set the tea on the coffee table, he sat and took hold of Sylvia's hand, and Rylee slumped in a side chair.

On the surface, they seemed happy. Did she have the right to play with his future? The moral dilemma thrummed from her head to her heart with each pulse. Yes. No. Yes. No? Was she even old enough to deal with such questions?

If he married Sylvia, then he might live—trading two lives for one. Her misery clamped on her, a steel weight holding her down as she watched them, sitting side by side, hand in hand, smiling and chatting about their future together while hers faded into the never-never.

* * *

The house was quiet when Jaxon returned from taking Sylvia home. He tossed his car keys in the foyer basket. As he crossed the hall, he slowed and watched Rylee, dressed for bed in an oversized T-shirt and drawstring pants.

She ran a hand over one of his model airplanes. Her touch was gentle, almost reverent as she slid her fingers along the gray plastic body. She stood, shoulders slumped, face crestfallen. She might have been crying. As he entered the living room, her sniffs grew louder, confirming his suspicion. He approached gently, careful not to startle her.

"You're up late."

She stiffened. Her hand stilled. She repositioned the model on the shelf and wiped her cheek while turning slightly toward him.

"Why are you so fascinated with those?" He moved closer.

"You'll just laugh." Her voice was husky.

"No, really. Tell me."

"They hold a special place in my heart."

What an odd thing to say. He shoved his hands in his pockets. "How so?"

"My grandfather used to build models like these. They remind me of him."

Quiet tears ran down her cheeks as he stepped closer.

"You can't marry her," she whispered in a desperate rush.

Was this simply her crushing on him, or was there something more here? He gripped her upper arms and turned her fully toward him. "Why?"

She hung her head. A sob broke from her lips as if she'd been trying to hold it in.

"Look at me."

Those red-rimmed eyes lifted to his face.

"Why?"

"I can't"—she hiccupped—"tell you."

The kid had to get a grip. "That's not good enough."

"Please trust me." She sobbed. "I know things. Isn't that obvious?"

"Any more talk like that, and you'll give me no choice but to call Child Services."

"Please don't marry her."

He gave her a gentle shake. "What can't you tell me?"

"I'll die if you marry her."

"Enough with this nonsense." She had to get over her crush. He put her from him. "Go to bed."

She gazed at him, all tear stained and puffy cheeked, clasped her lower lip with her teeth, and ran out.

He inhaled sharply in an effort to ward off the anger heating his chest. Then he strode across the room, yanked the glass stopper off the bourbon, and poured himself a drink. Since she'd arrived, that girl tied him in knots with her cryptic comments and blatant lies. Was Rylee Dean even her real name?

Worst of all, from their first meeting, he'd been drawn to her—and he had no idea why. She'd stirred a protective instinct he'd never felt, not even for his mother. One instant, he'd be driven to protect her—the next, to send her packing. If not for his mother, he'd have done that long ago. He tossed back the liquid, then poured himself another.

He slumped onto the couch, fat cushions pushing against him. She was adorable and a delight to his mother, who, since Rylee's arrival, worried less about him. His work was dangerous, and the risks were many. If something happened to him, Rylee would be a great comfort to the Dragon, which was one reason he'd allowed her to stay. But she had no history and no evidence she ever existed. Who wouldn't be intrigued by that?

Only someone with power could erase a person's records, so who had erased hers? Or maybe she was acting under a false identity. Maybe it's as simple as that. That said, she did know things, and he planned to find out how.

CHAPTER 21

Rylee threw herself on the bed and sobbed against the pillow, wishing this had never happened. A flash of loneliness stabbed at her. She missed her grandmother, but she really wanted her mom.

After a good cry, she sniffed, plumped her pillow, then slouched against the headboard. Boy, did she ever mishandle that! She groaned and swallowed a wave of anxiety. His patience was running out. She needed to either trust him with all the facts or leave.

So she'd leave.

She got up and sat at the little desk in the corner. She grabbed a sheet of stationery from the cubbyhole and wrote:

Dearest Miss Doris and Jax,

It's time for me to find my way back home. It's been difficult being stuck between two worlds. That said, I hope my being here has made a difference in yours. Only time will tell.

I love you both,
Rylee

When she finished, she stuffed the letter in an envelope, then propped it against her pillow. With a final glance at the bedroom, she tiptoed down the hallway to the front door.

Nothing had turned out as she'd hoped. Jaxon was engaged to the wrong woman, and Tessa seemed content to moon over him from a distance. Rylee refused to stay, only to watch him marry the wrong person sending her mom into oblivion. She had to get back, apologize to her, while there was still time.

She let herself out and eased the door closed. "He's wonderful, Mom," she whispered into the dark. "You would've loved him."

Across the yard, she paused and glanced back. In the dark, the house looked just like it did in her time. There'd been comfort in that.

Of all nights not to have a full moon! With a groan, she tripped over a fallen limb. Righting herself, she held up the flashlight and continued through the brush. What was it about the middle of the night that made *normal* sounds much more terrifying? Heart in her throat, she did everything but *will* herself to the Cessna. When the light fell across the fuselage, she almost shouted out her relief.

She climbed inside the cockpit and flipped on the overhead light. Forgoing the preflight check, she went through the motions to start the engine and began a slow taxi forward. She kept a watch on the special dial.

As she inched the Cessna into the clearing, the strange compass stayed still. After bouncing through tree limbs, thickets, and high grass, she broke into the open and headed for the runway, but still no movement from the dial.

Squeezing her eyes shut, she pressed the brake and shut off the engine. Who was she kidding? The only place she could go was back to 2021, but the compass refused to cooperate. And the only person alive who could help her figure this out was in 1981.

Sure, she could fly to another town, but what good would that do? Where would she hide the Cessna? She'd never get back home that way.

Complete and sudden exhaustion overwhelmed her. She rested her head back against the seat and tried to focus on her next steps.

* * *

Hip braced against the counter, Jax had just taken his first sip of coffee when Doris entered the kitchen. She crossed the room and shoved a note into his hand.

"Read this."

He scanned it.

Hands on her hips, the Dragon breathed her fire on him. "Did you say or do something to make her leave?"

"I came in last night and found her weeping over my model airplanes. She was distraught and told me I couldn't marry Sylvia. That if I did, she, Rylee, would die."

Doris's face softened. "The poor child. What did you say?"

"I scolded her and sent her to bed." He shoved his hands in his pockets. "Where every emotional teenage girl should be at one in the morning."

He pushed away from the counter. "Silly, stupid kid running off in the middle of the night." He tossed down the dregs of his coffee. "Don't worry. I'll find her."

The Dragon's hands lowered from her hips. One rested on his arm. "You have every right to be put out, but you feel it, too, don't you?"

He knew what she meant, but he wasn't about to admit it. "Feel it?"

A chill spread from her hand on his forearm. "This draw she has on us." Her voice dropped. "It's like a spell."

"Adorable and engaging—deceiving and infuriating. It's a spell, all right."

"What do you think she meant about being caught between two worlds?"

"She's led us to believe she has no home, but it sounds like she does and she's missing it. At least her cryptic answers to my questions now make more sense." Sliding away from her hand, he set his coffee mug into the sink. "In light of that, I'll do everything I can to get her back there."

Doris wrinkled her brow and clutched her robe. "Promise me you won't let anger dictate your actions."

"I am angry at myself for having brought her into our home in the first place. From day one, I knew something wasn't right about her story."

"She's sixteen and in trouble." She placed her hand to his chest. "I love this child, Jaxon, and I'm not sure why. But I'm drawn to her. That first night . . . the moment she stepped into my arms, it was as if she belonged here . . . belonged to us."

"I know." Her hand was a weight on his chest—or maybe her words were. He grasped it and squeezed it, moving it away as he tried to breathe.

"Find her. Then we'll both help her to get home."

* * *

Jax pulled up to the base entrance. Throughout the morning, he'd searched where she might have gone, but without success. It was time to get help.

As he got out of the car, sunlight glinted off a small aircraft on the runway. He hopped back in the car and headed toward it, then parked and stepped out.

It couldn't be? The registration number on the fuselage was his. He ran the last few yards, stopping at the propeller. Rylee was sound asleep in the pilot's seat. Heat rose in his belly. What had she done to

Dolly? Dings and dents, scratches and peeling paint marred his pristine beauty—the kind of damage he'd imagine years of neglect would achieve. And she'd done it in *hours*! "Sorry, baby," he whispered to his girl. "What did she do to you?"

Then he ducked underneath the wing and wrenched open the cockpit door.

Angry words rushed to his lips, but recalling his mother's plea, he stood silent. He took stock of the situation and of her—sound asleep, at peace, and oblivious to the trouble she'd caused. Pink rimmed her eyes, so she'd been crying.

Great. The last thing he needed was more drama.

He blew out a breath and tapped her shoulder.

She stirred, and her eyelids fluttered open. Then she gasped and sat up with a jerk.

"What do you think you're doing?" he asked.

She brushed a hand across one eye. "Sleeping."

"I can see that." He could also see the state of his aircraft. He stuffed his hands in his pockets more for her protection than anything else. "It's the *where* that has me puzzled."

She glanced sideways and bit her lip.

"While you sit there contemplating one of your ambiguous responses, think about this—Is this how you treat someone who's opened her heart and home to you? I left my mother sick with worry."

"I'm sorry, but I left a note explaining—"

"You mean that cryptic thing?"

She blinked and sat up even straighter. "I meant to be gone by now."

"In my airplane?"

"It's not your plane—well, technically it is."

His mouth dropped open. "Do you hear yourself?"

"I can explain."

"Get down. Now."

She climbed out and jumped to the ground, landing inches in front of him. Then she took an abrupt step back.

"Look at her." He threw up his hands and tromped to the back of the aircraft. "What did you do, taxi through the woods?"

She gaped at him, speechless.

"I haven't even finished paying for her yet." He raked his fingers through his hair, struggling to hold his temper.

"That's not what happened."

"Not what happened?"

"Your Cessna is still where you left it," she said. "It's safe. I promise."

"Then how do you explain this . . . and that . . . and that?" His voice rose as he stomped beside the fuse-lage, pointing out the dents and scrapes. He stopped and ran his hand across the back of his neck.

"Are you sure it's your Cessna?"

"Numbers don't lie. So, yeah, I'm quite sure." He blew out a sharp breath. "I keep that hanger locked. How did you get in?"

She glanced around as if searching for words. "It wasn't in the hanger. I'd parked in the woods . . . not far from here."

"You're unbelievable."

She scrunched up her face. "If I could just explain."

He folded his arms across his chest. "Fine. Go ahead. Explain."

A flicker of uneasiness twisted her features. She swallowed, fingering the edge of her blouse. "Well, I —It's . . ."

Her lame attempt and inability to explain said enough. He grabbed her by the arm and marched her to his car. He held the door open and stood at an angle to make sure she got in. Neither one spoke as they drove to the farm.

His mother stood waiting for them at the front stoop. "There's your welcoming committee. My mother has enough to worry about without you adding to it. Are we clear?"

"Yes. About the Cessna."

"Leave it."

As Rylee got out, he lifted the phone receiver from its cradle and punched in Rick's number. As it rang, he watched her walk toward his mother, who stood waiting, her face creased.

"Rick, here."

"My Cessna is on the runway at the base."

"How the—"

"I'll explain later. Right now, I need you to move it back to my hanger." He hung up, then caught up with Rylee in time to hear her apology.

"Miss Doris, I'm sorry if I worried you. I just—"

"Wanted to get home, I know." The Dragon pulled her into her arms. "It's going to be all right. Jaxon and I will help you." The look she shot him dared him to disagree.

CHAPTER 22

Jaxon found Rylee in the living room curled up on one end of the sofa stroking Redo's head. She hadn't said much since they'd gotten back and had refused to eat lunch, insisting she wasn't hungry. She watched his approach with a wary gaze.

"It's time you and I had a heart-to-heart."

As he sat in the club chair opposite her, the cat jumped from Rylee's lap, stretched, then sauntered out of the room. He imagined Rylee would love to follow her.

"I found the hanger key where I keep it, so how did you move my Cessna?"

She stared at him, pleading eyes, helpless posture.

He clenched his jaw. "While you're *contemplating* your answer, you need to know there's no record of you landing there. In fact, no one has landed there in weeks. So who helped you, someone from Leland Industries?"

"I don't know who that is." Closing her eyes, she rubbed the back of her neck—a mannerism she was picking up from him? "I know all of this looks bad to you. But it's not what you think." Those eyes opened, pled with his again. Man, they were such a deep violet. "I've made such a mess of things. Getting to know you has made it worse."

"Made what worse?"

"The loss. Having known you and spent time with you . . . it's so much harder."

He leaned toward her. "You keep holding back, and I can't help you unless I know everything. My mother opened her home to you. She loves you. As for me, well, you've been a royal pain more times than I care to count. That said, I've grown fond of you. If not me, then at least let my mom help you."

"Your mom can't help me." Her voice broke.

"Why not?"

Utter desolation slackened her features, her shoulders, her spine, until she looked ready to puddle up on the floor. "Because she doesn't know anything about time travel."

Time travel? Of all the ridiculous . . . Who did she think would buy *that*?

Her eyes closed again, her face contorting. "I have to get home." She clutched his forearm. "I *have* to make sure my mom is all right."

"I thought you said she was dead?"

"When I left, she was alive, but now, I don't know if she still is. You marrying Sylvia will change everything."

Sylvia again! This had to stop.

"It's going to be okay. I'll get you home. We'll find your mother. Just tell me where you live."

She continued to clutch at him as if he hadn't spoken. "If only it were that simple. Nothing is as it should be." Her fingernails dug into his flesh. "Nothing's like she told me it would be. It's all wrong!"

"Who told you how what should be? What's wrong?"

"Everything. I thought I could stay here—change your future."

"Change my future?" He eased from her grip, pressed his fingers to his forehead. "You're not making any sense."

"It makes no sense to me either. I didn't ask to come here. It just happened!"

"Rylee." He placed his hands on her upper arms with gentle care. "What is it you think you know? If you tell me, maybe I can change it—change my actions."

"What in the world . . .?"

Jaxon turned toward his mother and stood. "She's distraught. I'm not sure what to do."

The Dragon hurried over and wrapped an arm around Rylee's shoulder. "It's all right, honey." She beckoned him. "Help me get her to her room."

Soon, she had Rylee tucked in bed pressing a cool compress to her forehead.

"No, I don't need this." Rylee slapped Doris's hand away. "I need to get home."

Jax stood in the doorway. His mother always knew how to handle a crisis. Good thing she'd arrived when she did. He was getting nowhere with Rylee's ramblings.

"We'll do everything we can to get you home, but right now, I want you to sip on my special chamomile tea. I don't share it with just anyone, you know."

Rylee did as she was told like one of his mom's stray kittens.

"When you feel better, we'll talk."

Remarkably, she soon fell asleep. Jax motioned for his mom to follow him into the hallway.

"I heard some of what she said." She pressed her fingers to her furrowed forehead. "What did she mean by change your future?"

"I'm not sure. When she wakes up and is calmer, I'll talk to her."

"But—"

"You need to trust me." He moved his hands to her shoulders and leveled her with his this-has-everything-to-do-with-my-work look.

"How is that even possible?" She opened her mouth to say more, but let out a sigh instead.

"I'll find out what's bothering her. You keep making your calming tea." He glanced at the sleeping figure. "Something tells me I may need it, too."

* * *

Rylee lay on her side fully awake as Jax peeked around her door. When she spotted him, she sat up and swung her legs off the bed.

"May I come in?"

She nodded.

"Don't look so nervous. I promise I won't bite." He pulled out the oak desk chair beside her bed and sat. "How are you feeling?"

She snorted. Just how did he *think* she'd feel? "Like a crazy person."

One side of his mouth quirked up, and her heartbeat gave a hitch at the sight. She'd miss seeing that smile. "Do you feel up to talking?"

"Not really." She kicked her legs, focusing on their back and forth swing as she tucked hair behind her ear. "But it's inevitable at this point. I'm sure I said some things that need clarification."

"I agree." He held out his hand. "Let's take a walk. I don't want my mother listening."

Was she ready to hold his hand? So much of her ached for that connection, but would it be the last time? Shaking her head, she slid her fingers in his. Warm and rough, they closed around hers, that hitch jittered her heartbeat, and something heated the backs of her eyelids. But she couldn't let him see how much this meant to her, how much it *hurt*.

Outside, they walked down the back steps to the large oak tree. Coolness enveloped them in its shade where the old porch swing hung from one of its branches. She sat next to him, simply listening.

Birds skipped and fluttered overhead. The late after-noon breeze swished the leaves in its wake.

"I've always loved this tree," she said, breaking the silence.

He turned slightly, facing her. "You've been here before?"

She met his gaze. "Lots of times."

"Just great, more cryptic comments." He ran his fingers down the side of his neck as if trying to figure out what to say next. "You've laid a ton of stuff on me today, but I don't understand half of it."

She shifted in her seat, looking away from meadow grass waving in the field, and searched his face. "All right. Here it is." She let a deep breath fill her lungs, used it to push the unspeakable words out. "I'm from the future. And when I say the future, I mean right here." She pointed to the ground before them. "I live in a little white cottage, with a red door and green shutters, near this very spot." She ges-tured toward the open field to their right.

There. She'd said it. Out loud.

She held her breath, waiting for his reaction.

He raised a disbelieving brow. "You're telling me, you traveled through time and ended up right where you live?"

"Same place, only forty years earlier."

"So all this time you were already home?"

"Yes."

He barked a laugh and rolled his eyes. "I've heard some whoppers—"

"It's true. I held off telling you so I wouldn't mess up that time-continuum thing."

"Wow, you sure know all the right words. I can say that for you. Who coached you?"

"No one coached me." She slapped her thigh. "See. This is why I didn't want to tell you. I thought I could just figure it all out . . . somehow." Huffing, she folded her arms, dug her bare big toe into the soft grass, and focused on the tree, on the swaying leaves and dappled sunlight. It sure was smaller than in her time.

He clamped a hand on her shoulder, his brow creased. "Sitting there in a huff will not help the situation."

"Situation?" She jerked her shoulder free, her hands fisting in front of her. "*This* is much more than a *situation*. I'm in *real* trouble." She jumped up to pace. "I know you don't believe me. I wouldn't either. I totally get it." She waved her hands in the air, plopped back next to him, sniffed, and swatted at a tear.

"Rant and rave all you want, but I want to know what all that changing my future was all about?"

"If you don't believe me, then why should it matter?"

"Chalk it up to curiosity."

She took a deep breath. "Something happens to you. And I'm afraid my coming back may have altered more than your life, but mine as well."

"So *your* future's now at stake, too."

"Yes."

"What happens to me? What is it you think you know?"

Her hands shook as she tucked her hair behind her ear. "You go on some mission or some test flight and . . . and you don't come back."

"What, I die?"

"You disappear."

"How could you possibly know something like that?"

"I just do. Please don't do it. Don't go. Cancel. Tell them you're sick."

"I can see you're upset, but I can't do that. I cannot cancel."

"Is that odd compass thingy in your F-16?" she asked. "Wait." Her voice rose in pitch, and she bounced in place. "That's it. You don't die! You disappear, and you can't find your way back. Just like what's happening to me."

"Except that particular invention has nothing to do with my work for the military and is not in my F-16."

"Oh." She so wanted to cry. "Then you must double-check everything. You yourself told me how important it is for the pilot to make sure his craft is flight-worthy."

"An F-16 Falcon is a lot more complicated than a single-engine aircraft. I couldn't possibly check such a complicated machine. We have highly trained mechanics for that. They're thorough and I trust them."

Closing her eyes, she rubbed the pulsing points at her temples and focused on breathing. Then planted her elbows on her thighs and braced her forehead on her palms and sat perfectly still, feeling lost. More lost than any girl had a right to feel.

"Let's say, for argument's sake, I believe you," he said. "What else can you tell me about my future?"

She jerked upright to glare at him. "Now you're patronizing me. Why don't you pat me on the head while you're at it?"

His mouth quirked in a half smile—not *a* half smile, *his* half smile. And seeing it was killing her.

She folded her arms and leveled him with a frown. "You don't marry Sylvia, for one."

He waved a hand in a full circle. "So, we're back to her. I should have known. Fine, I'll play. Who might this fortunate woman be who takes her place?"

She wanted to spit on that humorous twinkle in his eyes. Instead, she spit out her words. "I can't tell you."

"That's what I thought. You make these outlandish statements, but can't back them up with facts."

"I'm not sure I should tell you. I mean . . . can you force yourself to fall in love with someone? Either you fall in love with her or you don't."

"According to you, I do." He laced his fingers in his lap. "I do love her, right?"

"Oh yes. And she loves you. Still does. In the future, that is."

He shook his head as if clearing cobwebs from his brain. "So, she's still alive—in your time?"

"She is."

"And she's my wife, not Sylvia."

If only she could make him believe her! She just stared at him, holding her mouth closed. Maybe when he found out there were two planes he'd believe her.

"Sounds like you two are close."

At least he'd figured that one out. "She's the one responsible for getting your Cessna flight-worthy for me."

"Really?"

"You're still being patronizing."

"Keep going." He folded his arms and rocked their swing with his foot. "This is all *very* interesting."

What would it take to make him stop looking at her like that? Hating feeling like a kid with a tall tale, she huffed again. "My mom and I live in a cottage on the same property as her. After school, I always stop by to see her before going home. We drink sweet iced tea, and sometimes, we look through her photo albums. That's how I know so much about you—from her."

"What else?"

"She makes the best fried peach pies in the county. Won the blue ribbon four years in a row at the fair."

"Is that right?" The humorous twinkle was back. Who'd have thought it could ever make her so mad?

"Melt-in-your-mouth delicious."

"I'm sure they are, but I don't think her pies are relative to my disappearance."

"Right."

"What else about my future?"

"You're involved with some secret project. Your wife didn't even know what it was. I tried to get her to tell me, but she clammed up, called you stubborn, then refused to say more."

"She did, did she?"

When she nodded, he spread his arm across the back of the swing and patted her shoulder, giving her a friendly jostling. "A woman who isn't afraid to speak her mind. I like her already."

"Go ahead and joke." She jumped off the swing. "If you go on that flight, this other stuff"—she waved her hand in the air—"won't matter anymore."

Her back to him, she stomped toward the house.

* * *

Jax's attempt at gentle persuasion didn't work with Rylee. She'd responded to his doubts with hard-headed resolve. At least she didn't have another breakdown.

He'd watched her face for subtleties in her expression, anything to signal if she were lying. He took note of her shaking hands and shallow breathing. In her mind, she was telling him the truth, a truth she believed.

He pushed off the swing. He was getting nowhere. Maybe the best thing was to let Child Services place her with another family. Let them deal with her cryptic comments and her time-travel illusions.

His beeper went off. He tugged it from his belt. Then he made his way to the house and dialed Rick's number to respond.

"Need you at the hanger, ASAP."

"What is it?"

"I'm standing here looking at two Cessna 172s with the same ID number."

Suddenly woozy, Jax grabbed the counter as the blood drained from his head. "I'll be right there." He replaced the receiver. Maybe she wasn't delusional after all.

Shortly later, he strode through the hanger opening and stopped midstride. As Rick had said, two Cessnas—Dolly and an imposter—were parked side by side. Each with the same registration number on their fuselage. He crossed the floor and joined his friend.

"This is incredible."

"As well as illegal," Rick said.

Jaxon yanked the pilot door open. His device was exactly where he'd installed it in the other Cessna. "It's safe to say the question as to whether or not someone knows about my invention has been answered."

"Looks like someone's planning a switcheroo—that's for sure." Rick ran his hand over the wing.

"This thing is years old—paint peeling off—scratches and dents all over the place. Whoever did this couldn't possibly think they could pass this aircraft off as yours."

His chest tight, Jax tried to keep his breathing even, his thinking straight. "Which makes an attempted switch unlikely."

"They'd have to do a bang-up paint job for this plane to pass muster. But why go to the trouble if they've already duplicated the ADD?"

He pressed his hand to the nearest wing as if he could feel the plane's pulse, hear its story. "Have you checked it out?"

"Yes, but I can't tell if it's the real deal unless I run some tests."

"It has to be a replica." He traced a dent. "Why else would you need to switch out the aircraft?"

"I still don't see how it got onto the base undetected? Nothing has landed there in weeks. If anything had flown in, we'd have picked it up on radar."

Jax brushed his fingers along the side of his neck. "Good news is, we now have them both. Check for fingerprints. Whoever did this has to have left something behind." He stuffed his hands in his pockets, unable to look away from the aircraft.

"I'll get right on it." Rick folded his arms. "There's something else, isn't there?"

Letting out a long breath, Jax nodded. "I found Rylee sitting in it."

"What?"

"Don't read too much into that. She ran away last night, and this morning, I found her sleeping in the cockpit."

"Still think she's not a spy?"

"She's not, okay?"

"You and your mom are starting to like this kid *way* too much."

"I know." He patted the fuselage. "There's just something about her."

"Yeah, you're probably right. Sounds like she simply stumbled upon a look-alike Cessna with the same ID numbers as yours."

"Forget Rylee." Jax strode ahead of Rick as they left the hanger. "I'll deal with her."

For certain, Rylee was some sort of link in this crazy chain of events, but instinct warned him not to give Rick any more ammunition. The guy already suspected her of being a spy.

Until Jax knew for sure what was going on, he'd play down her possible involvement. As much as he tried to deny it, something about her tugged at his heart *and* his mother's.

She knew there were two Cessnas—knew it before he did. At some point, she would figure out that he now knew it for himself. Then what?

As he climbed into his Chevy, he closed his eyes and then leaned his head back against the seat. Just how he should handle that information? Confront her or let her keep guessing? He put the car in drive.

This girl was a riddle he couldn't quite figure out. Her claiming she was from the future started to sound more and more plausible, which meant either she was crazy or *he* was for believing it. But, whatever was going on, Rylee Dean was right in the middle of it.

CHAPTER 23

June 11, the day of the test flight, Rylee and Doris accompanied Jax to the air base. She'd been in this time over a week—waiting, it seemed, for the inevitable.

Several men from the military were present, as well as some in business suits, likely from Lockley Aeronautics. While they waited, a uniformed man approached Doris and began chatting. Rylee focused on Jax who stood talking to a man in an olive-green jumpsuit near the F-16. He shook the man's hand, then made his way to her.

"You excited to be here?" he asked.

"I guess."

He bent forward at the waist. "That sounds more like a no. I thought you'd be thrilled." He tilted her chin with his hand. "Not everyone gets to see something like this. There's nothing like witnessing an F-16 take off."

"So, you're still going? Even after everything I've said, you're still going?"

His jaw hardened. "Yes."

"Why?" A cry echoed in her voice, and she didn't care who heard it.

"Because it's my job, and I love it. You, of all people, should understand. And if it makes you feel any better, the man I was just talking to is the mechanic. I had him run through another recheck yesterday, and he says everything's in order."

His mother touched his arm, claiming his attention, and Rylee stood by as they spoke.

"Godspeed," Doris said, hugging her son.

Jax turned to leave and had only taken a few steps when Rylee grabbed his arm.

"Don't go," she pleaded. "Don't leave us."

"We've been over this." He peeled her fingers from his arm. "I'll see you later at the house."

He saluted the crowd as he strode across the tarmac. Then he climbed into the cockpit.

So this was it—*the* moment. He would disappear, and her mother would cease to exist. Her coming had been more than in vain and would result in three deaths instead of one.

All she could do now was stand there and wait. It was impossible to change fate—life and death were in God's hands, not hers. She should have found comfort in that, but every bit of her screamed to run after Jax and beg him not to go.

Instead, she stood next to his proud mother and did her best to emulate the woman who'd opened her heart and home to her. She'd need to be extra strong for Doris when Jax disappeared. Maybe that's why she'd been sent back . . . to comfort her. After all, she was Doris's descendant. Except she would never be born, so after today, Doris would have no descendants.

Her brain stopped functioning. She couldn't think another thought. Maybe she was fading away already, and in a few hours, she would be gone, too.

Jax looked at her, violet-blue eyes to violet-blue eyes, then whoosh—he was gone—soaring up up into the sky like the speed of light. Feeling faint, she shook it off and watched until he was out of sight.

"I'm terrified every time I see him do that." Doris looped her hand through Rylee's arm. "My nerves are shot, and I can see by your pallor, you're affected, too."

It wouldn't be long before sorrow creased Doris's smiling face. A feeling of doom covered Rylee like a suffocating blanket.

"I know you're worried." Doris hugged Rylee's arm to her. "I am, too, but he'll be all right. Jax is the best pilot for the job. Let's go home. It'll be some time before he gets back."

The wait at the house was one of the most painful experiences of Rylee's life. Even Doris suggesting she eat something didn't help. All through dinner, she toyed with her food and checked the time on the wall clock.

This was Jaxon C. Scott's death date. According to the date scribbled under that last photo in her grandmother's album—6/11/81—her grandmother said he'd gone missing shortly after. Her chest tightened. They should have heard something by now.

She glanced at Doris, sitting in the club chair, her knitting needles flying around, her face pinched. She was feeling it, too. Rylee thought about how his death would affect this gracious woman and grieved for her. A tear slid down her cheek as she mourned the loss of her mom who would never be born. And what of her? Would she live the rest of her life here in 1981?

"Someone's coming up the drive." Doris jumped up and tossed her knitting aside.

Rylee sprung from the chair and rushed to the front door. She stopped next to Doris, who stood somber with her hands clutched to her breast.

A uniformed officer stepped from the black sedan. This was it. He'd come to the front door and announce his bad news.

Instead, he opened the back door. An arm emerged, then legs, and the officer bent to help Jaxon to his feet.

She heard the rush of breath as Doris released hers. The officer assisted Jax toward the front door. His injured arm tucked in a sling.

While Rylee pressed a hand to her mouth and stifled a sob, Doris flew down the steps. "Heavens, we thought you went missing." She opened her arms and hugged him with the Dragon's fierce affection.

Jax looked over his mother's head at Rylee. "Told you I'd be back."

"Of course you are," Doris said. "No one thought any differently."

He and Rylee locked gazes.

After the officer left, Doris remained at Jax's side, her arm around his waist. "What happened?"

"A bit of a rough landing, that's all. Knocked my elbow out of alignment. It won't even bother me tomorrow."

"Thank the Lord for that. Now let's get you inside."

"I can walk, Mom."

Ignoring his protest, she kept her arm around his waist as they mounted the steps. Once inside, she had him settled into one of the club chairs.

"My arm's what hurts, not my legs."

"Hush and let a mother take care of her son." She hovered over him, plumping the pillow at his back. "Rylee, put the kettle on."

"Yes, ma'am."

When Doris went to the kitchen to wash up, Rylee slid into the club chair across from Jax. Clasping her hands in her lap, she scooted forward. "How did you . . .?"

"Cheat death?" He winked.

"Yes."

"Acting on the information you gave me, I made a few modifications."

Her head went light as breathlessness swept her up. She clutched at the chair arms with both hands to keep from wobbling in her seat. "You changed something?"

"I had the flight time moved an hour later than scheduled, and I flew the test over the Gulf of Mexico instead of the Atlantic."

He stared at her as if contemplating his next words. "As you know, I had the mechanics run through another engine check yesterday. They found it was leaking oil. It was an easy fix, but if it had gotten worse, I could have gotten into real trouble up there. I may owe you my life."

"An oil leak?" She jerked back in her seat. They couldn't have lost Jaxon C. Scott to an *oil leak*! "*That was it?*"

His brow quirked. "You were expecting something worse?"

"I don't see how changing your departure time and your destination could make any difference. And an oil leak isn't all that serious."

"But it could have been, and thanks to you, I'm here."

"I don't know what to say."

"Well, I do. Thank you."

"You believe me then, about time travel?"

"There are other reasons you could have known about the oil leak besides time travel."

With a nod, she sat back. "I know." She couldn't help but stare at him, all safe and alive. Now all she had to do was get him to fall in love with Tessa and solve the mystery of how to get her back home.

Easy, right?

Doris returned, all smiles, beaming with obvious joy that this flight was behind him. Rylee glanced from one to the other and left the room, giving them a chance to visit alone.

She pushed through the screened door to the side porch and into the pleasantly cool night. Cicadas sang from the trees. The pungent, sweet smell from the honeysuckle vine wafted across the yard. Jaxon was safe and alive.

As she gazed out over the acres of farmland, she shivered. Jax would want to know more from her. How much should she tell him?

Until now, she'd held back about her identity because she had to. She so wanted to reveal all of it. Since her arrival, she'd wanted to throw herself against him and tell him everything. She needed help—*his* help. But there had to be a way to give him the information he needed to help her without letting him know she was his granddaughter.

How strange those words sounded. There were only eight years between them, and yet in her mind, he had been so much older. He'd always been part of the past and only recently part of her present, and that made all the difference.

But he was alive, and she—*Rylee Dean*—had helped to keep him that way. She'd traveled through time and saved a life. By some miracle, God saw fit to send her on a remarkable journey to save the life of someone she loved.

Love—maybe that was the key. Maybe love's what changes a life—even a past life. And in this case, the life of someone she'd never met. But hadn't she met him through her grandmother's words? Words were a powerful thing and when added to love, even more so.

Which brought her back to when and how and *what* to tell Jax.

* * *

Jax joined the girl standing by the porch railing. "Thanks for giving my mother and me a few minutes alone." He adjusted his sling, tilted his face toward the evening sky, leaned forward, and braced his free forearm on the railing. "Who are you, Rylee Dean?"

He studied her profile. "Who is this extraordinary girl who knows things she couldn't possibly know?"

She ran her finger along the railing edge, her shoulders edging upward. "What kind of things?"

There it was again—her avoidance. "That you knew to refer to my mother as the Dragon, for one, that I dusted crops when I was thirteen, and that I'd have engine trouble with today's flight. Who do you think sabotaged my aircraft?"

"What?" Her head jerked up. "No one."

"That's what I find odd. You seem so *sure* no one did it. How?"

"You think I'm working with someone and I'd participate in hurting you, maybe even killing you?"

He tipped his face to the sky, picking out constellations as he tried to keep the integration casual. "Of course not, but someone like Leland Industries could be using you. A company like LI has more power than you realize. Enough power to get you to spy for them."

Jerking back a step, she stomped her foot. "I don't know who that company is, nor am I working for them or anyone else."

"But you do know things."

Her arms crept around her middle. The kid did look like she needed a hug as she lowered her head and sighed.

"You say it's because you've traveled back in time. You do realize how difficult that is to believe, right? You talk about a cottage that someday will sit near the oak tree and about an old woman who knows me and claims to have married me, but you have no proof for such declarations." Just an old beat-up plane identical to his that materialized on the base with the ADD in it. That's all.

No. He couldn't let himself go there. He had to hold onto his sanity.

Turning sideways, she rested her hip on the rail. "And I can understand why it's easier for you to think I'm working for a competitor." She spread her hands wide. "But I'm sixteen. You really think I'm some kind of spy?"

"In my line of work, I have to consider every possibility."

Had she known it, the most compelling proof for her argument was the fact she did not exist, in any database, anywhere. Either she was a spy with a false name, or she was who she said she was. In light of recent events, he went with the latter.

So how could the girl standing before him not exist unless she was from the future? Easier to ask the question than to admit it outright. At least, not until he'd tested the area she claimed to have appeared in.

She stared up at him, gripping the handrail. "I came here in a Cessna 172—*your* Cessna 172. That's why there are two of them in this time with the same ID numbers on the fuselage."

So she was ready to address this. "There are indeed two, and they're both locked inside my hanger."

"I've been thinking about that strange dial thing on the control panel." The arms she'd hugged around herself tightened as she ducked her chin again. "I think that answers the *how*, and since you survived this day, then that must be the *why*. Now I have to get back home, and I think you're supposed to help me. Why else would I be led to the person whose plane I now own?"

The yearning in her voice begged him to believe her. Her upturned and hopeful face did the same. This entire experience was unbelievable—*she* was unbelievable. He straightened to a standing position. "Like I said, this go-to answer for difficult questions has got to go. There're more sound and stable explanations, and you need to start giving those."

Her whole body slumped. Tears filled her eyes.

"In the meantime, I have men working on the second Cessna to see if the dial, as you call it, is a fake or not. It's possible someone is trying to steal my invention and using you to help them."

"No." She shook her head so violently her whole body quaked. "I would never hurt you. I need you. I don't know how to get home! I've saved you—now you have to save me."

As a sob broke from her lips, he pulled her into his arms and held her. When her crying subsided, he eased her from him. Keeping one hand on her left arm, he placed his other underneath her chin.

She sniffed, lifting her head. "You created the dial. You must know how it works, how to get me back."

"There's one problem with your theory." His thumb swiped at the tears along her jaw. "The dial is not a time-travel device. It's an Anomaly Detection Device, ADD for short, and it detects anomalies in and on the planet's surface and possibly in the atmosphere. That's why I've created this one for my Cessna, but it hasn't been tested for the atmosphere yet."

She gripped his forearm. "That's it. That's got to be it."

"I'm afraid you've lost me." He tried to slide his arm free.

But she only tightened her grip, her nails cutting into his skin again as her voice rose and rushed out. "I spent most of the time taxying across a field. I was only airborne for about ten minutes. There was a huge lightning bolt seconds before I landed. The plane shook as I hit the runway. Then I passed out."

Something in him stilled, started listening. "You think something about the device detected an anomaly in the earth and brought you back in time?"

"How else did I get here?"

"Except the device is not a time-travel mechanism." He laid his hand over hers, and her grip slackened just enough to let his blood flow again. "I'm not even sure how that would work."

Her hopeful countenance deflated like air from a balloon.

"For the sake of argument, let's say my device did send you back in time. Could you find the exact spot where you showed up? I can at least test for anomalies there."

"I think so."

He nodded. "Then tomorrow we'll check it out."

The balloon filled with air again. She truly believed her story.

And he believed her. God help him—he believed her.

CHAPTER 24

Rylee waited in the living room for Jax. Last night's conversation had filled her with hope. She'd cleared the biggest hurdle when he survived the test flight. Now he was here to help get her home.

She'd continue to work on getting him and Tessa together. The dream of home was one thing, but if she didn't exist in the future, then what was the point?

With a smile, she turned at the sound of footsteps. Jax stood in the entryway, and he was anything but happy. Something chilling her, her smile faded. "What's wrong?"

Jax held something in his hand—her cell phone.

A gasp whooshed past her lips, and her hand reached for the wall to balance herself as she went light-headed.

He waved it. "I see you recognize this."

The phone had been opened to the most recent cover photo, the one of the compass from his Cessna.

"Handy little device. I had trouble figuring out how to turn it on, but as you can see, I was successful. Very high tech, and something a company like Leland Industries could manufacture. It's the kind of small electronic equipment a spy might use."

He took one step closer, turning it over in his hand. "It takes excellent photos—state of the art, in fact. I've never seen such clarity. Mom found it tucked beneath your mattress while she was making your bed. You can imagine what she thought."

"Okay." Rylee raised both palms. "I know this looks bad, but it's not what you think."

"Is Rylee Dean even your real name? Or did LI give you that as well?"

She huffed. "Rylee Dean is my real name, and until last night, I've never heard of Leland Industries."

"I'm most intrigued by these colorful little squares. I pressed on several of them, but nothing happened."

"I can explain what those are for if you would—"

"You almost had me fooled with your time-travel nonsense. I'd started to think there might be something to it. But this evidence says otherwise."

What was she supposed to say? To do? "Maybe. In a rational world that makes total sense, but my world is far from rational."

He shook the phone in front of her. "No way on earth could you have a device like this unless some high-tech company like LI gave it to you."

It was a high-tech company called Apple.

"And did they also give you your name? There's no record of a Rylee Dean—anywhere."

She threw up her arms. "That's because I haven't been born yet!"

She squared her shoulders and stepped forward. "That ADD thing is also in the Cessna you found me in, and when I saw it in *your* Cessna, I wanted to take a picture of it to compare the two. That's all I was doing. It's what brought me here and the key to getting me home."

He barked a laugh.

"Jax, I know this looks incriminating. But, listen, that device is more than a camera, and I can prove it." She extended her hand for the phone.

"Please do." He handed it over and leaned against the doorjamb.

As soon as the phone lay in her palm, it went dead. Oh no! "It died."

"How convenient."

"I can charge it. Liam is—"

"That's enough." He raised a hand and walked out. "We're done here."

"Have you forgotten I saved your life?" she yelled after him, but he was already gone.

Grandma was right—what a stubborn, stubborn man.

* * *

Rylee stood at the kitchen window. His last words played over and over in her mind. Maybe she should appeal to Doris for help. Or she could go to Tess. After all, she was her grandmother. That connection alone should count for something. One thing was certain—she'd never willingly enter a government institution. She'd run away first.

She gazed at the dead iPhone. She hadn't heard back from Liam yet about the charger, but she couldn't wait any longer. So she crossed the floor to the wall phone, lifted the receiver, and dialed his number.

"Hi! You've reached the Whitfield residence. Please leave your number after the beep, and we'll get back to you as soon as possible."

"Liam, it's Rylee. I wanted to check on that charger. Please call me when you get this. Talk soon."

Once she had the charger, Jax would have all the proof he needed.

While she waited for Liam to call back, she'd do some baking. Yesterday she'd spotted a roll of Toll House Cookie dough in the fridge. She found it on the second shelf, set the phone aside, grabbed a pair of scissors, and cut into the wrapper.

Thirty minutes later, chocolate, sugary baked goodness wafted in and around the kitchen. She opened the oven door to take a peek. Just about done. She rummaged inside several cabinets before spotting the cooling racks. After lining them up on the counter, she fit her hands into the cheery, floral oven mitts, then pulled the hot trays from the oven.

She'd just slid the last warm cookie onto the cooling rack when someone entered the house. "In the kitchen, Miss Doris," she hollered. As she removed the oven mitts, Sylvia joined her, followed by a middle-aged woman and Sheriff Carney.

"Hi, Sylvia. Miss Doris and Jax aren't home right now." Rylee gestured to the cooling racks. "Would you all like a cookie while you wait?"

"That's her." Sylvia spoke to the woman.

"Are you Rylee Dean?" the woman asked.

A chill went down Rylee's back. "Yes."

"I'm Mrs. Peterson with Child Services. We're here to take you to our facility. We've assigned you to another family." The lady's kindly tone and expression couldn't lessen such a blow.

Her heart racing, Rylee tried to gulp in enough air to respond. "I don't understand. I'm supposed to stay here with the Scotts."

Mrs. Peterson checked the paperwork in her hands. "According to my files, that was only temporary until we could find someplace permanent for you. So if you'll gather your things, we can go."

"But I'm safe here—there's no need for me to leave."

Was she imagining it? Or was Sylvia enjoying her discomfort?

"That's true, unless the arrangements were temporary."

"Does Miss Doris know about this?"

Mrs. Peterson and the sheriff cast glances at each other.

Rylee plopped down into the nearest chair. "I'm not going . . . not until I see Miss Doris. If she says I'm to go, then I'll go."

"I'm sorry, but that decision isn't up to her." The woman nodded to Carney.

He stepped forward and took Rylee by the arm. "I'm sorry, but this is out of my hands. Let's go."

She pulled away from him, but he tightened his grip. "Chin up, girl. You can do this." He led her from the kitchen.

"What about my things?"

"I'll make sure she gets them," Sylvia piped up in an obvious attempt to appear helpful. "It's the least I can do."

* * *

Rylee sat in Mrs. Peterson's back seat and watched the farmhouse disappear in her line of sight. Mrs. Peterson had looked more than once to Sylvia for direction. She couldn't blame Sylvia for trying to get rid of her—hadn't she done the same thing to Jaxon's fiancée?

To survive, she'd have to play her part long enough to lull the malleable Mrs. Peterson to sleep. At the police station, Rylee played complaint with everything asked of her. Still, she asked, "I thought you were taking me to your facility?"

"We will in a bit." Peterson gestured to the chairs. "Just take a seat until then."

Rylee sat on the bench she'd occupied that first night. After almost two weeks, she was back where she'd started. But she was braver now and knew a lot more. This Peterson woman may think she was placing her with another family, but Rylee had other plans.

CHAPTER 25

Jaxon arrived home to the Dragon in an uproar. Sheriff Carney stood over her with palms upraised. "Doris, you'll have a heart attack if you don't calm yourself."

"How could you drag that sweet girl out of my home?"

"I didn't drag her. She came with us willingly."

"I don't believe it."

"What the devil is going on?" Jax crossed the living room, stopping at his mother's side.

"Oh, Jaxon." Mom wiped her eyes with a handkerchief. "That woman is responsible for this—you mark my words."

"Calm down and tell me what happened."

"Sylvia showed up with someone from Child Services."

"What?"

"Nancy Peterson," Carney interrupted, "showed up at the station with Sylvia. I'm sorry, Jax, but her papers were in order. I had no choice."

He pushed back against the flush of adrenaline and spoke with forced restraint. "Are you telling me you took Rylee without informing us?"

"She had a court order."

"A call would have been nice, Carney." Jax ran his hand around the back of his neck. "I'll handle it from here."

"Walk me out, Jax," Carney said.

Once outside, Jax and Carney stopped on the porch.

Jax folded his arms. "Where'd they take her?"

"They're at the police station."

What on earth? "Why would they go there?"

"Peterson didn't say. I hung back here to wait for one of you to return. I didn't like how they insisted on Rylee leaving without saying goodbye, but listen." Carney held up a hand. "Your mother's right about one thing."

"And what would that be?"

"Sylvia." He adjusted his hat and wouldn't focus on Jaxon. "Sylvia Lockley spearheaded this. Just thought you should know."

Back inside, Jaxon poured himself a drink.

His mother dabbed her eyes, sniffed, and tucked her handkerchief into her dress pocket. Then the Dragon reared her head. "First thing tomorrow, Judge Carlyle is going to get a piece of my mind."

Taking a sip, Jax sat next to her and put an arm around her shoulder. "It's a shock to come home to something like this. I'll talk to the judge."

"You most certainly will not!" She sat up straight. "I've known Jeffrey since third grade, and I can handle him."

He stifled a smile. He hadn't named her the Dragon for nothing.

"Mom, listen." He clasped one of her hands. "We knew this day would come. Knew her stay was only temporary."

"But it should never have happened the way it did." Her voice caught in her throat. "I didn't get to say goodbye."

With his other hand, he touched her shoulder. "You were right about Sylvia's involvement. Carney confirmed it."

"I knew it."

"Tell you what—you take care of the judge while I handle Sylvia." He kissed her cheek. "I'll stop by the police station on the way. I'll find out Rylee's whereabouts, I promise."

Moments later, he headed down the driveway. If he could talk to Mrs. Peterson, he might convince her to let Rylee stay with his mother until she saw the judge in the morning.

As he drove up, a car was pulling away from the curb with Rylee in the back seat. He got out and tried to flag them down, but the car picked up speed.

"Peterson?" he yelled. "Hey. Slow up." He sprinted forward and slapped the vehicle with his palm to get the driver to stop. When that didn't work, he dove for the handle, missing it by inches. He stumbled forward and stood, watching the car drive away.

Heat seared his insides, and he clenched his fists. This was Sylvia's doing. The law may have boxed him in, but he could deal with her.

* * *

Jax stood at the Lockleys' massive front door. He'd gone over what he planned to say, and the sooner, the better. Over the past weeks, his relationship with Sylvia had begun to wane. He'd sensed it and felt she had as well. He'd already planned to break it off, but in a way that would make sense for the both of them.

But this latest move infuriated him. He'd kept those feelings from his mother since she'd had enough anger to fuel her own fire without him adding to it.

The rattling doorknob brought him back into the present.

"Darling, this is a surprise." Sylvia stepped back. "Come in. We're just finishing dinner. I'm sure Mom and Dad would love to see you."

He took her hand and drew her forward. "What I have to say is for your ears only."

She stepped onto the porch and closed the door behind her. She gazed into his face with nothing more than mild curiosity. As she looked at him, her lovely smile and fair complexion seemed cold and impersonal—artificial, in fact. No sign of real interest radiated from her. She was all surface and without depth of character.

She offered nothing in which to build a life together. How had it taken him this long to realize it? Everything of real substance and all the compromise had been on his side. He'd longed for a genuine, from-the-heart connection. Sylvia hadn't been capable of either. He'd always known something was missing, and it had taken a sixteen-year-old girl to make him see it.

"Why did you do it?" He held his tone relatively civil.

Her eyes widened before she wound her arms around his neck. "Well, *you* were never going to get rid of her. So . . ." She plucked at his collar. "I took matters into my own hands."

Something ferocious ripped through his core. "You had no right. I left my mother in tears."

"I'm sorry." Her lips pouted, her tone petulant.

"Have you any idea what Rylee is going through right now? Do you even care?"

"She's with a good family. I made sure of it."

"You made sure?" He grabbed her wrists and wrenched her arms away. "I don't know you, and frankly, I'm not sure I ever did. This engagement is off."

As he began to step away, she tugged off the diamond ring and threw it at him. With a reflex from years of flight training, he caught it midair.

As Sylvia slammed the door, he blew out a breath, tossed the ring into the air, and caught it with a flourish. He clipped down the steps, wondering if he could get his money back. No matter, the ring was a small price to pay for his freedom.

CHAPTER 26

Rylee sat with her head lolled against the back seat, a pounding in her temples and rebellion in every muscle as the car slowed.

"Here we are," Mrs. Peterson said. "Your family will arrive shortly. You'll like them, I promise. Can I get you something to drink while you wait?"

"No, ma'am."

"Make yourself comfortable. I have to make a quick call in my office. I won't be long."

After Peterson left the sitting area, Rylee approached a middle-aged woman at the main desk, trying not to let her outrageous shoulder pads distract her. "Excuse me, where's the ladies' room?"

"Down that hall on the right." The woman didn't even look up.

Rylee did her best to walk like a normal person. Once inside the bathroom, she rushed to the window. Unlocking it proved to be the easy part. When she pushed up, nothing happened. She tried again, but the stiff thing only moved about two inches.

Putting her full body weight into it, she pushed harder. Inch-by-inch, it gave way.

She cast a fearful glance over her shoulder, then gave one final shove. The window opened. She hoisted herself up and over the ledge, flung one leg through and then the other, and hit the ground running.

It was dark when she got to the Scotts' farm. The silhouette of two people occupied the lit living room. She slipped around the back of the house and through the back door, then made her way to Jax's room.

"Please be there," she whispered and went to the box holding the hanger key. Whew! It was right where she'd left it. Clutching it so tightly it pinched against her bones, she headed back outside.

Thank goodness for Doris's bike. It would've been a long walk to the hanger without it.

Once she arrived, she unlocked the wide doors and stepped inside. Both Cessnas greeted her like long-lost friends. What a strange and wonderful sight seeing them side by side!

She climbed into the cockpit and went through the steps to start the aircraft. When the propeller came to life, she hopped out, rushed across the floor, then opened the massive doors.

Back in the cockpit, she taxied out of the hanger and onto the tarmac. Drawing on everything Coop had taught her, she had the Cessna airborne in minutes.

She flew over the town and the neighboring farms to the Scott farm and crossed over the tree line, seeking the anomaly Jax had spoken of. She glared at the special dial. "Come on—*move!*"

Heat formed behind her eyelids, and a sob broke from her lips. She'd so hoped, but it was no use. The compass lay there, motionless.

Since her desperate attempt to get the ADD to move turned out to be an epic fail, she needed a place to land. About ten minutes later, she spotted an open field. She banked the aircraft, turned, then straightened out for landing.

It was rough going as the field had more bumps and potholes than she'd expected. At touchdown, her head snapped forward and slammed into the wheel. She fought off a dizzying sensation, pulled herself upright, and did her best to maintain control. The plane bounced and shuddered, then rumbled to a halt. She let out a breath, lifted a shaky hand to her forehead, and unclenched her jaw.

Shutting off the ignition, she sat back. Her head throbbed, and she closed her eyes against the pain. All she wanted to do was rest her head and breathe.

Both her solo flights had taken place at night, and not under the best of circumstances either, but she still felt pleased to have accomplished them.

Savoring the moment was short-lived. Jax or the police or both would be looking for her. Taking the plane had been rash and stupid. She should have gone to Tessa.

Her legs shook as she opened the door. She stepped to the ground, steadying her hand on the wing for support, then took off for a string of lights.

* * *

Jaxon sat in the oversized club chair, sipping a much-needed drink. When a knock sounded on the front door, he drug his body from the deep cushion, set his glass on the side table, and walked to the door.

A teenage boy stood on the front porch. "Is Rylee home?"

"Liam, right?"

"Yeah, that's right."

"I'm afraid she's gone."

Liam paled. "You mean like forever?"

"Child Services picked her up this afternoon. We're hoping it's a misunderstanding and she'll be back with us soon. We're seeing the judge in the morning."

"I hope so, too."

"Is there anything else?"

"No, I just brought back her—um, I brought her something."

"I'll take it for her."

After a slight hesitation, Liam withdrew a black cord from his pocket, then handed it over. One end had a standard plug, and the other had two wirelike prongs attached, like some sort of electronic charger —although clearly homemade.

"What's this?" Jax inspected it, turning it over in his hands.

"You should ask Rylee that question."

Huh. Jax eyed the teenager. "I'm asking *you.*"

Liam swallowed. "I'm not at liberty to say." He pivoted, but before he could take another step, Jax had him by the shirt collar. He led him inside to the chair he'd just vacated. "Sit down."

Liam sat.

"Rylee may be in trouble, so tell me what this is for?"

Liam hesitated and cast a wary glance up at Jax. "She has this device, and she left home without the charger. That thing in your hand is the one I made for it."

His heart rate kicking up, Jax slid the slender apparatus from his back pocket. "This device?"

The kid nodded.

"Show me how to connect it."

"I'll need a knife to pry off the back."

Jax grabbed a pocketknife from his pants. "Will this work?"

"Perfect." Minutes later, Liam had removed the back and hooked the charger up to the battery.

"Plug it in there." Jax pointed to the outlet near the base of his chair. Liam did so and then set the battery on the table while they waited for it to charge.

"How long will this take?"

"You'll have to leave it plugged in for a few minutes to get enough charge to turn on the phone. Five or ten minutes should do it. Once the battery is charged, we can reinsert it in the phone."

Phone? Jax crossed his arms. "How do you know this stuff?"

"I've been taking electronics apart since I was little." Liam shrugged. "Our entire basement is full of parts and pieces of just about everything you can imagine."

After five minutes, he reinserted the battery and turned on the phone.

"Looks like that worked." Jax bent over the table for a closer look. The screen had come on with the photo of the ADD Rylee had taken.

"Cool, huh?" Liam picked it up off the table. "You won't believe what else this sweet little piece of equipment can do."

"Sweet?" Jax eyed him with a raised brow.

"One of Rylee's words."

"I know. What else?"

"She's better at explaining it, but it's a tiny hand-held computer. As you can see, it's also a camera, and it stores tons of information. Like documents and photos. You scroll through the photos with a thing called an app. This one says photos. See?"

While Jax rubbed the back of his neck, trying to take in everything, Liam tapped the photo icon, and pictures filled the screen. "Glide your thumb over the pictures like this." He demonstrated by scrolling and clicking on individual photos. "Select one, and it fills the screen. Now you try it."

Jax took the phone and clicked on one of the photos, a picture of Rylee standing in front of the Cessna 172—his Cessna. He felt the blood drain from his face. "*Where* was this photo taken?"

"You'll have to ask Rylee."

"You say this is also a phone?"

"Yes, but it doesn't work because there are no cell towers here for it to connect to."

The home screen came back on, and for the first time, Jax noticed the date. June 3. The date she showed up at the base.

"Thanks. I'll have Rylee go over the rest of it."

He walked Liam out, and when he got to his car, Liam turned back. "For what it's worth, she wants to tell you everything. She just doesn't know how."

Jax sat in the club chair and picked up the phone device. He clicked on the app for the date. The year 2021 displayed on the screen. His heart nearly stopped—she'd been telling him the truth.

He stared ahead as another thought struck him. Then he reached into his pocket for his change. Rylee had given him some of hers the last time they were at Billy's. He ran his right index finger over the coins in his left palm to check the dates—2002, 1997, 2016. He shook his head. *Can this be possible?*

He reopened the phone and pressed the photo app. Earlier, he'd noticed a picture of a front-page newspaper article. Maybe it had a date to confirm her story further. He scrolled through the pictures to the one he'd seen before.

When he found it, it was almost impossible to read. He clicked on it, and except for a partial headline, the article was still too small to make out. He ran his finger across the screen, but nothing changed, then two fingers. He tried spreading his fingers apart. That worked.

The photo enlarged enough for him to read the headline—Granddaughter of Jaxon C. Scott Qualifies for Solo Flight. "Rylee Dean, the proud granddaughter of Jaxon C. Scott for whom this airport is named . . ." His heartbeat stuttered—heat rocked his inner core. He lowered the phone to his lap. He couldn't read another word even if he'd wanted to. The headline had been convincing enough. Rylee Dean, *his granddaughter,* traveled back through time to him.

CHAPTER 27

Jax stood on the front porch and inhaled the fresh night air. Rylee was out there somewhere, and he had to find her. The poor kid. He could only imagine what she must have gone through since her arrival. No wonder she was frantic to get home to her mother. The woman had to be sick with worry. The puzzle pieces called Rylee Dean started making sense.

The phone rang. He hurried inside to answer it.

"Got a minute?" Rick asked.

"Yeah, what's up?"

"Sorry to call so late. I'm on my way to the hanger, and I have some news."

With such enthusiasm in Rick's voice, Jax didn't need to see his friend's face to know the information would be extraordinary.

"This just came across the wire. NASA is tracking a growing anomaly in the earth's magnetic field."

Jax's whole body stiffened, his senses heightened, and his breathing slowed. "How big is it?"

"The word they've used is *vast*. It's much larger than the one you and I are tracking here."

"Something that massive could weaken the magnetic field causing a tear in space." Jax caught his breath. *Hurling an object straight through it.*

"Not at all what we thought it would do." Rick's voice rose. "Our research has been limited to what it would do on Earth, but not in the sky above us. This thing caused malfunctions in the space shuttle Columbia. Not only during launch, but while in orbit."

"So, if one that massive can affect the space shuttle and satellites in space, then a smaller anomaly like ours would also affect the atmosphere above us." With the receiver to his ear, Jax began to pace. "Which means the reduced magnetic field in the anomaly would affect technological systems onboard aircraft like . . . my Cessna."

"Are you saying flying your Cessna over one of these anomalies could cause a malfunction in the aircraft?"

"That's what I'm saying."

And most likely what happened to Rylee's aircraft, sending it and her through time and space.

"What kind of malfunction are we talking about here?" Rick asked.

"I'd say pretty extreme, and the last place I'd want to be is in an aircraft that short-circuits in flight."

Jax hung up and had taken only two steps when the phone rang again. He swung around and picked up the receiver.

"Jax"—Carney spoke fast as soon as Jax said hello —"Rylee ran away."

"She what?"

"Seems she escaped Peterson's clutches."

"When—how?"

"Climbed out of the bathroom window at Child Services."

"Okay, thanks for letting me know." He had no idea how to find Rylee, but he wouldn't sit here and wait either. He scribbled a note to his mother in case she woke up and found him gone. As he set the note on the foyer table, the phone rang again.

"I just arrived at the hanger and found the doors wide open!" Rick shouted. "The old Cessna is missing."

Rylee!

Jax hung up, sprinted across the lawn, and jumped into his Chevy. "Please be there." If the older Cessna was the same aircraft as his, then the tracking device should also be there. But after forty years would it still work? He turned on his GPS and held his breath.

A green light appeared on the screen. *Yes!* The signal was clear.

As he drove, he held his GPS in his left hand and followed the Cessna's signal. The tracker light had stopped moving which meant Rylee had landed somewhere near Beacons' Farm just outside of town. Only minutes away. He pressed the accelerator and headed west.

He spotted Rylee walking along the dirt road flanking the Beacons' place. As he approached, he flashed his headlights to get her to stop. He pulled up alongside the road and got out.

"Rylee, it's Jax!" While he ran toward her, she took a step back, eyeing him. Her usual adoring gaze was nowhere in sight, and her distrust hit him like an unexpected blow.

As he got closer, he noticed blood on her forehead. She blinked up at him as though questioning his intentions. He didn't say another word, just hauled her into his arms. "Are you all right?"

"A bit of a headache, that's all." When he released her, she touched her forehead. "How did you find me?"

"The Cessna has a tracking signal in the cockpit."

"It does?"

"It's for security. It would be a disaster if the ADD fell into the wrong hands."

"I'm sorry. I should never have taken it."

"Don't worry about that right now." He placed his hands on her upper arms and inspected her forehead. "That's some bump."

Again, she lifted a shaky hand to her temple. "It does hurt a little."

"Let's get you someplace where I can take a closer look."

She followed him to his car. Once inside, he switched on the overhead light. She squinted, turning away.

"Hold still." With her chin in his hand, he tipped her face to the light. "I think it's just a surface wound, but when I get you under better lighting, I'll be able to tell how deep the gash is."

He grabbed a paper napkin from the glove compartment. "Hold that to your head and keep it there. We only have a few miles to go before we get to the log cabin."

She held the napkin as he'd instructed. "What cabin?"

"It belongs to Rick's family. It sits on a nice little creek running along the back of the property."

He flipped off the overhead light and started the ignition, then pulled away from the roadside, heading south. Rylee leaned back against the seat and closed her eyes. A half a mile later, he veered off onto a gravel road. "Almost there."

She nodded, keeping her eyes closed.

"And . . . we're here."

He got out and walked around the car to open her door. As she swung her legs to the side, he caught her arm to steady her.

"I'm okay, really."

"That remains to be seen." Keeping his arm around her, he helped her up the steps. He found the key above the door and slid it in the lock, then opened the cabin, and flipped on the light.

The smell of leather and pine filled the space. Blue-and-red plaid pillows slumped on leather sofas. Family photos and old books, worn from many reads, stacked on a low wooden coffee table—an open checkerboard beside them.

He led her to the sofa. "Have a seat, and I'll get something to clean that wound." He returned with a washbasin of warm water, a white kitchen towel, and a first-aid box.

His hand on her shoulder, he gazed into Rylee's ashen features, taking in the deep shadows under her eyes. She seemed to be having trouble staying awake. He dropped down beside her, facing her, dunked the cloth into the warm water, then wrung it out over the basin. Swabbing the warm cloth to her forehead, he cleaned the area around the wound and the wound itself.

She winced when he dabbed her blood away.

"Sorry, I'm being as gentle as I can."

"It's okay."

From the first-aid box, he took out an antibiotic cream and spread it over the gash, then followed with gauze and white tape. "There. That should do it." Hand on her knee, he eyed her pale features. "How's it feel, now?"

"Much better, thank you."

She'd kept her eyes lowered, leaving him guilty for how he'd ended things. He'd left her, and then she'd been taken from what should have been a safe place.

"You look beat. Why don't you lie back against the sofa cushions while I fix us some hot tea?"

Two deep lines furrowed between her eyes. "Why are you being so nice? I stole your aircraft for crying out loud."

He stuffed his hands into his pockets. When she gazed at him with that sweet, little sincere expression of hers, as if he'd hung the moon, he finally got it. Got her.

She'd once told him she loved and admired him—loved him as a granddaughter loves a beloved granddad was what she'd meant. She'd grown up hearing stories about him, most likely embellished by the teller, of heroic acts he wouldn't recognize as himself. But tales that garnered hero worship from an impressionable teenage girl. It was all he could do not to take her in his arms and hug her like his grandfather used to hug him and assure her everything would be all right.

"I prefer to think of it as *our* aircraft." The corner of his mouth quirked. "We'll talk after I make the tea."

Soon, he returned with two mugs, each with a tea bag label hanging over the side. "I added sugar. I hope that's okay."

"It's how I like it, hot and sweet." She bent her head and blew over the rim of the mug. "Why are we really here? You could have taken me back to the farm or the sheriff's department."

"Carney contacted Mrs. Peterson, and she's agreed to let you stay with us until we can get the judge to reverse his order."

"Does that mean you don't think I'm a spy for Leland Industries?" Violet-blue eyes—*his* color blue eyes—gazed at him as she cradled the mug.

He sipped his own hot liquid. "About that. I'm sorry I didn't believe you. And I'm sorry for what Sylvia did to you."

Rylee ran her finger along the mug's rim. "Weren't you planning on doing the same thing?"

"No. I wasn't going to have you hauled away like some criminal and break my mother's heart. I'd planned to take you to Leland Industries corporate office, confront them with attempted theft, and then leave you in their care. I sure thought you were the daughter of one of their senior officers."

He set his cup down, then tilted her chin with his hand. "I'm not proud of the way I left things with you. I have no excuse for saying what I said and leaving you like I did, but some people would do just about anything to get their hands on my invention."

"Which is why you're very protective of it."

"So. Are we good?"

An engaging smile parted her lips. "We're more than good." She held her cup to her stomach. "I like it here. It's cozy."

"I like it here, too. Rick and I spent many summer afternoons fishing here."

"Which is how you got that scar over your left eye." As soon as she said it, she stopped, her eyes widening.

"True." He tapped his finger along his cup. "Did my mother tell you that?" When she didn't answer, he bent closer to her. "I hope by now you know you can tell me anything."

She still hesitated. Maybe the bump on her head was making her cautious. His actions earlier had given her reason to be. So he took a different tactic. "Liam came by this evening."

Her head snapped up. "He did?"

"He brought a charger for this." He slipped her phone from his back pocket.

"Oh."

"He showed me a little of how it works."

Her lashes fluttered as she fixated on the phone.

"Rylee, look at me." He waited for her to obey. "I believe you."

She closed her eyes, and when she opened them, tears glistened on her lashes. "You do?"

"Uh-huh." He inched forward on the chair. "I noticed an article in your phone. I couldn't see it very well due to its size, but I was able to make out my name and a couple of other things. I want to make sure it says what I think it says." He handed her the phone. "Can you enlarge the photo so I can read it?"

She brushed away a tear. "I can do even better." She pulled the newspaper article from her back pocket and handed it to him.

He eyed it, then her, took it from her hand, and proceeded to unfold it.

"I had it with me the night I left. And this photo." She handed it to him.

He held the picture between his fingers. "I don't recall having had this taken."

"That's because it hasn't happened yet. Tess took that. You were already married at the time."

Already married. Did hearing those words make it real? And did she simply mean he was married at the time or was she saying he'd been married to that Tess girl? His thoughts scrambled to understand. He handed back the photo, then focused on the article, published June 3, 2021. As he read, he periodically glanced at her. When he finished, he didn't say anything, just returned it back and stood.

He ran his hand over his mouth. She eyed him, half in anticipation, half in dread as if her life depended on his reaction.

He began to pace.

"You okay?" she asked.

He stopped and wiggled his fingers at the side of his head. "Just trying to put all the pieces together." Brow furrowed, he continued walking back and forth. "The woman you've been telling me about who owns the property where you and your mom live, is she your grandmother?" He paused and pivoted, pointing one finger at her. "Not just some sweet elderly lady you're fond of?"

"Correct."

He continued pacing. "And she lives here in town." He stopped in front of her and pointed toward the floorboards. "This town?"

"Yes."

"Let me get this straight. The article I just read . . ." He pressed his hands to the sides of his head. "I can't believe I'm going to say this out loud."

"You're almost there," she whispered.

He stared at her, trying to control the rush of emotions. "*I'm* your grandfather? The man you've been telling me about all this time is me?"

She nodded.

"And your mom is . . ."

"Your daughter and my mother."

"So, when you told me you'd die if I married Sylvia, you weren't being overdramatic."

"No. That's why I was so worried about my mom. If you marry Sylvia, then my mom will never be born."

"And if she isn't born, then you won't be, either."

Tears glistened on her heart-shaped face.

"Hey. It's all right." He plopped back in the seat opposite and folded her hands in his. "I. Choose. You. I have no idea how to convince this Tess woman, but I'll do everything in my power to make her fall in love with me."

Rylee swiped at her wet cheeks, a laugh jumping up her chest. "That shouldn't be too difficult."

"Knowing what you know, I'm surprised you didn't try your hand at matchmaking."

"Well, I did kind of interfere."

"How so?"

"Whenever Sylvia left a message on your answering machine, I erased it. And on the night she cooked, I, um, may have adjusted the temperature a bit."

"Of course, you did." He grinned. "And we both know the sprinkler going off was you."

As her cheeks glowed, he squeezed her hands. "Why didn't you tell me all of this before?"

"I wanted to, but I didn't want to mess up the—"

"Time-continuum thing," he said. "You're still worried about that, huh?"

"A little."

"You may be right." He clasped his hands together and rested his forearms on his thighs. "But there's something you need to understand—right here and right now—the future hasn't happened yet. Yes, you know things, and it's likely your presence has changed some of those things. Maybe for the better.

"As far as I'm concerned, none of it has happened yet. Think about it, everything we learn, experience, see, and hear can change our life's path in an instant. You coming back here is nothing short of a miracle. You're the kid sister I've always wanted. The daughter my mother never had. We've been given a gift. This might be selfish on my part, but I wouldn't change having had you in my life for anything in the world."

"So forget the time-continuum thing?"

He laughed. "We'd better not."

"What happens next?" She sniffed and swiped her cheek with the back of her hand.

"Now we have to get you back. I've been thinking about the anomalies and how they might be the key here. Tonight, I learned new information from NASA. I've got Rick and my crew working on it, and we should know something soon."

Her head tipped to one side, her lips pressed together, and the tip of her tongue sneaked past them. She seemed to be holding her breath, afraid to hope. "Okay."

"But listen, even though I know your heart's in the right place, you cannot change anything else. Whatever you change here could alter the future for people we don't even know. Do you understand?"

"I didn't think about that." She placed her half-finished tea on the pine coffee table.

"From here on out, I can't know what you know."

"But, Jaxon, what if there's—"

"No." He held up a hand, firm on this. "I know too much already. Any more and I'll be second-guessing my every action. As much as I'm tempted, I can't go there."

"I understand." Tears pooled in her eyes, and she threw herself against his chest, then sobbed out, "I'm so happy."

He wrapped her in his arms and held her close.

"I'll never forget you or my time here." She whispered the words into his shoulder, her hands fisting up wads of his shirt.

"Nor will I."

* * *

Rylee padded softly behind Jax into the farmhouse so as not to awaken Doris. He grabbed a letter from the hall table and crushed it in his hand.

"What was that?"

"A note I'd left for my mother. I didn't want her to worry in case she woke up while I was gone. Let's get some sleep. In the morning, Mom will take care of the judge's order, and you and I can make a plan to get you back home to my daughter." Smiling, he shook his head when he said it.

She threw her arms around his neck. "Good night . . . Grandpa."

"'Night, Kitten. Sweet dreams."

Sighing with contentment, Rylee climbed into bed. Tonight had been wonderful. Jaxon now knew who she was and believed her. She was at peace, finally having him as her ally.

As she settled deep under the covers, something important nagged at the back of her mind—something she had to tell him. But no matter how hard she tried, the memory eluded her. His life was still in danger—she knew that much. And she refused to come this far and risk losing him all over again. No matter what he'd said, she'd have to warn him as soon as she could remember.

CHAPTER 28

Two days later, Jax made his way across the lawn to join Rylee under the oak. "With as much time as you spend on this swing, people will be thinking you're a yard ornament."

"I like it here because it's my front yard."

"Right. How could I forget?" He sat next to her. "Good news. I'm close to figuring out how to get you home."

Slumping against the back of the swing, one foot idly kicking at the ground, she let out a sigh. "Will I have a home to go to?"

"That I can't say."

"You know how to fix it, don't you?"

"If it makes you feel any better, Sylvia and I are history. Your presence in my home irritated her enough to reveal a side of her I hadn't acknowledged until now."

She butted her shoulder against his. "You're welcome."

"After you're gone, I'll meet your Tess and see what comes of it."

"Like a spark?"

"Yeah, but that's all I can promise."

"No pressure, only my whole life depends on it."

"I'm twenty-four. Cut me some slack, will ya? A month ago, I had my entire life worked out. Then you showed up." His chest warming, he patted her shoulder and eyed her with amused tolerance. Hard to comprehend this girl was his granddaughter. "You could at least pretend I have some control here."

"You two were supposed to have a whole night together. Granted, you weren't alone, but still, that's a lot of time for—"

"Googly-eyes and meaningful conversation?"

She folded her arms and glared, reminding him of an angry little kitten his mother once fostered.

"You seem to have forgotten the future changed for her, too," he said. "She didn't meet and fall for me, either."

"Oh, you're right." She groaned, deflating like a balloon again. "And here I thought I only had to work on you."

"Tell you what. I'll see if the church plans to have another lock-in and—"

"They're not. I've already checked." She ran her finger along the edge of her blouse.

"You *so* think of everything," he squealed.

"Don't." A giggle burst from her lips. "It sounds totally weird when you say it."

"That's better." He grinned. "I didn't think I'd ever see that dimple again."

Shifting in the seat, he clasped her left hand. "You know, a part of me wants you to stay. You could grow up here. Mom would love it. Someday I could walk you down the aisle—try to make up for what you've lost."

"Don't think I haven't thought about it."

He pumped her hand. "Of course, no one could ever know of our real relationship."

"If I knew I had no one back home, I would *so* stay."

The sweet longing on her upturned face touched him. "But if they're alive, they're missing you something awful and doing everything in their power to find you." He tugged a strand of her hair. "As I would be."

"Grieving and heartbroken like when they lost you," she said. "I couldn't do that to them."

The sadness in her eyes pained him. "Then that settles it. You have to go back." He draped an arm over her shoulders and gave her a sideways hug. "I hope I make it. I hope I'm there for you."

"Why wouldn't you be?" She craned her neck to look into his face. "You didn't disappear."

"Forty years is a long time, and there are no guarantees."

* * *

Jax advanced along the area where Rylee had first appeared. If he could target the anomaly, then he might have a solution to get her back. She tagged along like a quiet mouse while he measured the space with his magnetometer.

"You're staring again," he said.

"You don't mind, do you? I know you did when we first met, but now that you know who I am and why I can't help but stare—"

"I know. Our time together is limited. But your staring still makes me feel weird, so stop."

"Fine." She kicked at the ground. "You sound more like an irritated older brother than a grandfather."

"Look at this." He paused midstride.

She stepped closer and bent over the readout on the meter.

He tapped the ground with a foot. "I think this is the spot."

"Except this isn't where I landed."

Still holding the meter to face her, he braced his free hand on her shoulder. "That's because the anomaly has moved."

"So, that's why I couldn't get any activity the other night."

The hands on the meter spun like mad. "This is definitely the spot," he said.

That wonderment in her eyes was a bit . . . intense. "How do you know all this?"

"The geniuses are all at the aeronautics firm where I work." He squeezed her shoulder and let go. "I'm their test pilot. That said, I'm not stupid. I've learned a few things while in their employ."

"Cool."

"Go get the hammer and stake from my backpack."

She sprinted over to the Jeep, yanked the pack off the seat, then ran back to him. He took the sack and dug out the items, then squatted down. After several firm smacks with the hammer, he secured the wooden stake. He gave it a final push to make certain it held, then stood.

"Step two complete." He grinned. "You know what this means, don't you?"

"I get to go home."

"Tomorrow soon enough for you?"

CHAPTER 29

As the sun hung low in the sky, Rylee took a seat on the yard swing. So this was it, her last night in 1981—her last night with Jax and Doris . . . and Liam. She couldn't forget him. He'd been her first kiss, her confidant, her friend, and the genius who'd come through for her. He'd promised to come by later to tell her goodbye. She dressed in one of the new outfits—white shorts and a brightly colored shirt worn off one shoulder and cinched with a wide patent leather belt.

She pushed off from the ground, setting the swing in motion. Tomorrow afternoon, with their final meal behind them, she and Jax would drive to the hanger.

As she began to swing, an overwhelming sadness weighed on her heart. Since the day of her return had arrived, she wasn't ready. Jax had only known her identity for a few days. Wonderful days spent planning and talking and dreaming of a future with him in it—hours reminiscing over all the family photos. He'd told her wonderful stories of his childhood, and she'd listened with an open heart, holding onto every nuance of his telling.

Doris joined them. She, too, had wonderful stories to share. Every once in a while, Jax caught Rylee's eye, his glance holding a thank you for the memories these moments would also give his mother.

They'd agreed he would tell Doris everything after Rylee left. She had wanted to tell Doris herself, but Jax was adamant. "She'll have too many questions, and we don't have enough time. Every moment from here until tomorrow afternoon is critical," he'd said.

Rylee squeezed her eyes shut. She couldn't allow herself to cave. Keeping her grandmother and her mom in her thoughts helped. They had to be grief-stricken by now, fearing the worst. She imagined their joy when she returned and the healing and recovery in having found her at last.

"Penny for them?"

"Jax. Sorry. I didn't see you there."

She paused the swing while he sat next to her. "What has you so deep in thought?"

"My family and my upcoming reunion with them and . . ."

A half smile quirked his mouth as he draped his arm over her shoulder. "And what?"

"The argument I had with my mom before I left."

"What was it about?"

Something stung her heart. She closed her eyes and whispered, "You."

"Me?"

"And flying and my safety. It's all wrapped up in one big ugly package."

"Airplanes and flying took her father from her. Then her only child took after him, complicating matters."

"Yeah, for me." She pressed her lips together. "Not a day went by that she didn't remind me that, if not for flying, her father might still be here."

"She'll be so happy to have found you that she won't care."

"I suppose." An overwhelming sadness nearly choked her. "I know I have to go, but I also want to stay."

"I know." He gazed at her, a glint in his amazing violet eyes. "I still can't believe this—you."

"Now who's staring?"

He threw back his head and laughed. "I'm going to miss you."

"See this empty space to the right of us?" Rylee held up her hands like a movie director. "Tomorrow, the Scotts' farm cottage will be right there with its red door and apple-green shutters. By now, my mom would've planted colorful annuals in the front beds."

"After you're gone, I'll have to sit here and imagine you there," he said. "You don't have any photos of it in your phone, do you?"

"Yes." Now, why hadn't she thought of that? Nearly bouncing, she scooted forward enough to pull it from her jeans pocket. She pressed Photos, then scrolled across the screen to the one she was looking for. She tipped the screen. "Here you go."

"Wow. It's a smaller version of the main house."

"That's what my mom wanted." She lowered the phone and continued to scroll. "Would you like to see a picture of her?"

They locked gazes, and he nodded. She found one a few swipes away. "This is one of my favorites. I snapped it when I was around ten."

This time, he took the phone from her. "This is my daughter?"

"Felicity."

"Beautiful name for a beautiful young woman. And she's got blonde hair. Funny, I'd assumed it would be dark, like ours."

"She takes after Tess in her coloring."

"It's like honey, all gold and shiny." Something tender and wistful twisted up his features. "*Goldie.*"

He'd nicknamed her. Her grandmother's words rang through Rylee's head—"He'd know it when he laid eyes on her." And wasn't that what just happened? She watched his face as he gazed at his daughter's photo. Both joy and sadness reflected in his eyes. She couldn't imagine the pain and heartache he must be feeling, the inexpressible loss at not having cradled her in his arms, sang her lullabies, or tucked her in at night.

"She looks somewhere in her early to mid-thirties," he said.

"I think that's right."

With one finger, he caressed the photographed face. "I look at her, and she's a stranger. It's heartbreaking to think I never knew her or saw her grow up, was never there for her birthdays or prom or wedding day."

"This time you will be. You *have* to be." The words escaped with great urgency.

Jax hugged her. "If I didn't have enough motivation before, then I do now. I want to see her more than anything. I'll do my best to be there for all of you." The hand on her shoulder offered a comforting squeeze.

In an abrupt move, she grabbed the phone. "Lean in." She sniffed and tilted her head toward his, and he did the same. She snapped several photos, then showed him them.

A low whistle slipped past his lips. "This technology is astonishing."

Wheels crunched on the gravel drive.

"Oh no! It's Liam and I look awful." She fanned her face.

Jax's lips curved upward. "You look vulnerable and sweet, and if you can keep that shimmer in those gorgeous blue eyes, I predict you'll be kissed before the night is over."

She gaped at him. "I can't believe you just said that."

"I may be your grandfather, but I'm twenty-four and well aware of what a teary-eyed beauty does to a man. Now go."

With his words bringing heat to her cheeks, she slid off the swing and hurried across the lawn. As she settled next to Liam on the screened porch's love seat, she breathed in his spicy scent.

"Are you okay? Have you been crying?"

She offered a watery smile. "It's all the goodbyes."

Nodding, he took her hand in his. "I've been thinking about this future grandson of mine and how to get you two together."

"Seriously? *That's* what's on your mind right now?"

He continued as if he hadn't heard her. "Maybe I should send you something and have him give it to you. He'll have to talk to you then."

"I can see it now." She spread her hand across the night sky. "Liam '81—matchmaker of the future."

He rolled his eyes. "You're right. Forget about him." He laced his fingers through hers. They sat perfectly still, their gazes saying what mere words could not. "Sure you have to go?"

"Yes." She closed her eyes and rested her forehead against his. "I have a family. They've already lost someone. If they should lose me in the same way . . ."

"It would kill them."

"It would."

He lifted his head from hers. "You know the part at the end of *The Time Machine*, when George takes three books back with him into the future?"

"Yeah?"

"If you could take three things back with you, what would they be?"

She laced her arms around his waist. "The book to remember our time together, um, a silver-covered Hersey's Kiss, and you."

"I like that last one." He hitched her closer. "I've been wanting to do this since you joined me on the porch." He cupped his hands to her face, and her heart hummed as the sweet warmth of his lips covered hers.

How do you hold on to a moment in time, a moment so sweet and so wonderful, that it's never, ever erased from your heart and mind? Tomorrow, God willing, she would be back in 2021. Wonderful, sweet Liam 1981 would be a fifty-six-year-old man. He would've lived much of his life, and she would still be starting hers. Whatever her future, she was certain of one thing—Liam '81 would always hold a special place in her heart, because a girl always remembers her first kiss.

As he raised his head, he placed two fingers against her mouth. "I hereby seal these lips for the Liam of the future—a promise of things to come."

She wound her arms around his neck. "I think Liam '81 is just fine."

* * *

After Liam left, Rylee found Jax watching *Dukes of Hazzard* in the den. When he waved her over, she took a seat next to him. "I've seen this before."

"Reruns?"

"Yeah."

"Well, don't tell me what happens."

She stayed quiet until he glanced at her, one brow cocked.

Scooting back in his seat, he folded his arms. "I'm not going to get to finish this am I?"

"I'm leaving tomorrow, and you're watching TV?"

"I was watching TV while you were with Liam." He picked up the remote and clicked the TV off. "What is it, Kitten?"

"I need to say goodbye to one more person. Will you take me?"

"Sure you're not trying to get us together before you leave? I told you, I have to do this part on my own."

Tears welled in her eyes. "I'm sure."

He tapped her nose. "When you look like that, how can I refuse?"

Snorting, she crossed her arms over her chest. "You do realize that, when you make it back to my time, I'll already have had you wrapped around my little finger, right?"

The humor of the moment was not lost on him, and he bit back the beginnings of a smile.

Ten minutes later, he stood in Billy's doorway as she approached the pretty waitress at the restaurant's opposite side. He hung back to give her privacy with her young grandmother.

She hugged Tess, and after they eased apart, Tess glanced at him. Rylee's heart warmed, even as he turned away and stepped outside to wait. After savoring the sweet peaches scent clinging to her grandmother, Rylee released her fully, walked away, pushed through the glass doors, and joined him. Her chest heavy, she sniffed and raised her gaze to his. "Let's go."

He took her hand and led her to his Chevy.

CHAPTER 30

Lunch had been . . . difficult. Ha! What an understatement. Knowing this was her last time with the Dragon saddened Rylee, as did hearing this sweet ferocious woman chat about how lovely it had been having her here and for her to be sure to keep in touch.

She'd have burst into tears had it not been for Jax's encouraging looks and timely interruptions.

Once in her room, Rylee took time to regroup emotionally while she dressed in the clothes she'd arrived in . . . except for the flight jacket. She left that hanging in the closet.

That done, she wrote Jax a note, then folded it under her phone on the bedside table. Her life was in there, and she wanted him to have access to all of it. She stood, took one last look around the room, and walked out.

Jax and Doris were waiting in the living room.

"I'll miss you, sweet girl." Doris hugged her.

"I'll miss you, too, and I'll always think of you when I smell lavender and mint." Snug in the older woman's fierce grip, Rylee pressed her face against Doris's wavy hair and breathed in deeply. "I hope someday you'll know what your hospitality meant to me."

"And of course you'll let us know you got home safely?"

With a half nod, half headshake that she hoped passed muster, Rylee glanced at Jax. She hated lying to her, but somehow a simple nod didn't seem quite so dishonest.

An hour later, they had the Cessna parked not far from where she'd arrived two weeks earlier. To save time, they both went through the preflight check.

Satisfied, they crossed the ground to the area Jax marked with the stake. He turned on the magnetometer to confirm the takeoff coordinates.

"Has the anomaly moved any?"

"No. It's still the same as yesterday and still near the runway, so this is perfect."

She lifted her gaze to his. "Jax, I need to tell you—"

"Rylee, no. I—"

She grabbed his arms. "I don't know what it is. I just know there's something else, something I've forgotten." She tapped the back of her head. "It's nagging at the back of my brain."

"What do you expect me to do with that?"

"Be careful. Test every mission—question everything."

"I will."

She gazed up at him. "So this is it."

"Yes."

She threw herself against his chest. "I love you, Jax."

He gathered her close. "And I you, Kitten."

"Don't forget me when I'm gone." She rested her cheek against his cotton shirt, the fabric scratching as her tears dampened it. Then she pushed away and sprinted to the plane. Without looking back, she climbed into the pilot's seat and began checking all instruments. The airspeed indicated zero, and the altimeter was good. She opened the throttle a quarter inch, then turned the key. The propeller fluttered, then came on full blast. She released the brake and taxied forward. When she got in position for takeoff, she took one last look at her amazing grandfather.

* * *

Jax approached the aircraft, signaling for Rylee to stop and step out. Her sobbing had ripped his insides. Flying while so upset would be too dangerous.

As she unlocked the door, he opened his arms wide. Her tear-streaked face lit up, and after jumping from the plane, she ran across the tarmac into his embrace.

With her tight in his arms, he breathed a silent prayer for her safety. After a long moment, he put her from him. Lifting his hand, he brushed her cheeks, kissed her forehead, then held her face between his hands. "I will always love you, no matter what my future holds."

She hugged him again with a fierceness that took his breath away, as if it would have to last her a lifetime. "See you on the other side," she whispered.

"Now go and make your grandfather proud."

She gave a nod, smiling through her tears, then ran back to the aircraft. Before she climbed in, she turned back.

"Go to Billy's!" she yelled over the propeller roar. "Sit at the counter!"

When she brought two fingers to her forehead in salute, he followed with one of his own.

As the aircraft moved forward, he hustled to the edge of the asphalt. The Cessna's engine roared. The plane sped down the runway. The next part was his favorite. The aircraft lifted, defying gravity. "You're doing great, Kitten."

He stood perfectly still, never once taking his eyes off the Cessna. "Godspeed."

A minute later, the Cessna banked right, then straightened. He held his breath as it flew over the coordinates. A shimmer of light caught the aircraft midair. Then she was gone.

His heart nearly stopped. His breath caught in his throat. Rubbing the back of his neck, he shook his head. The Cessna had disappeared. If he hadn't seen it, he wouldn't have believed it.

He drifted forward and continued to stare into the late afternoon sky. Had she made it back? Would he be there to greet her? If he didn't live, then he'd never know, but if he *did* live . . .

In that moment, he wanted to . . . very, very badly.

* * *

Around closing time, Jax entered Billy's. Except for two lingering customers, the place was empty. He took a seat at the counter and waited, but after several minutes, he got up and went to the swinging door leading to the kitchen.

A young woman in front of the massive oven door was pulling out a delicious-smelling pasty. With her blonde hair secured in a ponytail, she wore the familiar Billy's Dairy Dip pink-and-white uniform.

Jax leaned against the doorjamb and watched her carry the baking sheet over to the preparation table. As she yanked off the mittens, she closed her eyes, bent forward over the tray, and inhaled.

"Smells great," he said.

She spun toward him, her ponytail swaying with the movement. She gaped at him with the prettiest green eyes he'd ever seen. Remnants of white flour smeared on her left cheek and forehead seemed to enhance their glow.

How had he missed this—missed her? This woman was the most adorable thing he'd ever seen.

His insides churned in a wonderful way. When he smiled, she returned it with a shy one.

"Sorry. I didn't mean to startle you."

"It's . . . it's okay." She wiped her hands on her pink apron.

"You're Tessa, right?"

"You know my name?"

He bit back another smile. "It's written on your name tag."

"Oh . . . right." One of her hands fluttered to the tag as if checking if it was there—or on straight. "And you're Jaxon Scott," she added. "We were supposed to spend the night together." Her eyes widened, and her pretty cheeks flushed a rosy pink.

He tried his best to stifle a chuckle, but his wayward mouth still quirked upward.

"I mean . . . at the church . . . with the kids . . . during the lock-in. A few weeks ago." She mumbled a few more incoherent words and snapped up a spatula. "May I help you with something?"

"I was going to order a quick burger before you closed. I waited at the counter, but when no one came, I followed an amazing aroma."

"Sorry. I should have been out there." She pulled the order pad from her apron pocket, dropped the pencil in the process, disappeared behind the prep table, then popped up with the pencil poised over the pad. "What would you like with your burger?"

"On second thought . . . Are those peach turnovers?"

She brightened. "Yes."

"I've been here a thousand times, but never saw these on the menu."

"That's because this is one of my own recipes. Billy lets me use the kitchen after hours to test them."

"I see." He stood next to her.

She slid the spatula underneath one of the pastries and started transferring the sweets to a cooling rack.

"May I?" His hand hovered over the warm tray.

"Of course." She placed one on a plate, then handed it to him. "Careful, though. It's hot."

He picked up one end, then lowered his teeth into the peachy goodness. He eyed her, nodding, as he chewed. "Wow. I never knew peaches could taste so good."

"I can't take all the credit. There's a secret ingredient in the crust."

"Which is?"

"Promise you won't tell?"

"Cross my heart." He made a cross with his index finger over his chest.

"It's mace."

"Mace?"

"It's a spice. Rylee told me about it—said her grandmother used it in her peach turnovers and won the county fair with them four years in a row."

"Did she?" He couldn't help but smile. This guileless beauty had no idea she was talking about her future self.

He gazed at Tessa's upturned, flour-smudged face and slightly parted lips. His head spun with a desire to kiss her. In all the months he'd dated Sylvia, she'd never left him feeling like this.

He'd walked in here to make sure his daughter would be born, but as soon as he'd laid eyes on Tessa Blake, the last thing he was thinking about was his future family.

Standing before him was the girl he wanted to offer his coat to on a chilly evening, his shoulder to cry on when she was sad. He wanted to share every possession, every hope, and every dream with her . . . his very future. Did he *have* a future? As he gazed down at this woman, he certainly hoped so.

"And all because of mace?"

She nodded. "Speaking of mace, I hated to see Rylee go."

"Me, too."

"I learned a lot from that girl."

"So did I."

He took another bite of pastry. "You tell Billy to add these to the menu."

"I'll do that." She beamed.

He set the plate down and stuffed his hands into his pockets. "You, um, want to go out sometime? Like maybe tomorrow night?"

The corners of her mouth lifted, and her eyes twinkled. Her smile was sunshine itself. He took that as a yes.

CHAPTER 31

Tap, tap, tap. The repetitive, irritating noise followed by low voices penetrated Rylee's brain. As she awakened, the voices grew louder. She opened her eyes, and the past few hours clicked off in her mind. Liam, Doris, Jax, the meter, the goodbyes, the Cessna lifting into flight, and Jaxon disappearing in a flash. He was there one second, then gone. She closed her eyes against the sadness. *Please be here.*

Strangers clamored at the aircraft door. A man, a firefighter, opened it.

"Rylee Dean?"

"Yes?"

"Are you all right?"

Was she? She whispered, "I think so."

"She's all right!" he yelled over his shoulder to several others from search and rescue.

The firefighter unhooked her safety belt and helped her to the ground.

"What's today's date?" she asked.

"June 17."

"When? What year?"

"What year? Kiddo, you must have a head injury. You've been missing a while, but it's still 2021, of course."

She was back!

A gasp slipped from her throat, and her chest tightened. She pushed herself from the plane and fought to speak around the tightness. "Where's my mom? I want to see my mom."

"One of the men just called her. We'll take you home after we have you looked over."

Home.

Her mom stood on the cottage's front porch when she arrived. She'd barely made it down the steps when Rylee wrapped her arms around her.

"You're here. You're still here," she cried.

"Of course, I'm here. Where else would I be?" Mom eased back from Rylee's grip. "*You're* who's been missing."

"Grandma? Is she—?"

"She's fine. We're all fine."

"I need to see her."

"Okay, but—"

Rylee didn't wait, just jumped off the cottage porch, and ran to the big house. She burst through the front door. "Grandma!"

Tess rushed out of the kitchen and held out her arms. "Oh my!"

Choking back a sob, Rylee flew into her grandmother's warm embrace.

"I'm here." Tess rubbed Rylee's back, pressing her cheek atop Rylee's head. "I'm here, Kitten. I'm so thankful you're all right. We were all so worried about you."

Rylee pushed herself away and took her grandmother's hands in hers. "You're still so beautiful."

"What?" Tess laughed.

"I have so much to tell you. You won't believe where I've been."

"Two weeks is a long time, and it's enough that you've returned safe. We're all wanting to hear where you've been, but right now, someone else needs to set eyes on you."

"Hey, is that my girl?"

Rylee's heart stopped. She pivoted toward the familiar voice. In the doorway, with his left leg in a brace, stood her grandfather.

"You're here." The words whispered from somewhere deep inside her.

Tall and lean, with the same remarkable blue eyes, Jaxon Scott was just as she'd remembered him, only older.

Time slowed, she took a tentative step forward, then stopped. For a second, she couldn't move. Couldn't think. Only two words kept circling in her head. Then they escaped on a shuddered breath. "You're alive."

His head jerked up, his brow crinkling. "You had doubts?"

"Don't look so alarmed, Jax. She said the same thing to me." Tessa patted Rylee's shoulder.

"Well, don't just stand there, give your granddad a hug," he said.

But Rylee's brain wasn't functioning yet. Her feet wouldn't cooperate. But she had to be sure this was real—he was real. Somehow, her hand rose and pressed against his chest. Warm and hard and . . . and *real* his chest met her touch, his heart beating beneath her shaking fingertips. Something between a laugh and a sob broke from her lips, and she flung herself into his arms. "You're here—you're here."

He held her close as she sobbed against him. Then she stepped out of his embrace and searched his face. He patted her cheek. "You gave us quite a scare."

He doesn't remember. He has no recollection of all we went through.

She stared at him, a sinking sensation nearly bringing her to her knees. Yes, it was selfish, but for him not to recall all they'd experienced together broke her heart. What was wrong with her? Shouldn't she be beside herself with joy? After all, he'd survived whatever had taken him in the other timeline. So why was she feeling this . . . devastation?

"I heard how they found you. I'm sorry I wasn't there to help." He gripped her shoulders and eyed her up and down. "At least you aren't hurt. Leave it to me to jump from an airplane at my age," he said, tapping his leg.

"I told you," Tessa said.

"Nagged, more like." He winked at Rylee and mimicked Tessa. " 'And how do expect to find our girl with a bad leg?' " Then he ducked a playful swat for his trouble. His eyes twinkled lovingly at his wife. "If she said it once, she said it a million times. And as usual, she was right."

Tessa shook a finger. "You can take the man out of the air force, but you can't take the air force out of the man."

During her grandparents' banter, Rylee did her best to pull herself together. "It's wonderful to see you, Jax. It's okay if I call you that, isn't it?"

"Why wouldn't it be? You've called me that since you could talk."

Realization dawned. She had no memories of him on this side. The only ones she had were from her time in the past.

"Felicity is waiting for us on the porch," Tessa told them. "Come on, you two."

As they settled outside, Coop mounted the steps and entered the screened porch.

Mom smiled at him. "Coop, darling, I wasn't sure you'd make it."

Darling?

"And miss Rylee's homecoming? Never." He stepped over to Mom, bent down, and kissed her on the mouth.

Rylee gaped. "Coop?"

"Hey, you. I'm so thankful you're all right." He scooped her up, giving her a hug. Then he dropped into the seat next to Mom. "Listen, Ry, since it's been a while, I rescheduled your solo flight to next week, in case you needed time to go over your preflight information and to see if you had any questions."

"Speaking of your flight," Mom added, "your dad, Monica, and the boys are crossing the pond to be here for it. They're all so proud of you, honey."

All Rylee could do was stare—something she'd been doing a lot since her return.

"Who's ready for a cold drink and peach turnovers?" Tessa pushed through the connecting door onto the porch, balancing a tray in her hands, then placed it on the wicker coffee table.

"These remind me of the first time I saw you," Jax said.

"You mean the first time you took notice." Tess sat and gave him a peck on his cheek.

"They smell fabulous, honey."

"The secret's—"

"In the mace," Jax and Felicity said in unison.

Seems everyone now knew her secret. Rylee stared at her grandmother. Did she recall the girl who told her about the mace? Jax seemed oblivious to the connection as he helped himself to the pastry.

Waving a hand, Mom chuckled. "Some secret when the whole town knows."

"What do you mean the whole town knows?" Rylee blurted out. "I thought it was supposed to be a family secret."

"It's in my cookbook. You know that."

Rylee's jaw dropped. "You have a cookbook?"

"The Dip sells it, honey. You remember, don't you?"

"I . . . I . . ."

"Maybe Rylee forgot a few things while she's been away," Jax told them, his eye on her.

She looked right at him. That wonderful blue-eyed twinkle, the one she knew so well, was there and communicating the secret world they'd shared.

She caught her breath.

He does remember.

* * *

Rylee's heart soared. She'd received his message and had leveled him with a *look* of her own, confirming it. They'd talk later.

It was now later, and she made her way to the swing hanging underneath the old oak tree. Her chest warmed as she approached. Jaxon must have made sure there'd be one here when she returned.

She sat to wait, and soon, he left the house at the side door. He walked toward her, his booted leg not slowing him a bit. At sixty-four years old, he still had the physique and bearing of a younger man. He wore his hair shorter, and the gray at the temples made him look distinguished instead of old. When he neared the swing, she noticed the blue in his smiling eyes had not faded with age and their mild humor and piercing depths remained.

She stood, took two steps, and threw her arms around him. He caught her close and laughed. They pulled apart and laughed even more, then sat.

"You made it. You married Tess and you made it." She beamed up at him.

"I sure did."

"Which means you figured out the real date of your disappearance."

He nodded. "November sixth."

"Not June eleventh. By the time I realized it myself, it was too late to tell you."

"If I hadn't fully read the newspaper article about us, I'd have never known the date I actually disappeared."

"Instead of 6/11, that last picture of you was really 11/6," Rylee said. "I'd forgotten Tess wrote dates like the English. *That* was what bugged me. At the time, you wouldn't have known, but her mother was—"

"From England."

"So, what'd you do?"

"I canceled the flight and had maintenance recheck the aircraft. They found an issue with the hydraulics. Had I flown that plane, it would have had a complete hydraulic failure. I wouldn't have made it. Once they fixed the problem, I rescheduled the flight for a week later. I still had no idea if I'd make it. I figured when it was your time—it was your time."

"But it wasn't and you're here."

"Thanks to my brave, adorable granddaughter."

"You do realize I just left you this afternoon, right?"

"And yet a lifetime for me, Kitten."

"And I want to hear all about that lifetime," she said.

"Speaking of, the whole world is anxious to hear where you've been."

"I know." Frowning, she pressed her lips together, then sucked them between her teeth, chewing on the idea. "But what will I tell them?"

"We'll think of something . . . together."

She took his hand, wrapped his arm around her, and rested her head on his shoulder. "When I first got back and saw you, I didn't think you'd remembered."

"I know. Your disappointment was evident. I thought it best not to give anything away. It will always have to be our secret."

"It's enough that you know." She rose and kissed his cheek. "Thank you for getting me home."

"My pleasure. How are you handling the changes?"

"Well, Coop is a surprise. My dad and the boys—and *Monica*—getting along with Mom? Coming to see us?" She shook her head. "I did *not* see that coming."

She ran a finger along the edge of her blouse. "When I left here, my mom was a very unhappy person, and my dad hardly had anything to do with me.

Your presence—you being here—has made all the difference."

"For the both of us. Forty years is a long time, and a lot of living has taken place. As the time went by, your visit faded and seemed more a dream, than reality, until I wasn't sure it had happened."

He paused, tucked a finger under her chin, and tipped her face up. "After you were born and your parents named you, it all came back, and I remembered this." He reached into his back pocket and whipped out her iPhone. "I thought you might want it back."

"Sweet! You still have it."

"I'd misplaced it, and when I came across it years later, it reminded me of that other reality, the one with you in it."

She took the phone and pressed the power button.

"Your existence confirmed what happened all those years ago, and this phone was the evidence. And as you grew up, I began to recognize the girl who'd come back in time. As the day of your departure neared, I wondered if you'd still have to go back in order to come full circle."

"Timelines are a funny thing."

"That's one way of putting it." He shifted in his seat. "I got my answer when you disappeared two weeks ago, and I alone knew where you'd gone. I watched the town search, knowing they wouldn't find you. I shared in their anxiety because I didn't know if you'd make it back."

She tucked her hand in the crook of his arm. "I guess we both made it."

"I'm here because of you, Kitten." He kissed her on her forehead.

"I'm so glad you remember. I'd hate to be the only one to know what happened. But there's something I don't get." She scrunched up her face. "Why don't I have memories of you while growing up? The only ones I have are from our two weeks in 1981, and yet you recall all of it."

"I don't know. Maybe in time, you will."

"It's mind-boggling."

"All I know is you traveled back in time to me."

She squeezed his arm. "And we *both* know it happened."

"And I've had a long, wonderful life because of it." He took the phone and pressed the photo app. "You ready?"

When she nodded, he began scrolling through the pictures.

"You know, this all started with a photo album," she said.

"I seem to recall you telling me that, but we're high tech now."

She laughed. "I know."

He paused on a particular photo. "This one's a favorite of mine. You're about seven here, and you're helping me wash the Cessna." He ran his thumb over a few more and stopped. "And this one is when I took you up for the first time. You were twelve and so excited."

Enthralled, Rylee glanced from the photos to her grandfather's animated face and watched him tell her story after story, about her, her mom, and his beloved Tessa, well into the evening.

She had her grandfather, and he was right where he should be. And to have gotten to know him as a young man was a rare gift. How many people could say that?

CHAPTER 32

Rylee grabbed her favorite booth at the Dip and waited for Frankie and Lizzy to join her. As she perused the menu, Liam 2021 approached from across the diner, holding a wrapped package in his right hand. His hair still fell appealingly over one honey-brown eye. The last time she'd looked into those eyes they'd held an impatient boredom as he'd waited for her order, but today, an intense curiosity lit them.

Heart thudding, she held his gaze as he neared the booth. He stopped and stared at her as if struggling to find the words he wanted to say.

"Hello," she said, more to break the ice than anything else.

"Hey, Rylee." Without taking his gaze from hers, he slid into the bench opposite her and set the package beside him. "I guess you know the whole town searched for you, me included."

He had looked for her? Why? Her heartbeat gave a strange jitter flop. "I wasn't aware of that."

"My grandfather was one of them."

Her heart stilled. "That . . . that's so nice. I'd love to thank him."

"I wish you could, but he passed away just over a week ago."

"Oh." A raw ache hollowed her insides. Liam '81, her first kiss, had grown up and was now gone. "I'm so sorry."

"Thanks, but that's not what I came to say." Liam 2021 licked his lips. "He told me about you. And for the life of me, I don't know how he knew who you were much less the information he seemed to know."

"Small town—big mouths." She laughed and gave a nervous wave.

"I don't think so."

"Let me guess. You were twelve and—"

"What? No. This was a couple of days after you disappeared. He gave me something to give to you when you came back, not *if* you came back, but *when*. It was as if he knew. He was certain of your return."

Liam picked up the package and held it across the table.

She took it from his hands and unwrapped it. "*The Time Machine*." She ran her hand across the cover, then opened it. The manila envelope with the checkout card was still inside. She slid it out and caught her breath. Her signature was still there. She blinked, swallowed, and slid it back in place. She turned to the title page. There was a note.

Never forget,
Liam '81

Goose bumps prickled her arms. *I won't.*

How strange. It had been a week since he'd kissed her goodbye. In the minutes it took for her to come back, he'd married and raised a family, and then they'd had a family.

"Apparently, he bought it years ago at one of the library sales," Liam said. "It was very important to him that you got this."

She raised her gaze to his, closed the book, and held it to her chest. "Thank you."

"He, um, also wanted you to have this." Liam reached into his pocket and pulled out a small object. Hand extended between them, he hesitated. "This is just weird." He then opened his palm and placed a Hershey's chocolate Kiss in the center of the table.

She threw a hand to her mouth and tried to stifle a giggle.

Liam folded his arms and hit her with one of his to-die-for looks. "I know. I'm sorry. I can't imagine what he was thinking."

"I think you're pretty brave. It's not just any guy who'd give a girl he hardly knows a chocolate kiss."

Brown eyes, so much like his grandfather's, gleamed across the table at her, leveling a look that said there had to be more to this story.

For her, that chocolate kiss had occurred only mere weeks ago. For Liam '81, it was a lifetime.

She touched the top of the Hershey's Kiss, its peak poking her finger. "How did he die?"

"In his sleep. He'd been ill, lung cancer. He smoked for years. We knew his time was close and were thankful he died peacefully."

"I'm glad, too."

"I don't get it." Liam waved a hand in the air. "How did you two know each other?"

Laughter skittered up her chest and burst from her mouth. "We literally bumped into each other in front of the library. I had just checked out a stack of books on time travel, and he helped me pick them up off the sidewalk. He noticed my unusual interest, and we chatted about it in this very booth."

"You're kidding . . . my grandfather?"

"Yep."

"And the chocolate Kiss?"

"I'm afraid that's a story for another day." She fingered the candy. "It's a long one, and I'm not sure you would believe it if I told you."

"He told me there was a third gift and you would know what he meant."

She did. It was him—Liam 2021. Liam '81 had reached through time with his matchmaking skills after all.

"Look. I know there's more to this story than he told me." He reached across the table and took her hand in his. "And whenever you're ready, I'd like to hear it."

She gave him an assessing gaze. "I'll have to get to know you a lot better before that can happen." Liam '81 had given her confidence. She now saw *this* Liam in a whole new light and was no longer the quiet girl who'd crushed on him from afar. She liked the new her.

"I think that can be arranged." Expectation warmed his golden-brown eyes. He picked up the Kiss and twirled it between his fingers. "Maybe this isn't just for you. Maybe it's a sign of things to come. After all, Granddad left the rest of the bag with me." Liam held up a small bag of chocolates and shook it. "Said they might come in handy, if I played my cards right." He rested his forearms on the table and leaned toward her. "What do you think he meant?"

"Only time will tell." She smiled.

He smiled back.

EPILOGUE

A full moon hung low in the evening sky, shedding light along the pathway to the barn. Rylee took her time crossing the yard. The past week had flown by, giving her little time to reflect on her amazing journey into the past. At the barn entrance, she stepped through the wide doors and crossed the concrete floor to her Cessna. Coop had taken care of getting the aircraft back to the farm, but he'd insisted on having it checked out for safety first. Jax had agreed.

She ran her hand over the nose, along the prop, to the right wing.

"You always did love her."

Rylee spun at the sound. "Jax!"

The twenty-four-year-old Jaxon stepped out from the aircraft's other side, dressed in his flight suit. When she squealed and jumped into his arms, he caught her and swung her around, then set her on her feet.

"If you tell me I've gone back to 1981, I'll kill myself."

He laughed. "Don't worry. You haven't. I traveled here to make sure you'd made it and all was well with you. If it wasn't, I had strict orders from my mother to bring you back home with me."

"How is the Dragon?"

"Fine, but wishing she'd known who you were."

"I wanted to confide in her so many times. Please tell her that for me."

"I will."

"Did you come in our Cessna?"

"I upgraded. Bought a second plane, a Learjet 24. She's parked on the abandoned runway near here. It was built in 1966, and to use your words, she's *sweet.*"

"What I wouldn't give to fly in that."

"Someday, I promise. In the meantime"—he held up the special compass dial—"I made some modifications to the ADD. Like the original, this baby will plug right into the same opening. The only difference between the two is this one has been modified for time travel. It draws from every anomaly in a radius of ten miles, creating a compound effect by pulling them together into one large mass. It picks up the superanomaly, as we like to call it, then translates the data into beta waves converting it into—"

"Enough!" She threw up her hands. "You lost me at *modifications.*"

"Right. You don't have to understand it to know it works. I have one of the most brilliant young electrical engineers helping me. Any guesses as to whom?"

"I have no clue."

"Liam. He says hi, by the way."

"Wow, Liam. So he did turn out to be a nerd-genius. That doesn't surprise me in the least."

"He's impressive."

"Jax." Rylee tilted her head toward the farmhouse. "Will *he* know that you've been here? You know—have the memory of it?"

"Does he remember you being with me in the past?"

"He does."

"Then I'd say yes."

"Well, don't plan on too many trips back and forth. It could get confusing for him. He's not a young man, you know."

He grinned. "I'll take that into consideration."

She grinned back and threw herself into his arms. "Thank you for coming and checking on me. Now I have both of you in my life."

"Anytime, Kitten, and if you ever want to take a trip through time with me, let me know with this."

He presented her the modified dial. "This one's for your Cessna. Remove the screws from the other one and plug this one in its place, then hit this button. It'll send a signal to the one in my aircraft."

"Incredible." She took it from his hands as if he'd given her a rare jewel. "Would you install it for me?"

"Sure. Watch, so you can see how it's done." He climbed into the cockpit and began taking out the older model.

While he switched out the instrument, she gazed at his face, trying to keep her equilibrium while seeing the twenty-four-year-old Jaxon Scott here in her time.

He glanced down at her, and the side of his mouth quirked upward. "I have to admit it—I do miss your staring." He gave the ADD a final check. "There, it's in." He jumped down and secured the door.

"Hey, listen," Rylee said. "Tell Liam to stop smoking."

"He doesn't."

"Then tell him not to start."

"Will do." He opened his arms. "One more hug before I go?"

"You can't stay?"

He shook his head. "Better not. There could be ramifications we don't know about."

She stepped into his arms, breathing in the scent of pine needles and peppermint. "Love you, Jax."

"And I love you." He eased her away from him and tapped her nose. "Until next time." Then he gave her a lazy salute and strode from the barn.

Rylee stood perfectly still and watched him until he disappeared like a phantom into the night. Then she waited, listening. Minutes later, she heard the rush of a mighty wind, the high-pitched whistle, and the whir of a thousand wings as Jaxon Scott jetted through time and space.

"We all have our time machines, don't we?
Those that take us back are memories . . .
And those that carry us forward, are dreams."

— **H. G. Wells**

Thank you for reading!

Dear Reader,

I hope you enjoyed *Flight Time*. Dipping my toe into young adult, time travel fiction was so much fun!

I need to ask a favor. As you probably know, reviews can be hard to come by. And as a reader your feedback is so important. If you're so inclined, I'd love an honest review of *Flight Time*. It doesn't have to be long or fancy. :) One or two sentences is fine.

If you have time, here's a link to my author page on Amazon. You can check out all my books here:

http://www.amazon.com/-/e/B0077AG3ZM

In gratitude,
Darcy Flynn

About the Author

Award-Winning Author Darcy Flynn, is known for her heartwarming, sweet contemporary romances. Her refreshing storylines, irritatingly handsome heroes and feisty heroines will delight and entertain you from the first page to the last. Miss Flynn's heroes and heroines have a tangible chemistry that is entertaining, humorous and competitive.

Darcy lives with her husband and a menagerie of other living creatures on her horse farm in Franklin, Tennessee. She stargazes on warm summer nights and occasionally indulges in afternoon tea.

Although, published in the Christian non-fiction market under her real name, Joy Griffin Dent, it was the empty nest that turned her to writing romantic fiction. Proving that it's never too late to follow your dreams.

Follow Darcy on Instagram:
@joydarcyauthor

Twitter:
@darcyflynn

Facebook:
http:/www.facebook.com/DarcyFlynnAuthor

Visit her website:
darcyflynnromances.com

or feel free to drop her a line at:
darcyflynnromances@gmail.com

Also By Darcy Flynn

The Prince's Fake Fiancée
Stowaway
Double Trouble
Seven Days in December
Eagle Eye
Hawke's Nest
Rogue's Son
Sealed With a Kiss
Keeper of My Heart

www.ingramcontent.com/pod-product-compliance
Lightning Source LLC
Chambersburg PA
CBHW030800200726
48285CB00013B/312